Praise for The Asphalt Warr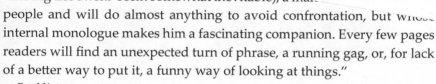

"Murph is a go-with-the-flow ph...
'The Big Lebowski' seem somewhat inevitable), a m...
people and will do almost anything to avoid confrontation, but who...
internal monologue makes him a fascinating companion. Every few pages
readers will find an unexpected turn of phrase, a running gag, or, for lack
of a better way to put it, a funny way of looking at things."
—*Booklist*

"Huge fun." —*National Public Radio*

"Reilly's genius lies in his ability to create a real, three-dimensional person
out of disparate descriptions and monologues strewn throughout the
story. In a way, though, it is not these 'facts' that fully describe Murph.
Rather, it is the breezy, almost constant running commentary on all that
happens or has happened in his life that brings Murph alive on the page."
—*Foreword Reviews*

"Reilly is a master wordsmith."—*The Denver Post*

What if the gloomy 19th century German philosopher Arthur Schopenhauer
drove a cab in Denver? What if Schopenhauer, crossed with Maynard G
Krebbs (you do know who that is, don't you?) by way of comedian Steven
Wright, chased fares in the Mile High City? You'd have this book. And you
need to read it...That Reilly. What a writer." —Barry Wightman, author
of *Pepperland*

:Gary Reilly is the kind of writer who leaves you smiling at the sheer
pleasure of his word choices. The Asphalt Warrior is a fun-filled read,
and you can't help rooting for the the book's taxi driving hero. If Murph
doesn't win your heart, it can't be won."
—Mark Graham, author of *The Natanz Directive*

"Gary Reilly's Asphalt Warrior is the tale of Brendan "Murph" Murphy, a
Denver Cabdriver of dead-pan hilarity and near heroic stoicism. In service
to his dream of finally publishing one of his novels, he has adapted a life

of simplicity that is Zen-like in its rigor: daily meditations on 'Gilligan's Island,' strict regime of frozen burgers, and most important, keeping the outside world's influence (ie, the affairs of his customers) to a minimum. Of course, the latter proves easier said than done, and his inevitable involvement with a fare's problems provides us with a highly entertaining read, throughout which Gary Reilly proves himself to be not just a gifted stylist, but a kind of Jedi Master of the understated."
—Fred Haefele, author of *Extremophilia*

"It didn't take long to snuggle back into a world that moves at the speed of Murph. Our insightful protagonist is a true minimalist. Not in some avant garde artsy form but as an honest-to-goodness way of life. Murph has perfected getting by and having just what he needs, never too little or too much but just right."
—*Manic Readers*

Varmint Rumble

A NOVEL

GARY REILLY

Running Meter Press
Mancos, Colorado

Published by Running Meter Press
Mancos, Colorado
Publisher@RunningMeterPress.com

Cover art by John Sherffius
Cover design by Jody Chapel

ISBN: 978-0-9908666-9-5
Library of Congress Control Number: 2020902836

First Edition 2020

Printed in the United States of America

Other Titles in The Asphalt Warrior Series

The Asphalt Warrior

Ticket to Hollywood

Heart of Darkness Club

Home for the Holidays

Doctor Lovebeads

Dark Night of the Soul

Pickup at Union Station

Devil's Night

FOREWORD

And so it ends. *Varmint Rumble* concludes The Asphalt Warrior series—nine wise and witty novels featuring the late Gary Reilly's alter ego, cab driver Brendan Murphy.

A.k.a., Murph.

My partner Mike Keefe and I continue to comb through the myriad computer files that Gary Reilly left behind when he passed away in 2011. From everything we can gather, *Varmint Rumble* is the final entry. But as we explore, who knows what we'll discover?

The series is primarily set on the streets of Denver—although Murph's adventures have taken us to Los Angeles (*Ticket to Hollywood*), Wichita (*Home for the Holidays*), and Boulder (*Doctor Lovebeads*). *Varmint Rumble* finds Murph in Commerce City as our cabbie hero and wannabe novelist gets tangled up with a motorcycle gang. As always, Murph tries hard to avoid getting caught up in the lives of his fares—but his instincts to do the right thing, this time, place him in a real life-and-death situation. Murph hides out in a bleak motel room, enduring a dark night of the soul in unique and colorful Murph fashion.

As the publishers of Gary's works—*Varmint Rumble* marks the 14th posthumously published novel—we couldn't be more pleased with the reception. Four of the novels have been finalists for the Colorado Book Award (*Ticket to Hollywood*, *Doctor Lovebeads*, *Pickup at Union Station*, and the standalone thriller *The Circumstantial Man*). Rave reviews have come from National Public Radio, *Booklist*, *The Denver Post*, The Vietnam Veterans of America website, *Westword*, and many others. More importantly, with each new novel, Gary's audience continues to grow. We can only assume that the fan base will continue to swell as we bring more of Gary's extensive stylistic range into print.

All of these books are the work of many hands. Thanks go out once again to Karen Haverkamp for her tenacious, precision editing with *Varmint Rumble*. Karen is an invaluable member of the Running Meter Press team. (And consider that she arrived on our doorstep as a Gary

Reilly fan!) Thanks to John Sherffius for another spot-on illustration for the cover. Thanks also to Jody Chapel for her work on the book design—inside and out. All these talented people donated many, many hours to shepherd Gary's electronic file into something you can enjoy.

So *Varmint Rumble* might close one chapter of Gary's works, but we all know Murph is out there. He's still deciding whether to write another soon-to-be-unpublished novel. He's working very hard at his peculiar brand of extreme minimalism, to make sure he doesn't earn too much money. He's planning another one of his trademarked "Spring Breaks." He's doing "the dish" after eating his burger. He's contemplating his next interaction with Rollo, Big Al, or a pair of nosy detectives who suspect him for murder or kidnapping. We all know the crow's nest is still there. So is the cabstand at The Brown Palace and the Twinkie aisle at 7-Eleven.

Welcome to *Varmint Rumble*. These might be Gary's last words of fiction about his most memorable fictional creation, but we all know . . . *Murph lives*!

And for that, to me, so does Gary.

Mark Stevens
Spring, 2020

CHAPTER 1

I was sitting in my taxi outside the Brown Palace Hotel eating a Twinkie and trying to get my transistor radio to work when a man came out of the hotel and climbed into my backseat—or rather—my taxi's backseat. English professors get upset if you talk like a normal person instead of a "literate person"—although not as upset as real people get when you interrupt a story to explain the psychological peccadillos of failed novelists, so let's move on.

The AM radio on the dashboard of Rocky Mountain Taxicab Number 123 had ceased to function two weeks earlier, and the top brass at RMTC had refused to get it fixed due to budget constraints, so I was forced to go transistor. The phrase "budget constraint" is business lingo for "this vehicle is a piece of junk and not worth pouring money into," and I was in agreement with their evaluation. I had been driving 123 long enough to know that it was a candidate for the Argo smelter (a Denver landmark), although anybody with nostrils could make the same evaluation without turning their back on a happy and fulfilling life by becoming a professional flesh porter, as I like to think of myself when I am either drunk or alone, my two favorite states of being. The honesty of the evaluation impressed me. I like the odor of honesty. It smells like victory, so I'm told. If any of you really knows what victory smells like, drop me a line.

Suddenly the back door to my taxi opened and a man climbed in. Taxi back doors open "suddenly" 62 percent of the time.

"Do you know where Brandywine Books is located?" the man said.

I gave up fiddling with my transistor radio. The battery was dead, but I was not to discover that for another three hours, the average amount of time that it takes me to grasp the obvious.

I set the radio on the seat next to me and glanced into the backseat. The man looked to be in his early fifties. He was wearing an overcoat and a full-brimmed hat of the type that everybody's father wore in the 1940s, assuming they did have a father. I gave up making assumptions a long time ago. I still think of things, but I try not to append the concept of "true" or "false" to anything I think of. Whichever way I go, I'm usually wrong, and when you realize that something is neither "true" nor "false" it can put a damper on your willingness to make a decision. I decided to give up making decisions the same day I decided to quit making assumptions—so, as you might expect, getting lost in traffic can be a nightmare, especially if your fare is late for a plane flight.

"Yes sir, I do know the place," I said, starting the engine and dropping my flag. Brandywine Books was ten dollars south of the Brown Palace Hotel, and I did not want to lose this customer. I had been waiting at the cabstand for an hour, hoping for a fifty-dollar trip to Denver International Airport, and an hour is as long as I am willing to wait before facing up to reality and accepting any piddling amount I can get my hands on. "Piddling" is taxi lingo for "Thank God someone got into my cab." It's the financial equivalent of twenty lira. An Italian tourist once explained this to me. Apparently, there are plenty of Italian taxi drivers who live lives of quiet desperation. I might retire to Venice when I turn sixty-five. I am charmed by the idea of living in a city where the streets are paved with water.

The man glanced at his wristwatch and said, "How long will it take to get there?"

"Ten to fifteen minutes," I said as I pulled away from the hotel.

I glanced at the man in my rearview mirror as we headed toward Broadway. He turned and looked out the rear window. He seemed nervous. This made me nervous for reasons that I will not go into, although it may become clear as we putter along. Whenever nervous people climb into my taxi, a pall of gloom settles on my shoulders based on precedent. I try to combat this unpleasant sensation by turning on my AM radio and searching for rock 'n' roll, but as stated earlier, neither of my two radios were functioning that day.

This is what is known as "foreshadowing" in literary circles, which was apt, because I was to discover during our trip to the bookstore that my fare was a writer. A published writer. Or to be more precise, a published novelist. He was going to a reading for his latest book. For those of you who have ridden in my taxi before, I don't suppose I need to explain to you why I was a nervous wreck by the time my cab arrived at the bookstore.

The presence of a published novelist has the same effect on me that red kryptonite has on Superman, since I am what is known in literary circles as an "unpublished novelist," the most dreaded and maligned creature known to the human race, i.e., the moral equivalent of a werewolf—to hear the members of my writers' group describe it anyway.

Yes. You heard me right. After twenty years of struggling to produce novels alone in the sanctity of the many apartments I had lived in from Atlanta to Kansas City to Denver, I had at last decided to join a writers' group. Twenty years of failure had convinced me that the time had come to ask somebody how to write a novel. This is one example of where my grasp of the obvious took more than three hours.

"Death is not a big deal," the man said. "If it were a big deal, it would not come so easily."

I nodded before glancing into my rearview mirror to check whether he was talking to me or himself or the phantom passenger who often sits alongside peculiar customers who climb into my taxi. I nod automatically when passengers speak aloud, but I remain silent just in case they are not talking to me. I don't want them to think I am listening in on their private conversations with nobody, while at the same time letting them know that I am alert to anything they say. I rarely have the slightest idea what they are talking about, but I have found that silence is the best response because the conversations usually work themselves out. Being a taxi driver is very much like being a politician or a diplomat or a doctor in a mental hospital. I was once a patient in a mental hospital, but I cannot go into detail about that dangerous and exciting experience because the security of the western hemisphere may depend on it. If you don't know what I'm talking about, just nod.

"Do you agree?" the man said.

"To tell you the truth, sir, I've never really given it much thought," I said.

This was Stock Answer Number 3 in my arsenal of taxi answers. The first two responses are "Yes" and "No."

"It's worth thinking about," he said, a statement that would confirm for me that he was a writer. Writers tend to think that everything they say is worth thinking about—especially if they have degrees in English.

At this point I gave the gas pedal a little extra toe. I was in no mood to become engaged in a conversation with someone who took themselves more seriously than I took myself.

I drove as far south as Louisiana, then turned east and began heading toward Grant Street where the Brandywine Bookstore was located.

I had been there many times before. As a reader, I know the address of virtually every bookstore in Denver, and as a connoisseur, I know the location of every used bookstore—did I say "connoisseur"? I meant "cheapskate." Brandywine is one of the few used bookstores left in Denver that sells all its paperbacks for a buck each. This was where I purchased my most treasured collector's item, a mint condition first edition paperback copy of *The Catcher in the Rye* with its shiny red cover. The spine is perfectly flat, which is to say it has never been cracked. I have never opened the book. On the day I bought it, I rushed home and put it into a plastic bag and sealed it tight. Not only is the book in mint condition, the air inside the bag is twenty years old. I hope someday to sell the air to research scientists who want to know what the atmosphere of the earth was like before the Green Party cleaned it up.

I parked in front of the store. It might have once been a grocery store because it had large display windows, and I could see a crowd of people inside.

"How much do I owe you?" the man said.

"Seven sixty," I said for the millionth time in my life. When I was a kid I never dreamed I would be speaking Mathematics when I grew up. I was an F student in arithmetic, yet here I was talking like a native, which goes to prove that learning has nothing to do with studying. It has to do with greed, corruption, and wealth. They don't teach that in Catholic schools. They teach practical subjects like Latin, so that when a Roman soldier climbs into a taxi he will be chauffeured by a well-rounded American.
I shut off the meter, making the digits disappear. "But I'll tell you what," I said. "Since you are a novelist, this ride is on me."

He raised his head and looked me full in the face. "I appreciate the gesture but I insist you let me pay," he said, plucking at his billfold. "There was a time in my life when a free taxi ride meant the difference between eating and starving, but those days are long past." He held out a ten-dollar bill and smiled. The creases in his face made him look like Tolkien. "I am going to stick my neck out and assume that you are an unpublished novelist," he said.

This was not the first time an older, wiser person had said this to me.

The last person was an old lady whose nephew lives in San Luis Obispo. He is a best-selling author, but I will not tell you his name because I hate him because he is a best-selling author.

"Consider this a tip," he said.

I took the money. I hate quibbling about money, so if you ever ride in my cab think twice about expecting me to reject your altruism.

"Thank you, sir," I said as I pocketed the "tip."

He began gathering himself together in preparation for climbing out of my taxi, pocketing his billfold, glancing at his watch, hoisting his briefcase, and I knew that it was now or never. This was the chance of a lifetime. I get these frequently but nevertheless I had a published author in my cab, and due to the fact that he could see right through me like everyone else in the world and knew that I was an unpublished novelist, I decided to go ahead and ask.

"Do you have any advice for beginning writers?" I said.

He grabbed hold of the door handle and paused. "Yes," he said. "Put it down on paper or shut up."

He yanked the handle and opened the door.

"What's the name of your novel?" I said before he got away from me.

"*Kremlin Bloodbath*," he said.

After I drove off, I lost track of time and place and eventually found myself cruising around the general area of Parker Road and Leetsdale Drive. For those of you who live in Denver, this should provide you with a good laugh. For those of you who live in New Jersey, this was like waking up in Vermont.

It took guts and grim determination, but I drove until I netted fifty dollars. I headed back to the Rocky Mountain Taxicab Company (RMTC) at 5 p.m. and turned in my vehicle. Otherwise I would have quit for the day as soon as I knew that I was in the presence of the man who had written *Kremlin Bloodbath*.

I had once given that paperback as a Christmas present to my rich brother who lives in San Francisco. It's a long story. Not *Kremlin Bloodbath* but my Christmas trip to Wichita. It involved relatives, Corn Huskers Lotion, and nuns.

I would rather not talk about it.

CHAPTER 2

After work I drove straight to Farb's Gymnasium on East Colfax Avenue. In the old days I would drive to the liquor store next door, but I had replaced binge drinking with binge pumping as a way to forget that I was a loser. It didn't work either, but it was better for my health. I kept my gym bag in the trunk of Blue Boy, my 1954 Plymouth. It made me feel like a yuppie on the go to have my exercise outfit close at hand. A jockstrap, a pair of fingerless gloves, and I was ready for action. This describes my dates when I lived in Philadelphia.

I parked up the block on a side street and walked down to Colfax Avenue, the reputed longest street in America in more ways than one. If you ever take the Number 15 bus, it becomes twice as long. I'm no good at math, so I don't know what twice as long as "longest" is, but I spend most of my time on the Number 15 moving from seat to seat to avoid the droolers, the sneezers, and poets.

There weren't a lot of people in the gym, but there were dozens of steroid geeks. Don't tell them I said that. I hogged one of the bench presses and shoved iron away from my face for about an hour. I had found that bench-pressing calmed me down best whenever anything in the outside world annoyed me. Given the fact that everything annoys me, I expect to look strange within a year. Perhaps "stranger" is a better choice of words.

My chest might match my gut in girth. I will look like Mr. Peanut. I really ought to work on my legs more.

After I left the gym, I walked up the street feeling light-headed. This is known as "the pump." When I used to binge drink to solve problems it was known as the "designated driver dance." I couldn't wait to get home and start drinking beer. When you combine the pump with the designated driver dance, it's like watching a *Gilligan's Island* marathon. The high is so great that it reminds me of streaking. But I try to avoid streaking when I watch *Gilligan's Island*. My landlord caught me doing that once after the neighbors downstairs complained about my footsteps. I don't know why I answered the door naked. I suspect the beer had something to do with it. It rarely doesn't.

I was halfway to my car when I heard the roar of motorcycles coming down the block. Three men on bikes passed at a velocity that irked me. They were violating the speed limit. They didn't even stop at the stop sign. They turned right onto Colfax and disappeared. As a professional taxi driver, I always get annoyed when people on vehicles violate the law. Aren't there enough fun things to do in this world without doing it where kids and elderly people walk? Go ride a roller coaster, thrill seekers. I have never understood speeding, because no matter how fast your car is going you are still sitting motionless on an upholstered seat. I have never understood the theory of relativity, algebra, or Spanish 101, so my opinion may not be valid, but I like to think it will be someday.

I climbed into my car and started the engine. It purred. I loved my Plymouth. I used to own a black 1964 Chevy with red doors. It was torched one night and burned to a cinder, but I can't go into details. The police haven't closed the casebook on it yet. I once drove a taxi that burned to a cinder. I've had my fingers crossed for a long time hoping the police won't make an erroneous connection and haul me in on charges of arson because I swear I did not set either of those fires, even though I was the only person known to have had access to the vehicles at the time they mysteriously burned up.

Let's move on.

I pulled out of the slot and drove toward 14th Avenue. I was halfway up the block when I noticed something out of the corner of my right eye. I have what is called "taxi eyes." Professional taxi drivers notice things that real people do not necessarily notice when they are driving, and this is because our livelihoods depend on seeing everything within our peripheral vision. Cab drivers live in a constant state of fear of losing their licenses, so we unconsciously scan the world "outside the cab" in order to avoid accidents, losing our licenses, and ending up with real jobs. I've had real jobs, and quitting them was no accident.

I saw what appeared to be a body lying between two parked cars.

I slowed and stopped, checked my rearview mirror, and backed up until I was adjacent to a human form lying on the asphalt between the bumpers. It was a man lying facedown. I put the gearshift into park, climbed out, and hurried around the front of my car and peered closely at him. This was not the first time I had done such a thing. You would not believe the number of bodies I have examined in my years as a cab driver, but only one of them was actually dead. This guy was breathing. I could see the rise and fall of his black leather jacket. Something stirred in my mind. I glanced at his feet and saw that he was wearing boots. He was dressed like the bikers who had zipped past me one minute earlier.

"Hey buddy, can you hear me?" I said. I squatted down near his head. I had long ago learned not to say "Are you okay?" to people lying facedown in the street. Victims informed me that it made me sound stupid, the last thing in the world I want to sound.

I eyed the asphalt for blood. I didn't see any.

I reached out and touched him on the shoulder with my right index finger, something I was loath to do. As far as I know, I don't like people touching me when I'm unconscious, so who was I to violate my own psychological tic? He groaned. I withdrew my finger with a sense of relief. Had he not groaned, I would have been forced to touch his shoulder with the palm of my hand. I don't know about you, but touching unconscious strangers makes me feel like a priest.

"Can you hear me?" I said. "Do you have any broken bones? Can you get up?" I recited a litany of possibilities in the hopes of hitting on a phrase that would focus his thoughts. I needed a response because I wanted him to be conscious when I left him lying on the road. I knew I would have to go up to a house and knock on a door and ask the people to call an ambulance, and I didn't want the victim expiring on me before I got back. It was at this precise moment that I finally admitted to myself that I had to stop being so goddamn "precious" and buy myself a cell phone.

I had been avoiding buying a cell phone for years because it seemed like something a yuppie would do. It's like the time in high school when I refused to read *Lord of the Flies* because everybody else was reading it. I wanted to set myself apart from the crowd. I wanted to feel "special." End result? Everyone laughed at me because I didn't know who "Piggy" was. I finally read the book in secret so I could learn who he was. It turned out that I was Piggy.

"Listen buddy," I said, "I have to go find a phone. I have to call the police and an ambulance. I'll be right back."

He raised his chin and grabbed my wrist. "No cops!" he rasped.

I had never heard anybody rasp in my entire life. I tried to draw my arm away from him but he held tight. His mouth was bleeding. He had a black eye.

"Do you want me to take you to a hospital?" I said.

"No doctors," he said, but it was not a rasp, it was a command. "No doctors, no cops."

"What happened?" I said.

"Help me." He raised himself on his elbows, then got up to his knees.

"You shouldn't move," I said. "You might have broken bones."

"Get me on my feet," he said.

I gave up. No doctors, no cops, just me. That would make anybody give up.

"Get me out of here," he said. The rasp was back. I sighed internally. I knew I would have to put him into my Plymouth and drive him somewhere. I thought about taking him to one of the free clinics on East Colfax. The free clinics are different from the hospitals. Informal, ya know? They might take him off my hands without any questions. I wanted to go home and eat. That may sound cold, but I had helped plenty of injured people during my years as a taxi driver, and I had learned that all you can do is procure medical attention as quickly as possible and then get on with your life. My "life" consisted of eating and watching TV, and I was behind schedule.

"I'll put you in the backseat of my car," I said.

He could barely walk. I maneuvered his left arm over my shoulder and walked him the few steps to my Plymouth. I opened the rear door and helped him inside. As he leaned down to crawl inside I noticed that he was clutching his belly with his free hand. Knife wound, I thought. I could see by the interior light that he definitely was a biker. His black leather jacket had the words "The Varmints" emblazoned across the back accompanied by a hand-stitched logo depicting a rodent skull engulfed in flames. Beneath that was a smaller hand-stitched phrase that said "Commerce City Chapter."

I began to get a bad feeling.

After I closed the door, I took a moment to look around for a motorcycle. I thought perhaps he had piled up his bike, maybe he had gotten tossed over the roof of a car and landed on the asphalt in between the bumpers. But I didn't see the wreckage of a bike anywhere. I wondered about the three men on bikes who had passed me earlier. I tried to visualize their jackets. It seemed to me that they were wearing blue-jean vests. Headbands. Engineer boots. Leather wrist braces. Speeding. Reckless driving. Endangering pedestrians. I shook it out. I had to get this guy to a clinic. I could reconstruct the images of those bikers after the police brought me in for interrogation. I had a feeling this was where it was all headed. That may sound unusual, but I had reconstructed images for the police plenty of times for such things as murder, kidnaping, assault and battery, armed robbery, all the things that cabbies like me encounter on a regular basis—although I am the only cabbie I personally know who is like me.

I climbed in and took my seat behind the steering wheel of Rocky Mountain Taxicab Number 1954, which is how I think of my Plymouth every time I have strangers in my backseat. So far I hadn't had any strange women in my backseat, but hope springs eternal.

I started the engine, reached up and lowered the flag on my imaginary meter, then stepped on the gas and drove to the corner of 14th Avenue. I crossed the avenue and went on up to 13th, which is one-way headed west. There is a free clinic not far from the Capitol building, but as I turned right the man in the backseat said, "Where we going, man?" He groaned it. He was sitting up but leaning back against the right-rear corner of the seat.

"A free clinic," I said. I assumed that a guy who rode bikes would not only comprehend but would be amenable to going to a place that offered free medical care. But instead he said, "Naw, hell man, you're going the wrong way."

As a cabbie this made me bristle, and as a hungry man this made me hungrier. I wanted to drop this guy off as fast as possible and get home. Mary Ann was waiting.

"What's the right way?" I said.

"Do you know the dog track?" he said.

I almost laughed. Did I know the dog track? I was the kennel club's best customer for one week ten years ago. I lost a hundred bucks betting on twin quins before a friend named Big Al dragged me out of the gutter, gave me a beer, and set me straight. One hundred bucks may not sound like a lot, but it was one-eighth of my entire fortune.

"Yeah," I said.

"Go there," he said.

A number of responses came to mind, i.e., "Do you live at the dog track?" and "I don't think there are any doctors at the dog track," as well as the obvious "Why do you want to go to the dog track?"

But instead I said, "Listen, I can drop you off at a free clinic or a police station." I don't like taking orders from nonpaying customers.

"No cops, man," he said, then he fell over sideways and lay on the seat groaning.

I quietly reached out and turned off the switch of the imaginary TV set that I always watch on my way home. I saw Mary Ann fading into the sunset. Just before she disappeared, I saw Gilligan being chased around a palm tree by a gorilla. I took a deep breath and sighed, then stopped thinking about the two hamburgers in the sack at my side that I had intended to heat up before watching my real TV back in my apartment. I made the proper attitude adjustment that taxi drivers are especially good at, i.e., I gave up all hope.

"Where exactly do you want to go?" I said.

Since he had forbidden me to take him to a doctor, all I could do was ask for directions and take him wherever he wanted. I had never held an actual conversation with a biker before, but from what little I had gleaned about their personality characteristics from movies, bikers were extremely focused people who lived on the cutting edge of existence and brooked no nonsense from people who did not know an Indian from a Harley. An "Indian" is a model of motorcycle they stopped making years ago. The throttle is on the left handle grip. They say it is a very awkward bike to master, but I can't speak from experience because I have never mastered anything.

"Vasquez," he said.

I got the message. I wheeled right and went back down to 14th Avenue. I turned right again and drove toward Colorado Boulevard. I didn't speak *bikerese* but I knew what he meant. When you've driven a taxi as long as I have, you know that when a man says "dog track" and "Vasquez," he is telling you to go to Vasquez Boulevard, which is the ancient road that runs northeast past the kennel club in Commerce City.

It was going to be a long night.

This thought passed through my mind for many reasons but mostly because I had driven a cab for so long that I recognized the signs even when I wasn't in my cab. The first time I showed up at Rocky Cab in my 1954 Plymouth the garage mechanics came out to look at it, then offered to paint it green and install a two-way radio. Which is to say, they offered to turn it into a taxicab. I was touched. When garage mechanics get creative, you almost feel like you are on the cutting edge of evolution. But I politely declined. If "Blue Boy," as I called my Plymouth, became an authorized taxicab, I would have to go out and buy another used car and, believe me, I went through a hell of a lot of trouble getting my mitts on Blue Boy. This was in conjunction with the burning of my '64 Chevy, the torching of a three-story mansion, veiled death threats, and a desperate run through a graveyard—in other words, a typical cab shift.

CHAPTER 3

I drove with one ear attuned to the backseat. The man kept making painful noises on a low-voltage scale. As long as he was groaning I figured things were okay. I dreaded the moment when the sounds of suffering in the backseat might stop. I tried not to think about how I would explain to the police that I happened to have a dead biker in the backseat of my Plymouth. That may sound paranoid to you, but I had a lot of experience during the past few years trying to explain peculiar situations to the police, and a dead biker would not be considered outside the norm—not by the detectives who knew me. Six detectives at the Denver Police Department know me fairly well. Their jobs range from homicide to missing persons, which seems almost redundant but isn't really. I mean, once you're dead, who knows where the hell you are? But I had gotten so good at explaining peculiar situations to my buddies in blue that I didn't think they would go too far in their criminal investigation before throwing up their hands and saying, "It's only Murph—let's drop it."

We crossed over Interstate 70 at Colorado Boulevard and pulled onto Vasquez. I glanced back and said, "I'm on Vasquez, where do I go from here?"

"Right at Fifty-Eighth, man," he said. He squeezed it out of his throat. I started to feel edgy. A professional taxi driver knows when it's time to feel edgy, and I was right on the mark. I stepped on the gas. There were a lot of junkyards and factories in that part of town. You could go back in time fifty years and that stretch of Vasquez would look the same. I think of Commerce City as "The Land That Time Forgot On Purpose."

I broke the speed limit racing toward 58th. Everybody was breaking the speed limit. Call me a cynic, but I think the cops cut people slack on their way to lose money at the dog track. Maybe the big boys at the kennel club paid the cops to look the other way when it came to excessive speed. Or maybe the cops looked the other way because it sickened them to see people hurrying to lose money. Or maybe—just maybe—the cops didn't feel like ticketing two hundred cars per minute every night.

I made the right turn, then glanced back and said, "We're on Fifty-Eighth. Where do we go from here?"

At this point he reached up with his left hand and grabbed the top of the seatback. He was holding onto his stomach with his right hand. He pulled himself erect and looked out the windows, his head swiveling like a guy surfacing in a lake and looking around for sharks, which is a fairly apt analogy.

He began directing me along backstreets, turn here, turn there, all the time holding onto the seat like a man clinging to the side of a boat. "Down this alley," he finally said.

We were in a cheesy neighborhood. Shotgun housing thrown up after WWII, inexpensive clapboard homes for veterans back in the days when a man could own his own castle for five grand. I would say that the houses in the neighborhood had risen in value to six grand.

"See that garage?" he said.

I didn't have time to answer.

He collapsed onto the backseat and went silent. This sent a chill down my spine. It was an exact duplicate of the chill that went down my spine when I saw the garage. Or more specifically, the bikers standing outside the garage. I did not know it at the time, but I was coming up on the headquarters of the most notorious outlaw biker gang in Commerce City. Perhaps the only outlaw biker gang in Commerce City. Most biker gangs do not officially proclaim themselves to be outlaws, they leave that up to the police.

When they saw the headlights coming, all twenty bikers turned and faced my Plymouth. But they didn't just watch. They started closing ranks and moving toward me at a slow pace like characters out of *Night of the Living Dead*. I could hear the crinkle of beer cans being crushed. I could see foam dripping down fists. These characters knew how to put on a real horror show.

"Show" is exactly what they were doing too because I was approaching their "turf." I'm going to cut down on using quotation marks here because it gets tiresome, and when you describe the world of outlaw bikers you tend to use a lot of quotes because there is quite a bit of esoteric jargon connected with the world of people who build, drive, and maintain "hogs." Excuse me—hogs.

I made a quick calculation. Either stop thirty feet away, or else drive slowly forward in order to make them believe I wasn't afraid. I decided to go with Door Number 2, if for no other reason than fraud is my middle name.

I reached overhead and switched on the interior light so they could see what was inside. I instinctively felt that this was a good move, even though I usually avoid my instincts. I rolled down my window so I could begin explaining the situation as quickly as possible. The herd of Varmints came to a halt, but I kept rolling. I was idling toward them at a rate of less than one mile per hour. I felt I was in a Zone Of Acceptable Speed measured by men who do not like being approached rapidly by strangers.

I knew I would have to stop before I hit any of them with my bumper. This too was instinctive. But I was wrong. The crowd began to part like the Red Sea, and I do mean sea, as I rolled along. They allowed me to go as far as the open garage door before they moved in front of my hood again.

I stopped.

I was now surrounded by leather-clad men leaning down and peering through all my windows. If you've ever seen a Roger Corman movie, then you have seen these men. I feel no need to describe their physical appearance any further. If you have never seen a Roger Corman movie, then I pity you almost as much as I pitied myself when they recognized the body of their brother Varmint lying unconscious in the backseat of my car.

"It's Moochie!"

Both back doors opened. I looked around and saw extended arms reaching toward the man in the backseat. The driver's side door opened and an arm reached in, shot past my face, and grabbed the ignition key. The engine died. The hand withdrew holding the key. My door closed and I sat there listening to Moochie being lifted out of the rear.

I heard things like "Is he breathing?" "Hey, Moochie!" and "Who the hell are you, man?"

This may sound odd, but I wasn't interested in answering the last question. It was directed toward me by a biker with long hair and a beard who was leaning down into my window. I was thinking about the Fourth Amendment and how the Founding Fathers had written it into the Constitution in order to avoid situations like the one I had just experienced, which was an invasion of my private property. I had always thought of the Fourth as applying to cops and soldiers, but until this moment it never occurred to me to wonder if it applied to civilians. I couldn't help but feel that it did. These bikers had trespassed on my car without a warrant. It irritated me to the extent that it almost smothered the adrenaline that shot through me when the hijinks began. The operative word there is "almost."

You may not believe this, but for someone who spends most of his time watching TV, sleeping, and sitting on an upholstered chair, adrenaline plays a large role in my life. I can't tell you how many times it had raised its electric head in the past few years, often when I was accused of murder or kidnaping or some other ridiculous mistake on the part of the police. Ergo, I was able to focus on the constitutional aspects of my current situation even though my nerves were being spindled by hits of adrenaline fired like machine-gun bullets. I felt like I was in the presence of Morlocks—I'm talking the Morlocks of George Pal's *The Time Machine* and not the lame remakes.

"Is he dead?"

That one caught my attention. I looked past the biker who was interrogating me and saw a group of men carrying Moochie into the lighted garage. One of them knocked a clutter of tools off a workbench. They laid him out on the table. While they were busy trying to resuscitate him, my door opened and the bearded biker leaned in. "Climb out of there, man."

I decided to drop the legal nuances of protocol and do what he said. I had come here to deliver the injured man and to explain to whomever needed the information exactly what had happened. "I found him lying in the street up the block from Colfax Avenue," I said after I climbed out.

"Where's his bike?" someone said.

"I don't know."

"Was he in an accident?"

"I don't know."

"What happened to him?"

"I don't know."

I could not help but feel that my answers were falling into the category of "dissatisfying." The bikers who weren't attending to the victim were roaming around my Plymouth sipping beers and eyeing me with suspicion. Three of them were standing directly in front of me looking my body up and down.

"Who the hell are you?" one said.

"How did you find this place?" another said.

I glanced around and saw two men squatting down and examining the front of my car the way insurance adjustors examine cars that have been in accidents. They were squinting and rubbing their thumbs against random scratches.

"I didn't hit him with my car," I said.

One of them glanced at me with a surly expression. But they all had surly expressions. I hadn't been around so many surly expressions since my first sergeant canceled a weekend pass for the entire company. Which first sergeant doesn't really matter. They all canceled the weekend pass after I blew the inspection.

"How did you know to come here?" another man said.

"Moochie told me how to get here."

"How did you know his name was Moochie?"

"I just now heard one of you say 'Moochie.'"

This quieted a few of them down even though the surliness remained in their eyes.

"He's alive!" someone shouted.

Everyone glanced at the garage. Beer cans were tossed. Men wandered into the garage to look at Moochie. The rest looked at me. A quick glance at the group indicated that they all had curled fists. I started to get annoyed because, after all, I had brought their friend back to them. But then I realized that curled fists were probably part of the "persona" of bikers and not to be taken seriously.

I may have to start using quotation marks again.

"What's happening?" a hard voice said.

Everyone glanced toward the garage. A man had stepped through a doorway that led into what I assumed was a backyard. He was not as tall as the rest of the gang, but he carried himself with an attitude that indicated he might be the leader of the pack.

CHAPTER 4

"Moochie went down and this guy knows something about it," a voice said.

There seemed to be a group gestalt here where virtually anybody could pipe up to speak for the mob as a whole.

"What guy?" he said.

The group parted so he could see me. I got a better look at him. He wasn't wearing a black leather jacket. He had on a T-shirt and blue jeans and tennis shoes. He looked like a taxi driver. My heart sank. I hate to meet drivers "outside the cab." It's a psychological thing, like seeing your teacher in a grocery store. I don't know about you, but it always made my skin crawl to think that my teacher was a real person.

He passed through the garage, glancing over at Moochie as he walked up to me. He looked thirty-five years old. He was clean-shaven and his hair was styled, razor-cut, natty. His eyes were as dark as those of a shark. He held a vague resemblance to Al Pacino—but that's also true of Dustin Hoffman and Harvey Lembeck, so you'll have to work with me here.

"My name is Spinelli," he said softly. "Who are you?"

I sensed a subtle surge from the crowd as they leaned in to hear my answer.

"My name is Murph."

He didn't nod or acknowledge my answer in any way. He just said, "What happened here?"

"This dude came driving down the alley—"

A bearded man snarled, but Spinelli glanced at him with a quick snap of the head. That shut him up.

Spinelli looked at me. "What happened?"

I told him that I was driving up a side street off Colfax Avenue when I saw someone lying between two parked cars. I described the ensuing activity. As I spoke he kept staring at me. He didn't blink or turn his head.

I felt like he was peering into the depths of my soul. I was used to that. Cops do it all the time.

After I told him about helping Moochie into my backseat, he said, "What were you doing up at Colfax?"

"I had just been at Farb's Gym," I said. "I was—"

"Do you know Moochie from Farb's?"

"What?"

"Is that where you met Moochie?"

"I've never met Moochie before."

Spinelli looked around at the gang, then looked back at me. "Moochie pumps iron there."

I nodded, then shook my head no. "I've never talked to anybody at Farb's except Vic. I never noticed Moochie."

He gazed at me for a while, then nodded.

"Where's Moochie's bike?"

"I don't kn . . . oh, wait a minute," I said. "I left something out."

I was used to this too. I was always leaving things out when cops interrogated me. It got to be embarrassing, if not incriminating.

"Three guys on bikes rode past me while I was stashing my gym bag in my car trunk."

"What kind of bikes?"

"I don't know," I said. "I didn't get a good look at them. They were speeding."

"Think," he said.

"What?"

"Think. Did one of the bikes have ape-hangers?"

I knew what ape-hangers were. All real Americans are familiar with ape-hangers, even girls.

"Yes," I said.

"The other bikes, what did they look like?"

"Just bikes. They didn't have ape-hangers."

"Think," he said. I saw a change of expression on his face, a slight bulging of the eyes like a hypnotist in an Ed Wood movie trying to see into my mind. I also felt that he was getting exasperated.

"I can't tell you anything more about the bikes, but the men riding them were wearing blue-jean vests."

Curses ranged around the mob. Men began mumbling back and forth.

Spinelli raised his chin and squinted at me for the first time. "Did you see their logo?"

"No."

"Think," he said. "On the back of their jackets, did you see a dragon head?"

"I didn't get a good look. They were speeding. They took me by surprise. I saw them shoot past me. I looked around and saw them turn right onto Colfax without stopping at the stop sign, which pissed me off."

"Why did that piss you off you?"

"Because I drive a taxi for a living and I obey all traffic laws, and you're supposed to stop at stop signs."

A silence settled over the crowd.

"Who do you drive for?" he said.

"Rocky Cab."

"Hubcap!" he barked.

A man moved out of the crowd and stood next to Spinelli.

"This guy drives for Rocky."

The man was clean-shaven, but clean-shaven like a biker who shaves. He nodded but did not otherwise show any emotion. Spinelli spoke: "Hubcap here is a garage mechanic over at Metro Taxi."

Hubcap and I looked at each other. A Rocky driver and a Metro mechanic had virtually nothing in common. Hubcap might as well have been a nuclear physicist, which is to say, I know as much about subatomic particles as I know about carburetors.

"Do you know Earl Cozart?" Hubcap said.

"Foreman of the night crew at the Rocky garage," I replied.

He nodded, then turned away and disappeared into the crowd.

"I want to talk to you," Spinelli said. He tossed me the keys. "Park your car over there." He said it like a man used to giving orders. I obeyed like a man used to taking orders.

I climbed into Blue Boy and drove over to a cleared space beside the garage off the main thoroughfare of the alley. I glanced at the shotgun seat, then climbed out. Spinelli was waiting for me just inside the garage. His body was backlit against the light so I could see only his silhouette. He had an odd stance, as if he was leaning into a hard wind, one knee cocked slightly. Behind him the gang was standing motionless looking at Moochie, who was sitting up on the bench and holding his stomach with both hands. The room was lit soft yellow by the single bulb hanging from the rafters. The scene had the quality of a painting by someone who understood light, color, shadow, and form better than I understood novel writing. "Come with me," Spinelli said.

I followed him through the garage, through the doorway, and into a backyard. We went along a sidewalk to the back porch of a one-story clapboard house.

Spinelli pulled the screen door open and led me into a kitchen where a pretty blonde woman was washing a large pot. The house smelled like chili. Homemade. Mass-produced.

"This is my old lady," Spinelli said.

She smiled at me. She had a wide mouth. Her close-lipped smile took up the bottom half of her entire face. "Annie, this is Murph," Spinelli said.

"Hi, Murph," she chirped.

I don't know if he gave her some kind of secret signal, but Annie suddenly stopped scrubbing the pot, dried her hands on a towel, and exited the kitchen without further word.

Spinelli opened the refrigerator and pulled out two bottled beers. He held one toward me, the glass neck pointed like the barrel of a pistol.

"No thanks, I don't drink and drive," I said.

"Coke?" he said.

"I'm fine."

"Have a seat."

We sat down at the kitchen table. It had a red checkered tablecloth. A single lit candle was stuck in a wine bottle resting in the center of the table. Spinelli leaned forward and blew out the flame.

"That was the Denver Dragons that blew past you tonight," he said. "They jumped Moochie." He took a swig of beer, set it down, crossed his arms, and laid his elbows on the table. "Did they see you?"

"I don't think so," I said. "My trunk lid was up when they drove past. I doubt if they could have seen me."

"That's good," he said. "That's good."

He took another swig of beer and set the bottle down. "I'd like you to do me a favor," he said.

"What's that?"

"I want you to tell me everything that happened tonight starting with the moment you saw the bikers go past you."

I recounted it all. He watched me like a hawk, or a cop, or a bird dog—take your pick. He cocked his head slightly as he listened, and he never blinked. I noticed that the pupils of his eyes were only a shade darker than the irises. For some reason this gave me the creeps. I had to consciously force myself not to look away from his piercing gaze as I spoke.

When I did look away, I looked toward the ceiling. This was in conjunction with his mandate to "think," which he said often. He was like a schoolteacher admonishing me to concentrate hard on a boring arithmetic problem. But is there any other kind?

When I finished, he looked down at his beer, picked it up, and took a swig. He set it down.

"Were you followed here?" he said.

This surprised me. I didn't have an answer, except "I don't know."

He nodded. He looked me up and down. He did this frequently. I had the feeling he was "sizing me up." Most people who size me up do it discreetly, such as salesmen in stereo shops. But this guy was "up front" with his rude behavior.

"So you never noticed Moochie before at the gym?" he said.

"No."

"Did you ever see any other bikers hanging around the gym?"

"No."

"You never heard of the Denver Dragons?"

"No. I never heard of The Varmints either."

A flicker of the eyes, like someone who couldn't believe he had never been heard of before. I wondered if he felt slighted. But he didn't say anything about it.

"Can I ask you something?" I said.

He nodded.

"Are you the leader of The Varmints?"

He nodded again, then said, "Thanks for bringing Moochie here. That was a righteous act. You didn't have to do it."

"He needed medical attention," I said. "I thought maybe he was stabbed."

"Don't worry about it. We got it covered. Doc is taking care of him."

I almost asked who "Doc" was, then changed my mind. I started to get a funny feeling. I got this same feeling one time when I accidentally walked into an EM club on an army base in Kentucky. The place was filled with Green Berets. Not musical Green Berets but Vietnam veteran Green Berets. They made it clear to me by the looks in their eyes that I had wandered into the wrong publicly funded watering hole. I was not a part of—nor welcome in—their world. I turned around and marched back out of the club. Call me a coward. I'm used to it.

"Moochie got kicked in the ribs," Spinelli said.

How he knew this I did not know. Maybe someone ran into the house and told him as soon as we arrived. Or maybe this was a group of telepathic bikers. I suddenly got the urge to go home, fire up my word processor, and begin applying for rejection slips.

"I got another favor to ask you," he said.

"What's that?"

"Forget all this. Don't mention it to anybody. After you leave here tonight, it's like it never happened."

I was flabbergasted. I had long ago perfected the art of treating things as if they had never happened. I got excited. I wanted to tell him he could count on me. But instead I said, "It's forgotten."

"Thanks, Murph."

"You're welcome."

"Let's go," he said. He stood up from the table.

"I have a problem," I said.

He slowly sat back down. All expression left his face the way it does when people assume I am going to borrow money from them. "What's the problem?"

"My hamburger has disappeared."

"How's that?"

"When I got into my Plymouth to park it by your garage, I looked at the shotgun seat and noticed that my sack of food was gone. It had two hamburgers in it."

He slowly closed his eyes, then opened them.

"Let's go," he said.

We got up. I followed him out to the garage.

We stepped through the doorway into the yellow light where everybody was standing around looking at Moochie seated on the edge of the bench. A guy with his sleeves rolled up was injecting him with a syringe. I assumed this was Doc. I looked away. I did not ever want to have to identify him, even though he was slightly balding, had a Screaming Eagle tattooed on his left hand, was wearing spectacles, and sported a well-groomed mustache. I caught only a glimpse of him, but I have "taxi eyes" so my glimpses are fairly all-encompassing if the lighting is right.

"Who stole this man's burgers?"

Everybody froze.

I heard the subtle crackle of paper.

Spinelli stormed across the room and grabbed a man by the front of his jacket. A Burger King sack dropped to the floor behind him. Spinelli stared at him for five seconds, then the man bowed his head and pulled out his billfold. He removed a five-dollar bill and handed it to Spinelli.

"I oughta make you eat that paper sack, Mutha," Spinelli said. "This dude brought Moochie here."

He turned and crossed the room and handed me the money. "Sorry, man. You'll have to buy a new meal. Mutha ate your hamburgers."

"Thanks," I said, keeping it as short as possible.

Spinelli turned and looked at his gang. "This man's name is Murph. He's good people."

He looked back at me.

"Time for you to get out of here."

CHAPTER 5

I'll admit it. Coming in contact with a gang of outlaw bikers prompted me to review my life and change it as quickly as possible. I do this every time I come in contact with any organization. The army comes to mind. Now that I had become "friends" with a biker who worked out at Farb's, I knew I would have to quit going to Farb's. I had visions of Moochie asking me to be his lifting partner, to spot him as he did four-hundred-pound bench presses. His life would once again be in my hands. This was completely beyond the pale.

I sat in my apartment that night with the TV turned off, which was beyond the pale in its own way, and listened to the sound of thunder outside. It was raining hard. The thunder sounded like motorcycles. The patter of rain sounded like blood dripping onto the asphalt. I thought about Moochie lying in the gutter, stomped by a rival biker gang. What if Moochie came to like me so much that he decided to recruit me to his gang? I would have to learn how to ride a motorcycle. I would have to learn how to participate in gang fights. Perhaps I would be required to own a zip gun, and to wield a bicycle chain like a lasso. What if I showed up late for a rumble? Would there be some sort of penalty? A fine? Perhaps The Varmints had a demerit system. Maybe they would make me do push-ups like the sergeants did when I showed up late for formations. Spinelli reminded me of sergeants. Lots of sergeants, as well as a few officers. And worst of all, if I became a renegade outlaw, when would I find time to watch *Gilligan*?

No, the prospect of being pulled into their world was too intimidating. I would either have to give up weight lifting altogether, or else find a new gym for my workouts. But where would I find a place as rustic as Farb's? It was unique in Denver. It was the cheapest gym in town. That was one of the things that had drawn me to Farb's when I decided to tighten up the ol' abs before it was too late.

My decision to stop weight lifting was ironic since it was the first time I ever gave up something that was good for me. I gave up cigarettes a long time ago. I still write novels though, which is not good for me. And believe me, pal, I've given up writing plenty of times. The first time I gave up writing occurred after the first time I received a rejection slip. I was shocked that there existed someone in New York City who was not impressed with me. I was already spending my first million on the day I received a letter that started off with the word "Sorry . . ." I didn't read the rest of the letter. I know when I'm not wanted. I threw the rejection slip into the trash along with the manuscript and swore off writing forever. I celebrated by lighting a cigarette, popping a brewski, and turning on the TV. I don't know what happened, but when I woke up in the morning I found sheets of typing paper scattered all over the living room with notes for a novel titled "Draculina." Apparently, I had gotten drunk and broken my vow. That is how most of my vows break. The rest get broken through forgetfulness. I eventually wrote *Draculina*, but I did it with a sense of shame, like I do everything. It didn't help. The book was rejected. It was about a stewardess who becomes a vampire. Can you imagine what it would be like to travel on an airplane with a bloodsucking stewardess? A transatlantic flight would be a real white-knuckler.

I seem to have gotten off the subject here.

I did not go to Farb's Gym on the following Monday evening. I normally worked out three days a week, which coincided with my taxi-driving days: Mon-Wed-Fri. I had gotten into the Mon-Wed-Fri habit in college. I never went to school on Tue-Thu. Tue-Thu was my "day" off. I never did homework, had sex, or drank on Tue-Thu. Nothing has changed. If I ever go for a master's degree in English I'll be psychologically, physically, and sexually ready to do nothing. Who knows? This might be the real reason I drove a taxi only on Mon-Wed-Fri for fourteen years. Maybe I was subconsciously preparing to go back to school, get a teaching certificate, find a real job, and give up writing. This is how all my college buddies succeeded in giving up writing. There seems to be some mysterious connection between money and writing. As soon as you get money, you stop writing, which is why I live in fear of the day I will become a millionaire. Think of all the songs in me that won't be sung. Bummer.

I admit it. After work I drove past Farb's Gym just to see if there were any motorcycles parked out front. Deep down inside I wanted to do some bench presses, but I was afraid Moochie might be there, and I simply did not want to get sucked into the strange and violent world of outlaw motorcycle gangs. This was ironic because on the following Tuesday morning I did something that sucked me into the strange and violent world of outlaw motorcycle gangs. Two, to be exact. The Varmints and the Denver Dragons. Let me explain. This might take a while. Perhaps sixty thousand words. But I want to demonstrate in precise detail just how badly I can screw up when I kick off the traces, pull out all the stops, and try to do someone a favor.

I woke up Tuesday morning feeling "edgy." I attributed this to the fact that I had not gone to the gym the previous evening. My muscles were whining for exercise. By the time I had shaved, showered, and eaten breakfast, they were bawling for exercise. My muscles are like spoiled children. I have to discipline them. I have to deny them. Whenever they wanted to bench-press four hundred pounds at the gym I told them no! And how did they react? "All the other pecs get to press four hundred pounds, why can't we?" The logic of children is both charming and exasperating. It's similar to the logic of adults. "What if all the other pecs wanted to jump off a bridge . . . ?" I said. I never finished that sentence. I smugly let them finish it in their minds, like an artistic writer who doesn't provide pat endings to short stories because there are no pat endings in real life, not counting WWII. But I could see it in my muscles' eyes. They were humiliated by my brilliant logic. My pecs slouched off to their bedrooms and pouted. Normally I do not tolerate the sulking and self-pity of pectoral muscles, but I wanted to teach them a lesson. There will be no bench-pressing four-hundred-pound barbells as long as I am the boss of this carcass. So you can just stay in your T-shirts and don't come out until you're ready to say you're sorry.

That may sound cruel, but I do not approve of bodybuilders who let their muscles run around like wild animals. I always say, Spare the rod and spoil the bulk—as if there weren't enough muscles in this country hanging around street corners chewing steroids, intimidating pedestrians, and listening to motivational tapes. And don't even get me started on our lenient court system.

I seem to have gotten off the subject again. I do that as often as possible. It's better than confronting reality, and the memory of the events that took place on what I now refer to as "Black Tuesday" usually sends me lurching violently to the nearest liquor store, so I want to keep my mind clear. I want to reproduce with absolute honesty and clarity the sequence of events that led to some of the most frightening moments of my life. Later on, when you and I have come to the end of this bloodcurdling ride, I will get back to my regular lying. This will include making up things that never really happened, bragging about heroics that never took place, and disparaging everybody who doesn't genuflect to my greatness. But I assure you that every word of my bone-chilling tale is practically true. You can take dat to da bank, as Baretta used to say. I've always wondered why Robert Blake, a child star raised in La La Land, talked like a poyson from New Joisey.

I arrived at the Rocky Mountain Taxicab Company at five minutes to seven that Tuesday morning in good spirits. This was so abnormal that I began to worry. What was wrong with me? Why could I not stop smiling affably at everyone I encountered? How could I possibly have paid the man in the cage my seventy-dollar taxi lease without hurling sarcastic remarks like so many mortars aimed at Dien Bien Phu?

The man in the cage is named Rollo. He and I get along about as well as most people. Yet there I was, grinning at him and taking my key and trip sheet and sauntering out the door like a man holding the world by the tail. For one moment I feared I might leap up and click my heels. What the hell was wrong with me? My unfettered joy had the quality of a bad omen. This forced me to do what I always do when dark clouds begin forming on the horizon: I ignored them, got into my cab, and drove off. This tactic never worked, but if I wasted my time trying to make anything work I wouldn't have time to read paperbacks in front of the Brown Palace.

A cab driver always expects a lucrative trip to the airport when he parks at a hotel cabstand, so when a passenger comes out of the hotel, climbs into your cab, and says "Convention Center," it is like a knife in your heart. Not a big knife though, but a little knife, like one of those three-inch Swiss Army knives. Small but effective. It draws just enough blood to remind you that you ought to be taking calls off the radio instead of sitting in front of a hotel playing Russian roulette with the revolving door. The fare paid me four bucks for a two-dollar trip. I decided not to return to the hotel. In a rare state of personal admonishment, I began taking calls off the radio.

I will not bore you with the details, but during the next ninety minutes

I picked up forty dollars rushing around Capitol Hill taking one call after another. It almost killed me. Jumping contiguous bells is a method of profit-taking that is referred to in cabbie jargon as "working hard." I have never cared much for jargon, and when it comes to profit-taking I am completely out of my element, so I am always surprised when I find my T-shirt pocket bulging with fives and tens. Working hard is such an easy way to make lots of money that I sometimes fear the gods are setting me up for a big fall. I hate it when the gods toy with my shirts. I can never shake the feeling that I must be doing something wrong. Who the hell makes lots of money in this world? The whole concept of rolling in dough leaves a sour taste in my mouth. But on that day I just went with the flow. What else can you do when the gods are stuffing five-dollar bills up your kazoo?

Then came The Call.

I get a lot of those. Around twelve a year on average. They sometimes leave me bloodied but unbowed. This is good because I simply can't afford to be bowed. I have to keep on driving in order to make the money to buy the food that gives me the energy to keep on driving to make the money to buy the food, etc. It's a regular Möbius nightmare. Just think what the world would be like if we didn't have to eat food. I suspect that the majority of the human race wouldn't do diddly-squat. This is ironic because that is my ultimate goal in life. Instead of taxi driving I really ought to devote my time to figuring out a way to stop eating. But into each life a little rain must fall.

"One twenty-three, pickup."

I lifted the microphone off the dashboard, pretended to be Vic Damone crooning in Vegas, punched the button, and said, "One twenty-three."

"You've got a personal, Murph."

"I didn't set up any personals," I snarled.

"This is a woman named Maureen who requested your service. I told her I would pass the word along to you."

"What's the address?" I said.

"It's in Commerce City," he said. He told me the address. I frowned like a baffled lounge singer. You see a lot of those in Vegas. Mostly Elvis imitators.

"Okay, I'll take it," I said.

I had no idea who the woman was. I did not recognize the address. But

I was intrigued by the idea that a woman had personally requested my service. I bet you are too. Why would any woman request anything from me? And just what, precisely, was her definition of "service"? This was the intriguing part. The odds were good that she wanted a taxi ride, but there was a 2 percent chance that she wanted something else. I had learned this from experience. In Vegas you have a 2 percent chance of beating the house at blackjack if you play your cards right. When I am in Vegas I spend most of my time crossing my fingers and whispering impromptu prayers. This works about as often as it doesn't. Some people call it "breaking even." I really ought to try playing my cards right just to see if it really works. It sounds like an old wives' tale to me, but my friend Big Al always plays his cards right in Vegas, and he comes home rolling in dough. He is one of the most irritating people I have ever borrowed money from.

I hung up the microphone and aimed my taxi for Commerce City. There is a biker gang in Commerce City, as you well know, but I had no intention of making a detour past their headquarters just to give those little rascals a hound-dog howdy. I had business to attend to. A woman wanted me. This is what I love about the English language. You can pretend that what you are saying is true, even when it is true. Lawyers know what I'm talking about. So do chronic liars.

I made my way to Colorado Boulevard, headed north, then got off at the Vasquez Boulevard exit. This took me on the same route that I had taken when I brought Moochie to the headquarters of The Varmints, except that I made a left turn on 52nd Avenue and drove toward a residential district that had remained relatively unchanged since the early twentieth century. I don't know who named Commerce City but he certainly was an optimist. Maybe he believed in the magic of language, as I do. There are a lot of factories and refineries and junkyards in Commerce City. It makes me think of New Joisey, even though I have never been to the East Coast. But I have seen a lot of Joe Pesci movies.

I pulled up in front of a small wood-frame house. It reminded me of a dump where I once lived when I was in Kansas City. That's a long story that involves getting run out of town by a pack of angry parents on Halloween. I won't bore you with the details save to say that the message the parents howled at me with shaking fists had to do with the fact that children cannot eat paperbacks.

I shut off the engine and prepared for the long walk up to the concrete porch to knock politely on the front door. No honking. The idea of honking at a paying customer leaves me cold, yet many cabbies do it as if they are big shots impatient to get going and can't be bothered with tardy fares. Get your ass out here! seems to be their message. I hate those bastards. They ruin it for the rest of us impatient big shots. But I didn't have to worry, I barely had my seatbelt unbuckled when the front door opened and a beautiful woman with long, dishwater-blonde hair stepped out onto the porch lugging a large leather purse. She was wearing boots, tight faded blue jeans, and a blue-jean jacket covered with colorful hand-stitched patterns. She was sporting sunglasses. She seemed to be in an awful hurry to lock the door and get down to my cab. This pleased me to no end. You cannot imagine the willpower it takes for me to resist pounding on the horn with an angry fist. I am a secret bastard.

She walked with a slight bow, as if the contents of her purse was heavy. She hurried up to the back door, opened it, and slipped in. She seated herself comfortably, dragged hair out of her eyes with her fingertips, and smiled.

"You're Murph, right?" she said. She had a slightly ragged, sexy voice. I have encountered a lot of women with this raggedy voice, as if the woman cannot quite get her throat cleared. It charms the hell out of me. It makes me think thoughts. But let's move on.

"Yes," I said. "Are you Maureen?"

She paused a moment before replying, then she nodded, which technically isn't a reply but you know what I mean.

"Where are you headed?" I said.

She dug into her purse and fished around, then pulled out a scrap of paper and handed it to me. I took it and squinted at the printing, which was like that of a child who had failed penmanship. I could barely read it. It looked like my own handwriting. In my youth I had been the shame of the Palmer Method. When my Maw opened my very first report card and saw that bright red angry-nun F in the penmanship column, she busted out laughing. I remained mute and took notes. I had expected a whipping. My Maw's definition of "whipping" was to make me eat ALL of my vegetables. "Sure, and you are your father's son," she said, handing back the report card. I had to take her word for it.

"3609?" I said, although I did not say it in numbers. I'm not sure that numbers really qualify as words, but I use them anyway when I write. I'm too lazy to type "three six zero nine." Why bother? The Rocky Mountain Taxicab Company doesn't grade my prose, and me ol' Dad died nine years ago.

"That's right," she said.

The address was in Five Points. I have noted in my travels that a lot of cities have districts that are referred to as "Five Points." That is where five streets intersect at the same spot. In Denver, Five Points is the heart of the black district. As with Globeville, another district of old Denver, real estate developers have left Five Points alone. They had never "clear-cut" the structures of Five Points the way they did with Larimer Street back in the 1970s, thus destroying some of the most beautiful examples of nineteenth-century architecture west of the Mississippi River. If you ever want to know what Denver looked like in 1901, take a drive through Five Points. The architecture will blow your socks off.

"All right," I said, putting Rocky Mountain Taxicab Number 123 into gear and driving away from the little white wooden house with the weed-filled yard and the 1956 Ford up on blocks beside the cracked two-track concrete driveway and a rusted tricycle lying on its side next to a hose coiled below a faucet that was slowly leaking water at the corner of the house, making a permanent mud puddle. This, too, is a legacy of old Denver.

I wheeled around and made my way back in the direction I had come. We were not very far from Five Points, but then Denver is not so big that you are very far away from anything at any time. The suburbs are another story, but this is true of all cities, especially Los Angeles. For those of you who have never been to LA, the actual city itself consists of four blocks near East 7th Street and Gladys Avenue. The suburbs consist of the entire west coast. Let's move on because I have a couple of lousy memories associated with Los Angeles—but who doesn't?

I glanced into the rearview mirror as I headed toward Vasquez Boulevard. The woman had removed her sunglasses and was rubbing at her eyes with thumb and forefinger. She looked tired. I thought about striking up a conversation but I usually leave that futile task up to the fare. If a customer wants to talk, I go with the flow. If a customer seems to want to be left alone, I obey the body language. When a customer is a beautiful woman in tight blue jeans, I am torn. Should I pretend that our conversation will evolve into a manic love affair, or should I accept the fact that it will lead where all of my conversations with beautiful women go? My apartment. Alone. With a can of beer and the TV tuned to Mary Ann. If you don't know who Mary Ann is, stick around.

"How's your day been going?" I said, reaching into my sack of smooth lines.

Her head jerked up and she squinted at the rearview mirror, then quickly slipped her glasses back on.

She remained motionless for a few moments, which gave me the creeps. Had I inadvertently insulted her? You would not believe the number of times and the number of women I have angered by simply reminding them of my existence.

"You don't remember me do you?" she said.

Oh Christ. Now what do I say? Women can be mighty touchy about their own existence. I quickly accepted the fact that this conversation was blown sky-high the moment I said "how's." I shook my head no and began the slow descent into Female Hell.

"I probably should remember you, but I get so many customers in my taxi that I kind of lose track of faces," I said.

She touched the rim of her glasses, pressing them closer to her face, then smiled. "I'm not a former customer," she said. "But I know you."

Yep.

Female Hell.

I took a deep breath and exhaled. Before I finished emptying my lungs, I made a list of all the jobs I wished I was doing instead of cab driving. I could not think of a single one except millionaire novelist. But I don't think that really qualifies as a "job." Some people call it "Fantasy Island."

"Where do you know me from?" I said.

"I was there the night you brought Moochie to the clubhouse," she said.

The smiled melted from my face and dripped onto my lap. I looked down and noted that my fly was zipped closed. Remind me to tell you some hilarious "open-fly" stories from my youth. If you ply me with enough scotch, I will tell you the mortifying versions.

I glanced up at the rearview mirror. Maureen had removed her sunglasses again and was looking right at me with her chin raised as if to demonstrate her face.

"I'm sorry but I don't recognize you," I said.

"I'm not surprised," she said. "We didn't come face-to-face. I was at the back of the crowd in the garage drinking a beer with my boyfriend."

The girlfriend of an outlaw biker was sitting in my backseat and here I was thinking about my fly. I really do need some kind of goddamned therapy.

"Oh, I see," I said, nodding and hoping that my feeble reply would put an end to this gut-wrenching journey through Lady Hades.

She kept smiling. She put her glasses back on and looked out the side window. We were turning onto Vasquez. From there I intended to drive to York Street and make my way down to Randolph Avenue. The avenue was named after Daddy, a legendary pit master who served the best ribs and threw the best Thanksgiving parties in Denver out of his BBQ shack in Five Points. He was originally from the Ozarks, one of my favorite words. His motto was, "God loves you, and so does Daddy."

We turned left onto York Street and headed south. My eyes kept flickering to the mirror. Now that I knew she was dating a biker I was reluctant to turn on the ol' charm, but at the same time I did not want to snub her. If I didn't talk to her, she might tell her boyfriend. This is how my mind works when it isn't working very well. I tried to keep my mind off the fact that I couldn't keep my mind off Maureen. She was extremely attractive. I wished she would leave her sunglasses off. I liked looking at all of her face, not just the lower half—but that's me, Mister Mona Lisa.

As we came up on Randolph Avenue I switched on my right blinker.

"Why are you turning?" she said.

I froze. How does a cabbie answer a question like that? Logically? Or is there some less direct way of explaining why one is turning right at the right place to turn right? I was thrown for a loop. All the signs were converging.

"This is Thirty-Sixth," I said, modulating the desperation in my voice.

"Keep going, keep going," she said, removing her glasses and looking at the houses and then the storefronts as they appeared. Five Points has the kinds of small business blocks that checker Denver: grocery stores, bars, music stores, laundromats, places where the people leasing the redbrick buildings thrive and die on the vine. I kept going. Pretty soon we were at the intersection of York and 26th Avenue.

"This is ten blocks south of the address you showed me on the slip of paper," I said, trying to jog her memory. I was beginning to feel uneasy.

"I just want to see something," she said as we rolled past a barbershop.

Black men were lounging around outside the shop. As we cruised by, Maureen twisted around in her seat and looked back. "Turn right at Twenty-Fifth Avenue."

I turned right at the next intersection.

"Circle on back and drive past that barbershop again," she said.

Something inside me twitched. It was the cabbie reaction to not arriving at a destination. By telling me to circle back it meant that the cab ride was now open-ended. We were supposed to be at 3609, and we were nowhere near it and I was driving in circles. This meant I was losing money. Cabbies do not make money driving people around town, they make money getting people in and out of their taxis as quickly as possible. Each time a customer gets into my taxi I automatically earn $1.50 on the meter. If I get fifteen customers a day, I get paid $22.50 for doing nothing. As you might guess, this is a government rule. It was designed, I presume, to keep idiots from climbing in and out of taxis without going anywhere. It's a type of "fail-safe" device. If someone gets in and goes one-quarter of a mile, they owe me $1.60 no questions asked or I call the cops. I like the rule—free money and armed police swarming my cab, handcuffing freeloaders. It makes me feel like the star of a TV show about a cab driver who has exciting adventures. My co-star is a wisecracking dame named Mary Ann. Our relationship is platonic, but the audience knows that one day I'm going to sweep Mary Ann . . . I'm sorry . . . I seem to have gotten off the track again. I do that a lot, especially when I'm irritated by reality.

"Turn right here," Maureen said, interrupting my trip to *Gilligan's Island*.

I swung around and made my way over to York and drove again past the barbershop.

"Slow down," she said.

I glanced back. Maureen was eyeing each of the men lounging around outside the barbershop. I knew enough to keep my mouth shut. Whatever she was up to was none of my business. I fell easily into the role of Outside Observer, like Timothy Bottoms in *The Last Picture Show* where he is watching a high school football game. Last year he was a sports hero and this year he is just a schmuck holding the ten-yard marker for his old coach. He is wistful. That's me. Standing on the sidelines watching life pass me by—and I wouldn't have it any other way.

Maureen sat back and put her sunglasses on. "Take me up to Thirty-

Sixth," she said.

I turned right at the next intersection and drove toward what I hoped would be the end of the ride. In some ways, it was.

"Slow down, slow down, slow down," she said. A tall black man was walking along the sidewalk. I slowed. Maureen pressed her face to the window and studied him, then sat back and said, "Keep going."

I started to get a bad feeling, but I ignored it. Opening my eyes in the morning gives me a bad feeling. If I paid attention to every bad feeling that comes down the pike, I would be too distracted to watch TV, eat, or watch more TV.

I made a few right and left turns and eventually we were at 3609 on a street in the heart of Five Points. It was the address of an old house, not well kept up. Dead lawn. Rusted wheelbarrow lying upside down near the porch. Hose covered with dirt. "Stop here, I'll be right back," Maureen said.

I bit my tongue and let her get out of my taxi without paying. I usually demand a small stipend, like five bucks, if a customer wants to leave my taxi before the full fare has been paid. This often involves liquor stores and pawnshops.

Maureen hurried up to the door and knocked, then waited. I won't describe her wait in detail. You've waited before.

She waited and waited, but nobody answered the door. Then she did something I was afraid she was going to do. She began making a circuit of the house, peering through windows and gently tapping on the glass.

I glanced at my watch, noted that this ride had lasted twenty minutes so far, then I closed my eyes, sat back against the seat, and whispered, "Jaysus."

The right-rear door opened, and I opened my eyes and sat up. Maureen was climbing in. She settled on the seat, removed her sunglasses, wiped at her eyes, and mumbled something to herself.

I made a quick decision not to ask her to repeat what she had said. She looked none too pleased about something. She looked like she was going to cry.

"Nobody home?" I said, trying to both distance myself from the situation yet find out what the problem was simultaneously.

She shook her head no, put on her glasses, and said, "I want to go back to that barbershop on York Street," she said.

At this point I did what I had done many times in my taxi-driving career. I groaned inwardly and set about making an attitude adjustment. I knew that this ride would last a long time and that I had to accept the fact that it might be another hour before a new customer climbed into my backseat. The situation had all the earmarks of a long trip, and to a certain extent I was legally required to make that trip and go wherever she told me to go. As long as she paid me the meter fare, and as long as she didn't get violent in the backseat or break any laws, I was obligated to be her slave. Being the slave of a beautiful blonde was not the worst-case scenario I had ever been involved in, but her boyfriend was an outlaw biker and I was getting bored and hungry and blah blah blah, so I put the taxi into gear and set into motion what would turn out to be one of the longest rides of my life.

CHAPTER 6

We drove past the barbershop. Maureen was now turned on her seat facing west, touching the sill of the window and peering at the men in front of the shop. I noted that half of the men were different from the men I had seen when we first drove by.

"Slow down," she said.

I couldn't have gone much slower than I was already going. Men glanced at the taxi with blank faces. I looked in the rearview mirror and—based on the flickering of her eyes—I sensed that Maureen was looking at the face of each man, trying to find one that she recognized.

We passed on by.

Maureen twisted around and sat back, pulled her glasses off and rubbed at her face, then put them back on. "I know where to go," she said, as if I was no longer a taxi driver, a stranger, a cipher, but a friend who was helping her to find another friend. "Go over to Daddy's place."

I knew the address. I was relieved. I stepped on the gas and made my way there, but after I pulled up outside and Maureen got out, she did not go inside, she entered a phone booth at the edge of the property and dropped a coin in the slot. I had thought she was going in to buy some ribs. Maybe she would even buy some for me. But instead she spent one minute on the line, then hung up and hurried out to the taxi. I peered at the doorway wondering if Daddy was in there. I had seen him a few times, mostly on Thanksgiving when he threw what the local papers called a "shindig," which is about as hip as Denver journalists ever talk.

"Go up to the corner and take a right," Maureen said. She seemed revitalized. I followed her directions. She guided me further north until we came to a residential neighborhood thick with green shade trees. A group of men were lounging around beside an old green Dodge in front of a house that had a cyclone fence encircling the front yard. Two pit bulls were chained to a tree. The dogs had water bowls, chew bones, and slack in the chains. The men watched us as we drove toward them.

"Park here," Maureen said.

I pulled over and parked and looked at the men. They looked at me. Maureen leaned into the front seat and said, "Here, keep this for me will you? I'll be right back." It was a wad of twenty-dollar bills. She slipped out of the cab and walked toward the men.

I gave the wad a quick flip and calculated that she had given me three hundred dollars. I leaned forward and slid the money beneath the seat, then watched as Maureen walked up to the group of men and started talking to them. One of the men smiled and held out his hand. Maureen took his hand, and together they entered the yard, walked up to the front porch, and disappeared through the doorway.

"Shit," I mumbled to myself. I knew what was going on by now. I had been hoping it wasn't going on, but I had been around the block enough times to know a drug deal when I saw one coming down. I had been around the block in Atlanta, Pittsburgh, Cincinnati, Philadelphia, Kansas City, San Francisco, and Los Angeles. It's a mighty big block. It runs through every city in America. I felt bad. The three hundred dollars was vibrating beneath the seat like a wad of kryptonite. Maureen had given it to me so that she would not get ripped off. Whatever she was buying inside that house, she had taken just enough money to pay for it and no more. I hated this. I hated being part of a drug deal, even if I was only an innocent outside observer. I hated to see money being thrown away on something as pointless as drugs when it could be spent on more pointless things, like giant-screen TVs. But — "Que sera, sera," as Doris Day shrieked in *The Man Who Knew Too Much*. People will live their lives the way they want to live them, in spite of my efforts to manipulate every individual I come in contact with. It's a terrible thing to be a compulsive busybody in a free country. You feel so darn powerless.

Maureen came out of the house followed by a man I did not recognize from the Dodge group. He opened my right-rear door and Maureen climbed inside. He followed.

"This is Murph," Maureen said, pointing at me. "He's good people."

I truly wished she had not said that, but the damage had been done.

"Hi, Murph," the man said.

"This is Paul," Maureen said.

I twisted around and looked at him. He was hatless, wearing a Hawaiian shirt, khaki chinos, black loafers. A slight smiled was affixed to his face. "Hi, Paul," I said. "Where are we going?"

"Just up the road," he said. "Just up the road."

I silently put 123 into gear and pulled out onto the street and began driving west at twenty miles an hour. I glanced at the meter. The fare was coming up on twelve dollars and there was no end in sight. "Turn here," Paul said, pointing the way.

I turned right and drove north. I glanced into the rearview mirror for one reason only that I am going to confess here. I was looking to see if my taxi was being followed by a cop car. That's all I want to say on that subject.

Paul gave me directions. We turned left, right, left, until we came to the middle of a block. "Pull over here, Murph," Paul said.

I pulled over and parked.

"Gimme a few minutes," he said. "I'll be right back."

He climbed out, shut the door, and walked further up the street to the intersection. He turned right and walked out of sight.

I looked at Maureen in the rearview mirror. Her eyes were fixed on the spot in the distance where Paul had disappeared.

"How long do we have to wait?" I said.

She looked at my eyes in the mirror and said, "Just a couple minutes. He said he would be right back."

"Where is he going?" I said, but she didn't answer that one, and I didn't ask again. I didn't ask if she wanted her three hundred dollars back. I didn't ask anything. I felt myself metaphorically receding into the middle distance, becoming as much of a neutral observer to this situation as was legally possible. I knew that if the DEA swarmed my taxi I would have nothing to worry about. I would be cleared of any involvement rather quickly. I was just an innocent taxi driver, an oblivious schmuck who was being used by other people to get what they wanted—which is the actual job description of a taxi driver.

On top of that, I was personally acquainted with a half dozen detectives down at DPD who would be willing to act as character witnesses if I was hauled into police headquarters draped in chains. Some of them would be disgusted and some of them would get a real kick out of seeing me cuffed, but all of them would eventually help me to get a reprieve. I doubt if they could live with themselves if they allowed me to be sentenced to a nickel in Cañon City. They all believed that I was as pure as the driven snow. What a pack of fools.

The silence in the back of my taxi became unnerving. I couldn't take it anymore. "How is Moochie doing?" I said.

Maureen looked at me in the mirror, then smirked. "He's okay. The gang is going to help him get his bike back this weekend."

"Where is his bike?" I said without one iota of interest.

"The Denver Dragons ripped it off."

I nodded and decided not to pursue this line of disinterest. No way I wanted to get involved with an event that might result in violence. For instance, I haven't done any Christmas shopping in a long time.

Paul suddenly came around the corner striding fast, one hand jammed into his right-front pocket. Without being told, I instinctively started the engine and began coasting forward. Paul yanked open the right-rear door and slipped in. "Let's go, let's go, turn left up ahead."

I followed his orders.

When we got around the corner, I saw Paul turn and look out the rear window. He turned back and looked at Maureen and started to pull something out of his pocket, then he looked at me.

"Are you writing a book?" he said quietly.

I almost busted out laughing. I knew what he was implying: "Mind your own business." But in fact I was writing a book. Part of it was lying in a steamer trunk in my apartment on Capitol Hill. The irony of his question was so charming that I almost tried to explain it to Paul, but I had found that absolutely nobody on the planet earth has any interest in the fact that someone they know is writing a book. Nobody gives a damn. Nobody cares. It is only writers who think that other people care that they are desperately trying to make it in the literary world. Writers think that everyone is in awe of them, when in fact people are in awe only of unpublished taxi drivers. I'm not bragging—I'm just stating a scientific fact.

"Where to now?" I said, desperate to get this ride over with.

I knew that some kind of drug deal had gone down, and I wanted to get back to reading paperbacks in front of hotels. The seamy side of life comes with the territory of cab driving, but I try to avoid it as much as possible. This includes not working nights and not working the bars, but occasionally a cabbie finds himself enmeshed in a situation he would rather not be in, and the only solution is to just ride it out. It's like life itself.

"Just keep driving," Paul said.

Maybe the ride wasn't coming to an end. I began backtracking in my mind trying to figure out how I had gotten into this situation so I could avoid it in the future, when I heard Paul whispering something. Maureen replied, "No, no, I don't think so," a little bit louder than Paul was talking.

"Come on now, I gave you what you wanted, how about giving me what I want?"

I looked in the rearview mirror and saw that Paul had placed his arm along the top of the backseat. He wasn't touching Maureen but his arm was close to her neck.

"No, I can't do that," she said, leaning forward a bit and grinning at him, and in that moment I knew I was getting involved in an entirely new situation.

"Why not?"

"I have to get home to my kid," Maureen said. She still had the grin on her face, was still being affable, but I recognized it for what it was. She was trying to be nice, trying to keep things on an even keel, trying to maintain a sense of humor in what was becoming an untenable situation. I recognized the words and the body language. I myself had been in dozens of untenable situations just that week.

"Aw, come on."

"I can't," Maureen said. "My kid is sick. I really have to get home."

I took a deep breath and sighed. I knew what was coming. At some point within the next few minutes I would have to act mature. Just the thought of comporting myself like a grownup irritated me so much that I looked around and said, "Do you want me to take you back home right now, Maureen, or do you have somewhere else to go?"

They both looked at me.

"I want to go home," Maureen said.

Paul raised his chin and peered at me.

"Where can I drop you off, Paul?" I said.

Paul kept his chin raised and studied me for a moment. I plucked the microphone from the dashboard, pressed the button, and said, "One twenty-three, time check."

"Eleven seventeen, Murph," the dispatcher replied.

I glanced back at Paul but kept the mike an inch away from my mouth. "Where do you want off?" I said.

Paul looked at my eyes, looked at the microphone, looked at my two-way radio, then raised his arm and moved it away from Maureen.

"Right here . . . Murph," he said.

I pulled over to the curb and stopped. Paul gave me an enigmatic smile, then opened the door and climbed out. He ducked his head back in and looked at Maureen. "Maybe I'll see you next week, huh?"

Maureen grinned at him. "Yeah."

Paul shut the door and started walking east. I put the car into gear and pulled out, drove past Paul, and turned north at the next intersection.

We didn't say anything for a while. It was a funny thing about the unpalatable incident that had just occurred. Every character in the scenario knew exactly what was going on, and yet no one made any direct reference to it. I could feel the tension inside my taxi evaporating like morning fog. I decided it was best not to say anything at all, just head on back to Commerce City, drop Maureen off, take the money she would pay me, drive back to the Denver city limits, and never again take a personal call as long as I lived.

Like any good woodsman or cabbie, I took note of where I was and began plotting my return trip to Maureen's house. I was in the middle of Five Points and needed to get back to Vasquez Boulevard, which meant I had to work my way north and east and . . .

What's that smell?

I stopped plotting and looked at the dials on my dashboard. For one moment I thought my taxi was on fire. This had happened to me before—ironically, on my way to Vasquez Boulevard—and that taxi ultimately burned up. This created a psychological tic that hopefully will never go away. It is sort of like my own DEW system. That's Distant Early Warning system for those of you who have never seen paranoid movies produced in the early '60s about attacks by the Russkies. The DEW system warns of nuclear warheads as well as burning taxis. It must have cost trillions of dollars during the Cold War; however, my personal DEW system was free, if you don't add the cost of a taxi turned into a charcoal briquette.

After I had ascertained that smoke was not boiling out of my hood like Vesuvius vapor, I glanced at the rearview mirror and did not see Maureen. This fit in so perfectly with everything that had ever happened in my lifetime that I was not the least bit taken aback. Maureen had disappeared and a strange odor was wafting through my cab. Doubtless it was spontaneous combustion. Dickens writes about this in *Bleak House*. I had to assume that Maureen had disintegrated in a puff of smoke, which meant I wasn't going to get paid.

These thoughts went through my mind rather quickly the way most of my thoughts do, like little kids running through a cemetery at night. My thoughts don't like being inside my brain, which is fine with me, but it didn't resolve the fact that somebody owed me close to sixteen dollars.

I heard a cough and saw Maureen rise from below the seatback. To be perfectly honest with you, I'd had the feeling she was still inside my taxi, I just didn't know where. She was holding what I might as well admit I recognized as a small glass bong. She was smoking whatever she had bought. I did not recognize the odor. I do recognize the odor of marijuana and not just because I once made the mistake of letting two hippie girls smoke pot in my taxi. It's a long story.

Maureen began coughing.

Let me finish up quickly: I recognize the odor of pot because I used to go to a thing called the Underground Cinema 12 where hippies and myself watched short, avant-garde films. That's not the only reason I recognize the odor of pot, but I've probably said too much already. Let's move on.

Maureen sat back against the seat. She was not wearing her sunglasses. Her eyelids were clamped shut and she was breathing fast and heavy.

"Are you okay?" I said.

She opened her eyes and nodded.

The fact that she had not asked me if it was okay to light up told me something about drug users that I already knew: the rules do not apply to them. I recognized the phenomenon. I practically invented it.

Maureen leaned forward so that she was below the windows, spun the wheel on a lighter, and lit the stuff in the bong. She took another hit, then sat back and held her breath. I had genuinely mixed feelings about this scenario, but I have that feeling about everything so I just let it ride. If she wanted to smoke a drug in my cab, I would simply take her home and try not to think about it. Part of being a cab driver is denying the reality of terrible things, and I had gotten good at it. Plus, I'm Irish/Catholic, so I have a head start on the rest of humanity.

If I was a praying man I would have been pleased by what happened next, because Maureen began disassembling her bong and putting everything away in her leather purse. My unspoken prayer had been answered. She was finished "toking" or whatever smokers of hard drugs call it. Maybe they just call it "smoking." I don't know. I've been out of the loop so long that I've lost touch with jive lingo. Maureen zipped her blue-jean jacket up to the neck and looked out the side window with a complacent smile on her face. She acted as if I wasn't even there. I wished the rest of humanity would do that. It would make my life less interesting.

"What's wrong with your child?" I said.

Maureen slowly turned her head and looked at me. "What?"

"You told Paul that your kid was sick. Does he have a cold or something?"

A smile cracked her entire face. She reached up and began rubbing her face with her palms. "No," she said. "I don't have a kid. I just told Paul that so he would lay off."

I nodded.

"He seemed to know you," I said.

"He doesn't know me that well," she said. "I see him once in a while. We're not friends. I just know him."

I breathed a deep sigh of relief and almost choked on the heavy atmosphere of drug vapors. I rolled the window down. I was relieved because I was afraid I was dealing with a "latchkey" situation, which automatically made me feel bad. Now I felt better. Whatever Maureen was doing to herself, at least she wasn't doing it to anybody else, especially a child. I immediately edited that scenario from the movie that runs perpetually through my mind and concentrated on getting back to Commerce City.

By the time we were on Vasquez Boulevard Maureen was leaning against the door on the right-rear side of the cab. Her eyes were closed and she was humming to herself. It sounded like "Amazing Grace." I know a few people who dislike that song intensely. I don't understand why anybody wouldn't like a song that mentions "a wretch like me," but each to his own I always say.

CHAPTER 7

I pulled up in front of Maureen's house and hit the meter. The fare came to $17.80. I glanced at my watch. The entire ride had taken more than an hour and a half, which was exceptionally long for a taxi ride. Believe it or not, I once had the supervisor of the sewer system of Cologne, Germany, in my taxicab. He and his wife were touring America. They wanted me to drive them around Denver to see the sights. It took three hours. During the ride I learned more about the sewers of Cologne than most cabbies ought to know. One interesting fact I learned was that Cologne was properly pronounced "koln!" and not "coe lone!" He was a pretty big guy, so I took him at his word.

I know what you're thinking: Denver has three hours' worth of sights?

"Seventeen eighty," I said to Maureen.

She leaned forward and handed me a twenty and a five. "Keep the change, Murph," she said. She must have had the money at the ready, which indicated to me that she was an experienced taxi passenger. No time wasted digging through a purse or a billfold. Hand over the money, say "Keep the change," and climb out of the cab. That's the way I like it—a word to the wise if you ever ride with me. And please remember to enunciate when you say "Keep the change." Poor diction can lead to embarrassing misunderstandings.

"Thanks," I said.

Maureen yanked the handle and climbed out. She shut the door and began walking up to the porch, but her walk was unsteady. I debated whether to get out and escort her to the house to make certain she got inside okay. It was one of those small dilemmas that confront cab drivers occasionally, especially if you work the bars on weekends. Not everybody who gets out of a taxi at 2 a.m. on a Saturday night can walk. A learned thing.

But she made it to the front door. I felt bad. I knew she was bombed, or stewed, or whatever smokers get when they opt for hard drugs over tobacco. But she was a biker, her boyfriend was a biker, and I could not help but feel that she had enough experience with this type of situation to know how to handle it. I say that only because of my own history of drug usage. If the military had based promotions on the ability to function effectively in a combat situation while under the influence of beer, I might have achieved the rank of general by the time I was discharged—or "drummed out," as I like to think of the ceremonial termination of my triumphal army career.

I stayed long enough to watch Maureen enter her house. I filled out my trip sheet during the wait. This had been a round trip that came to $17.80. I wrote "RT" in a blank space, then filled out Maureen's address, and the 3906 address. When I was finished I went back to work. I put 123 into gear and drove off. I made it almost to Vasquez Boulevard when suddenly I slammed on the brakes. Sweet Jaysus! Three hundred dollars! I reached down and felt around under the seat and came up with the wad of bills that I had forgotten because I had more intense things on my mind, like the possibility that a woman was smoking crack in my backseat. I knew nothing about crack except that it was epidemic in America among addicts, so the thought did occur to me that she was smoking the stuff. But I had put it in the back of my mind where I keep all the baggage that I cannot do anything about. As an Irish/Catholic, the one thing I knew for a fact was that you cannot control another person's addiction. The road from Dublin to Denver is littered with the bones of do-gooders who tried to stop their boy-os from tippling. I don't mean to make light of a terrible truth, but what can you do when all else fails?

"Damn," I hissed.

I glanced around for cops, then whipped a louie right there on the avenue. I wondered if Maureen was already frantically calling RMTC demanding to know where the hell Murph the taxi driver was. That put me in mind of a time when I shortchanged a blind man who didn't waste a second phoning RMTC. It's an embarrassing story that sounds so phony that I'm not going to plead innocent by reason of insanity, my excuse for everything.

I sped back to Maureen's house, pulled up at the curb, and hopped out of my cab with the long green in my hand where she could see it if she peeked out the window with the phone in her ear. I walked up to the porch fast, something I had never done in my entire taxi career. I knocked on the door before looking for a doorbell. That's how anxious I was about the prospect of being accused of stealing three hundred dollars. In the past I had been falsely accused of such things as stealing one hundred thousand dollars, kidnaping three girls, and murdering two men, so my angst had a precedent.

I raised the three hundred like a bouquet of flowers so it would be the first thing she would see. She had obviously forgotten it in her drugged state, and maybe this would serve as a pleasant reminder.

I waited for thirty seconds, then looked again for a doorbell but didn't see one. It was an old house, probably built in the 1920s before dinging became widespread. I knocked again and waited. No answer.

As an experienced professional taxicab driver, I knew exactly what to do. There were a number of tactics, but I decided to go with the most simpleminded. I reached down and twisted the doorknob. I pushed the door open an inch and simultaneously said, "Yoo-hoo!" Please don't tell anybody I actually said that. Only the most unhip dork would say *yoo-hoo* to another human being, but I did not want Maureen to be afraid. I wanted her to think Howard Sprague opened her door.

"Maureen? This is Murph. You forgot your change."

I said that to be funny. Incorporating humor can sometimes take the edge off housebreaking.

No reply.

I pushed the door open a little further and peered into the darkness. Maybe she was in the bathroom. I decided to wait a few minutes, and while I was thinking this my pupils dilated to the point where I saw a pair of legs stretched out on the floor of the living room.

The world stopped turning. I pushed the door all the way open so sunlight filled the space, allowing me to see clearly that Maureen was lying faceup on the floor. Her eyes were wide open and a bit of drool was spilling from the side of her mouth.

"Maureen!" I shouted as I rushed into the room. "Oh Jesus!" I kept saying "Maureen" and "Oh Jesus" throughout the entire ordeal, so I am not going to repeat it here. Just think of it as background noise. Terrible, dreadful, gut-wrenching background noise.

I dropped to my knees and leaned down to her face. Her lips were blue. Stop the bleeding. Protect the wound. Treat for shock. These were the rules of aiding a wounded buddy in combat that I had been taught in the army. This wasn't the first time but it was the worst time those words had come back to me like a superhero traveling through a time warp. I yanked two cushions off the couch, lifted her legs and shoved the cushions underneath, elevating her feet above her head, grabbed her nose, squeezed it, cleared her mouth, and began blowing oxygen into her lungs. Due to the fact that the next thirty minutes reminded me of the first time I delivered a baby, I will have to piece the series of events together like a jigsaw puzzle. I looked around for a telephone but didn't see one. I ran to my taxi and grabbed the microphone. "Code twenty-two, this is Murph. I need an ambulance." The RMTC system shut down and the radio opened up for me and me alone.

"What's the address, Murph?" the dispatcher said.

I gave him the address, then told him I was going back into the house. I dropped the mike and ran to the house. Maureen's eyes were closed. This seemed like a good thing. It was the first sign of physical activity she had demonstrated. I couldn't tell if her lips had lost any of the deep blue hue.

I could hear the background noise as if someone next to me was chanting. I began artificial respiration again. I didn't know what else to do. Stop the bleeding. Protect the wound. Treat for shock. There was no bleeding that I could see. There was no wound to protect because her brain had taken the hit and it was hidden inside her skull. I could only treat for shock. I grabbed her hand and felt for a pulse. It felt like a mitten plucked from a winter sidewalk. I got no pulse. I unzipped her jacket and opened her collar, slammed my ear to her chest, and listened for a heartbeat. I heard nothing. I began breathing into her lungs again. In and out—in and out—to the accompanying Gregorian chant.

That was how the medics found me. Kneeling over the inert form of Maureen, blowing in and out and mumbling incantations. I remember the palm of a hand touching my shoulder. Then I was standing in a dim corner of the living room watching the professionals at work. Tubes and masks and white coats and a stretcher and yelling and motion and uniformed policemen walking in and out of Maureen's house. I followed the dolly as it rolled down the sidewalk toward the open doors of an ambulance. The doors closed and the ambulance sped away, its siren screaming like a banshee flying across the rooftops of Commerce City.

Then everything grew quiet.

CHAPTER 8

"One twenty-three, pick up. One twenty-three, pick up."

I heard this dim chant and could not interpret it because I was thinking of Maureen lying on the stretcher. At least her face had not been covered up. This told me that she was not dead. That is the difference between life and death: a foot of white cotton fabric.

"One twenty-three, pick up. One twenty-three, pick up."

It's strange to hear the English language and not know what is being said. The dispatcher was calling and I was standing ten feet from my cab, looking at the empty road where Maureen had disappeared. I didn't understand the language but I recognized the tinny, harsh sound of a two-way radio. My two-way radio. My lifeline to RMTC, which can mean the difference between life and death when a cab driver is alone in a deadly situation. Usually a robbery. Sometimes an actual shooting. Many years ago a wounded taxi driver was found by the police with his microphone gripped in his fist. He had been shot in the back of the head. He could not talk, so he held onto the microphone and pushed the button over and over with his thumb until the police found his taxi parked in an alley.

"One twenty-three," I said into the microphone.

"Murph, what's the status on the emergency?"

"It's over. You can cancel the lockdown. I'll be coming back to the motor in a little while," to confess my sins.

"Check. Mr. Hogan has been apprised of the situation. He wants you to come up to his office as soon as you get here."

I wasn't able to reply. My Adam's apple got in the way. I hung up the microphone and got out of the cab and walked up to the house, where a policeman in a dark blue uniform was waiting for me.

I knew it was all over for me. I knew that Mr. Hogan would be firing me for the last time. I had lost count of how many times I had been fired from the Rocky Mountain Taxicab Company. In the past it had always been due to ridiculous misunderstandings, and I was always allowed to return to work. But those days were gone. Even after I got out of prison I would not be able to get a taxi license. Not in Denver anyway. I don't know how the cab companies in other cities feel about accidental manslaughter, but I imagine the rules are the same everywhere. They usually are, starting with the Ten Commandments and working their way down to leash laws. I could have used a few leash laws in my life, but it was too late now.

The cop was big, taller than me and with a barrel chest about the size of my beer belly. He reminded me of a character actor whose name I could not remember because I was not able to think very clearly at the moment, but he was the cop who rousted Rambo.

"Sir, I'm Officer Grogan," he said, nodding and giving up a small smile. "What's your name?"

"Brendan Murphy."

"I need to ask you a few questions, Mr. Murphy. First off, can you tell me how you happened to be here when this girl overdosed?"

"She was a passenger in my taxi," I said, a sentence that was completely meaningless in this context. In order to give it the surface appearance of meaning, I added, "I had just dropped her off here."

He nodded and wrote something in a notebook. Then he looked up at me. "Can I see your trip sheet?"

"I'll go get it," I said.

"And bring your Herdic too," he said.

I walked back to the taxi feeling as if I was about to produce Exhibits A and B at my trial. I picked up the sheet off the seat, pulled my Herdic license out of my plastic briefcase, and carried them back to the house. I handed the incriminating evidence to Officer Grogan. He signaled me to come inside. He studied my trip sheet as I entered the living room. I deliberately avoided stepping on the spot in the middle of the living room where Maureen had been lying.

"This girl's trip, it's the last one at the bottom, correct?" he said.

"That's correct, sir."

He read Maureen's address out loud, then the 3906 address. At that point I realized I had juxtaposed the numbers. This did not come as a surprise to me. Numbers and I had been archenemies since the day I entered grade school. I had written 3906 instead of 3609.

"Uh . . ." I said, the most common undefined word in the English language. It is said hundreds of millions of times a day in America, mostly by people who are slightly confused, yet it does not appear in the dictionary. I would imagine that there are equivalents to "uh" in all foreign languages and they too are probably not defined. Maybe the human race is ashamed of its confusion. I would define it as follows: "Uh: Ÿh —a verbal form of hesitation used by people who are not quite certain what they want to say but are compelled to make a random noise in order to let the listener know that something of potential significance is going to be said in the immediate future."

"So this was a round trip?" Grogan said before I could expound any further on my "uh."

"Yes sir," I said. "I took her—" I started to say "to a house in Five Points," but I stopped suddenly. A voice inside my head told me to stop, and it wasn't Joanne Woodward. For the first time in my life I realized a lawyer lived inside my head along with all the other entities crowding my brain.

It would take too long to explain what I mean by that, so let me just say that I realized I should not say anything until a real lawyer was standing by my side. In turn, he would probably advise me never to say anything to anyone unless I was on the witness stand under oath. I decided to take his advice and cut this short.

"— on a round trip."

"To this address at 3906?" Grogan said.

There are times in a man's life when he wishes he was living in his mother's house in Wichita. I'm sure it's happened to you. I leaned in and looked at the trip sheet just to make certain that I had written down the wrong address. Then I nodded, confirming that I had made another classic blunder in a long line of Academy Award winners. Was it my fault that he interpreted the nod to mean I had taken Maureen to the 3906 address? I'll let you be the judge. Later on, you can be my executioner. A good time will be had by all.

"That's in Five Points, correct?" he said.

I nodded.

He proceeded to write something down in his notebook. I wished I could see what he was writing. I wished I had the power to point my finger and make things disappear through spontaneous combustion, starting with that notebook and ending with the entire past week. This made me think of The Varmints and Spinelli. I then realized that I had a lot more to worry about than a ten-spot in Supermax. There was a boyfriend in an outlaw biker gang whose girlfriend was lying on a bed in the ICU because she had made the mistake of asking me for a ride in my big green taxi. Suddenly the idea of standing next to a cop the size of King Kong had a certain appeal. I glanced at the .38 caliber service revolver attached to his web belt. This made me feel even better. Right at that moment the illusion of safety was more vivid and intense than the illusion that I would someday be a published novelist.

"Here you go," Grogan said. He held out my trip sheet and license.

I took them and said, "Do you want me to make out a written statement here, or should I come with you down to the police station?"

"No need for that," he said. "If we need a written statement we'll get in touch with you."

I started to open my mouth, but Perry, as I began to think of the lawyer inside my head, kicked me in the ass. I waited for the policeman to haul out the handcuffs. You would not believe the number of times I have waited for such a thing, unless you know me well.

Officer Grogan flipped his notebook closed and looked at me. "All right, you can go back to work, Mr. Murphy. We're going to seal off the house."

Again I had the urge to speak, but Perry began slapping me left and right. If it wasn't for the fact that I was not paying him to defend me, I would have fired him. As I stood there recovering from the various shocks of the day, I wondered if suing a lawyer would be considered frivolous by a judge.

I walked outside and floated down to my cab, insofar as I could not feel my feet. I am not talking exhilaration or relief. I don't know what I'm talking about. But that's how I felt. Light-headed and floating, and expecting the sting of hot lead to rip into my spine. I walked around the front of my cab and stood for a moment looking at the house. The front door was open and two cops were walking around in the living room. I felt as if I had come to a moral nexus, that my future and my fate hinged on whatever action I would take within the next five seconds. Fortunately, I feel this way every time I wake up, so I knew how to handle it. I climbed into my taxi, started the engine, adjusted the rearview mirror, and lifted the mike off the dash.

"One twenty-three," I said.

"One twenty-three," the dispatcher replied.

"R-two. Ten minutes." This meant I was going to return to the taxi company within the next ten minutes. I love those quickie codes. R-2. R-5. R-9. Sometimes I wish everybody spoke the language of R. It would certainly cover up my deficiencies as a prose stylist.

I drove away from Maureen's house following in the wake of the ambulance. Perhaps "wake" is a poor choice of words. After I drove up Vasquez Boulevard, I turned right and took the old 48th Avenue road that runs beneath Interstate 70. I always feel wistful driving along 48th. Before the interstate was built, this part of town was nothing but wide-open spaces. Now it is eerie, the massive gray concrete columns supporting the roadbed dwindling in a geometric perspective like the bleak and sterile setting of a science fiction movie. At any moment, I expected Winston Smith to stagger out from behind a column, flag me down, and beg me to take him to 1984.

By the time I got back to the motor, I was Winston Smith. In the past, whenever I was faced with metaphorical annihilation I would simply walk off the job and move to another state. But now I was trapped. I had helped a woman buy hard drugs, and for all I knew she was dead, if not dying. There was no place to go except Hogan's office. In the past, whenever I told a foreman to take this job and shove it he did not send out federal agents to track me down. He did not send an outlaw biker gang to run me to ground. He just laughed and told me to put my broom in the supply closet and hit the road. There is a dull predictability to warehouse supervisors.

I parked 123 in the dirt lot behind the headquarters building, gathered up all my taxi accouterment for what I knew was the last time in my life, and climbed out. I stood for a moment looking across the green sea of RMTC cabs parked in the lot. They blended nicely with the foothills of the Rocky Mountains, which rose in the western distance. I wanted to remember this moment. By the same token, I will never forget the moment I left Cincinnati for good—but who can?

I walked into the on-call room and decided to go see Hogan before handing in my key and trip sheet for the last time. As a consequence, I walked through the room without looking at Rollo, who was seated behind the thick plexiglass window of the cage. I did this because I did not want to look at Rollo twice in the same afternoon—but who can?

Rollo didn't say anything as I walked by without acknowledging his presence. I knew that he knew that I had screwed up and that Hogan wanted to see me. The cage man knows everything that goes on at RMTC. The cage man is like the red-hot core of a nuclear reactor. If you mess with the cage man, you can get burned. He holds the power of life and death over your billfold. If you commit the slightest infraction of the rules, he can deny you a key to a taxi. He can send you skulking in disgrace to the lowest limbo of squaresville.

Okay, I'll admit it. I got that last line from a Donald Duck comic book. But I like it so much that I say it as often as possible, which isn't often. It basically depends on how many times per month I annoy Rollo. In the comic book, Donald Duck teams up with Gyro Gearloose to pull a cruel prank on Huey, Louie, and Dewey—except the prank backfires. It's a real knee-slapper. I often think about Donald Duck when I get into trouble. I have never really understood Donald Duck. He constantly torments his nephews. He has the personality characteristics of a bipolar manic-depressive. If Gyro Gearloose was a real friend, he would invent a device that would secretly put Donald Duck on a permanent regimen of lithium. But I digress.

I climbed the staircase to Hogan's office and knocked on the door.

"Yuh," Hogan responded with his signature grunt.

I opened the door and stepped inside for the last time. I never thought I would miss being reamed out by my taxi supervisor, but I consoled myself with the knowledge that the guards at Supermax would endeavor to make me feel at home. Their simulated reamings would be the wind under my stripes.

Hogan's eyes lit up. "Murph!" he said with such delight in his voice that I could not help but feel that he was pulling a prank as cruel as anything conceived of by D. Duck.

He stood up and moved around from behind his desk and held out his hand for a shake. I quickly scanned his palm for a joy buzzer, then I took it and shook it. To my knowledge, this was only the fifth time he and I had ever touched. I won't go into the details of the previous four touchings, save to say that they involved greetings and salutations.

"Good news, Murph. I just got word from the hospital. That woman who overdosed is going to live. She has recovered, she is conscious, and she is talking."

As I stood there shaking hands with Hogan, I wondered what part of the word "good" he didn't understand. The fact that Maureen was "talking" struck me as "bad." But then Hogan had no way of knowing this. Only I had a way of knowing. I and Maureen. I was experiencing mixed feelings about the fact that she was talking, and the fact that she had recovered, and the fact that her boyfriend was probably racing to the hospital at that very moment on his hog. Based on every Roger Corman movie I had ever seen, I doubted if he was obeying the speed limit.

"That is good news, Mr. Hogan," I said with as much courtesy and humility as I could muster. I sensed that he would not feel good about firing me. For some reason he never felt good about firing me. But then he wasn't a warehouse supervisor, he was a taxi supervisor. Taxi supervisors are completely unpredictable, which is why cabbies tread lightly around them.

"It's a damn good thing you were there," he said.

"What?" I said.

"If you hadn't been there she might have died."

"What?"

"The doctor told me that whoever started CPR saved her life."

"What?"

"He told me that forcing oxygen into her lungs and keeping her feet elevated were without a doubt the only two things a person could have done to keep her alive before the ambulance showed up."

I will not bore you with another "what." I lost count of the "whats"—that had happened before and I assumed it would happen again, so what's the point of keeping count? That would be like keeping old love letters, or Putt-Putt golf course free passes, when you know you will never score a hole in one again as long as you live. In my case the hole in one was named Mary Margaret Flaherty, although I never even made it to the first dogleg with her. I lost my balls in the sand trap—but let's move on.

"I just called you in here to warn you about something, Murph," Hogan said, which made so much sense that I returned to a state of reality. I knew what was coming. I just wondered if my taxi supervisor was authorized by the city to handcuff pure evil.

"Do you remember Gordo Klein?" he said.

"Yes I do, Mr. Hogan."

"After he saved that girl from drowning he was given a medal of commendation by the mayor. If things work out the way they normally do, you better buy yourself a suit and make yourself look pretty for the paparazzi."

My bag of "whats" was empty, so I just stood there with my jaw hanging open. A bit of drool began to form at the base of my lower lip, so rather than spit I swallowed it and frowned at Hogan. What in the hell was he talking about? Didn't he know that he was standing in the presence of THE embodiment? What's all this medal jazz?

For those of you who don't read *The Denver Post*, Gordo Klein was a cabbie who was driving around an apartment complex in southeast Denver looking for a fare who had called a taxi. He noticed a little girl floating facedown in the residents' swimming pool. He hopped out of his cab, pulled the girl out of the water, gave her CPR, and saved her life. It was probably the most heartwarming story that ever came out of RMTC, whereas mine was probably the most vile story ever to slouch its way into Colorado.

"Just a heads-up," Hogan said. "I imagine somebody will be getting in touch with you in the next day or two. This story is going to make it to the papers, so brace yourself for your allotted fifteen minutes of fame, my friend."

His eyes were shining when he said this. Taxi supervisors love it when a driver does something that reflects well on the company. On the other hand, they hate it when taxi drivers are involved in bank robberies, kidnapings, and murders, which is why I got fired so often. I suddenly had the urge to tell him the truth. It was such an odd feeling that I didn't trust it. It is true that I had told the truth in the past, but it was never the result of an "urge." It was the result of police interrogations.

"You've still got about six hours left on your lease," Hogan said. "But if you would rather call it a day, I'll write it off and let you drive for free tomorrow."

By now I was tangled in a web coated with sticky chocolate and I did not know which way to futilely struggle. So I did what I had always done in similar situations. I called upon my old army training. I stood perfectly still and did nothing. You would not believe the number of times this tactic saved my life. It works much better than doing something. I would have to say that all the problems I was ever forced to deal with in my lifetime were the result of doing something. It's been my experience that people who do things generally regret them. But that's just a layman's observation.

"Thank you, Mr. Hogan," I said. "Maybe I will knock off for the day. I don't know if I will be driving tomorrow, but . . ."

"The next time you come to work I will make sure that Rollo knows you've got a free lease coming."

Damnit. I didn't want Rollo dragged into this. I never want him to know about anything I do. It makes me feel vulnerable just to know that Rollo knows I exist. God only knows what he plans to do with that information. He and I have been engaged in a colossal battle of the intellects ever since the first day I drove a taxi. Remind me to tell you the upshot of our first legendary "meeting of the minds." The old pros at RMTC who were around fifteen years ago still talk about it when they have run out of other subjects at the taxi stands. It's like listening to veterans of Gettysburg talk about the last days of Pompeii.

"Thank you," I said.

"You've had a rugged day," Hogan said with a smile. "Go on home, kick off your shoes, and watch *Gilligan's Island*."

"I'll do that," I said with a frown. How did he know I was addicted to watching *Gilligan's Island*? I thought that was the best-kept secret of Murph's cabana. Was it possible that Rollo had leaked the information? But how had Rollo found out? He was always the prime suspect when any of my shameful secrets were splashed all over the taxi company.

As I made my way down the staircase to the ground floor, I began to feel like the invisible man. Not the H. G. Wells character but a plastic model I bought when I was a kid. It was a human being made of transparent plastic. You could see the insides, the skeleton, the heart, the lungs, the liver, the kidneys, my God, even my Maw was appalled when I got it assembled and proudly showed it to her. Remind me to tell you the upshot of that event. I have had more than my share of upshots in my life. If I could bottle that stuff I could make a fortune off people who are bored with the D.T.'s.

I entered the on-call room and took a deep breath, walked up to the cage, and set my key and trip sheet on the counter. Rollo was reading a comic book, but he quickly set it aside, which I assumed was out of a sense of shame, but he dispelled that idea when he slid his arms through the small hole cut into the base of the plexiglass window where we cabbies slide things in and out. I thought he was going for my throat. But instead he grabbed my hand and shook it. "Good work, Murph. Hogan tells me you saved a woman's life."

Have you ever touched a cage man?

I'm not even going to bother recounting that experience. It would take an entire library of nonfiction books just to describe the feel of his . . . his . . . . well . . . I suppose "flesh" is the best word.

"Thanks," I said with a lump in my throat.

He let go, thank God, then took my key and trip sheet. "Hogan usually gives a free lease to drivers who save lives, so I expect I'll see you bright and early tomorrow morning," he said with a smile so hideous that he looked like Victor Buono. But he always looks like Victor Buono. If you have ever seen Victor Buono smile, you know the uneasy feeling it evokes in theater audiences.

"Maybe," I said. "I'm not sure when I'm going to drive again."

"I'll keep one twenty-three on ice just for you, Murph," he said.

I nodded and slunk out of the on-call room. On ice? Wasn't that prison terminology? Was he hinting at something? Was he sticking it to me? Was he tormenting me again? Then I realized that I myself kept beer on ice, although not when I was in prison. Technically, I have never actually been in prison. I may be splitting hairs here because I have been hauled down to police headquarters in quite a few cities, but I have never actually heard the clang of a door slamming shut in an iron-bar motel. I have heard door latches click shut in small rooms, but never a clang. I never did know for certain but I sensed that the soft click was a lock. Your guess is as good as two of mine.

I glanced at my wristwatch. I wondered who the genius was who named the wristwatch. It was a little after two. Where had the time gone? I could not even remember what time I had picked up Maureen. But one thing I did know was that I had written it down on the trip sheet that I had given to Rollo. In the past I had forgotten to write down the times of my trips on the sheet, which really annoys homicide detectives, but fortunately I had written this down while I was watching Maureen stagger toward her front door. I was relieved to know that when the DEA finally got around to grilling me, I would not have to fumble and fib my way through an explanation as to why I had not written down the start time and the end time of a drug deal. It was all right there in black and white. For some reason, I began to think of it as "Exhibit C" but I couldn't remember why.

My mind felt cloudy. I know you are not going to believe this but I have never had any trouble thinking. This may be the source of most of my troubles. I think too much. A taxi driver named Big Al has counseled me on this many times. I suppose I should listen to him. My mind usually wanders when Big Al starts lecturing me about the size and effectiveness of my brain. It gets old.

CHAPTER 9

I wandered around the dirt parking lot of RMTC for ten minutes looking for Blue Boy, my 1954 Plymouth. Not only could I not find it, I kept forgetting that I was looking for it. I was thinking about Maureen's face, the cold blue lips that I had touched with my guilty lips, the feeling of horror when she did not respond, and the fact that she was worse off than I was, which is my handy metaphor for death.

I kept telling myself that it wasn't my fault. To my knowledge, I was the only person who ever said that about me. Every time someone dies in my general vicinity I tend to fade from the scene until the excitement blows over.

Habit.

But this time I began telling myself that it was my fault, that I had helped Maureen buy drugs, that I could control another person's addiction, and that she had been lying stone-cold dead on her living room floor because she had made the mistake of bringing me into her life. In turn this made me realize that Moochie had first brought me into her life. In turn this made me think of the Harley-Davidson people. If the Harley motorcycle had not been invented, Moochie's bike would never have been stolen by the Denver Dragons. I was getting way out on the limb of blame shifting here when I realized that Moochie would simply have owned another brand of hog. Perhaps an Indian, one of the coolest motorcycles ever built. It has a left-handed accelerator. I read a book about it once. Very awkward to get used to if you're not a southpaw. If I rode an Indian I would accidentally run every stop sign in town until Fate stopped me. Or a cop.

But I digress.

A horn honked and woke me from my dissembling trance. I nearly dropped my load. I thought Saint Peter was coming for me again. But it was only Jacobsen, who was pulling in to park his cab for the night. He had a grin on his face. My heart sank. I knew that he knew my story. You couldn't fart at RMTC without the dispatcher sending out the word.

Jacobsen climbed out of his taxi, leaned back in, and brought out two cups of joe. He walked up to me and handed over one of the steaming cups.

"Good work, champ," he said. That's all he needed to say. We cabbies often speak a kind of shorthand. No need for excessive verbiage. The nature of taxi driving is the reason. Drivers are always cutting conversations short, so unless we're stranded at a cabstand with no sign of customers, we tend to converse on the run, sometimes at a red light.

"Thanks," I said, smiling as my heart fell from the heights of the Royal Gorge. The coffee was my reward, the Nobel Prize of taxi driving. You know that you have fooled everyone when you receive this honor. I took the symbolic sip. It tasted terrible, but not because it was 7-Eleven joe. 7-Eleven joe can't be beat. It's the force that through the green fuse drives RMTC cabs, as Dylan Thomas may have once said.

Jacobsen grabbed his accouterment and walked away. Conversation over. Everything that could have been said, had been said, except the part about me being a total fraud.

I looked around wondering where I was. There were so many taxis surrounding me that I thought I was at Denver International Airport waiting for the green light that would allow me to drive uphill to the circus tent. Then I wondered what Blue Boy was doing at DIA. I was standing right in front of him. For one moment I was overjoyed. I thought I had recovered my stolen car for the first time in my life. The cops usually find it parked within a mile of my crow's nest. After giving it a test drive, the thieves always leave it parked at the spot where they got disgusted. This had happened approximately one million times with Ol' Betsy, my 1964 Chevy, which burned up one night when I was not minding my own business. But Blue Boy had been stolen only six times since I had bought it from Satan.

I then realized I was not at DIA but in the real world. For those of you who've never been to Denver, the real world consists of four square blocks of property near the northern viaducts. It's full of taxicabs, and that's about as real-world as my life gets. If it wasn't for taxi driving, I wouldn't know any homicide detectives on an uncomfortable basis. I had the feeling that I had once again come to within a hairsbreadth of being grilled by the boys down at homicide, and this time for real.

I went through the difficult process of opening my car door with a cup of hot coffee in my hand, climbed in, and settled behind the steering wheel. I set my cup in a plastic holder that I had purchased at Venice Beach awhile back when I was out in LA not minding my own business. I was a murder suspect at the time, but I won't bore you with the details.

I started the engine and drove out of RMTC. I headed south toward my apartment on Capitol Hill.

Usually when I drive home after a long day of sitting still for twelve hours, I head for a hamburger joint to rejuvenate myself in time for sitting still in front of the television for a minimum of four hours. I need the protein to climb the stairs to my crow's nest. But for some reason I wasn't hungry that day. Maybe it was because I had knocked off early. Maybe I had tricked my body into thinking that I wasn't going home. I've always been suspicious of hunger. I find it odd that human beings get hungry just about suppertime. It is as if something else is going on, and that we are being programmed and controlled by some mysterious force that wants to distract us from what is "really" going on. It's as if the gods want all of us to go into dining rooms and restaurants while they perform mysterious activities outside the building that they do not wish us to see for reasons that must be kept secret. I envision gods with hard hats and pickaxes "doing" things in fields while we make clanking noises on our plates with silverware. When the clanking stops, the gods hurriedly put their tools away and fade from the scene. What it is they are "doing" is not entirely clear to me, but I am certain that my theory is true. Someday somebody is going to get up from the table and go into a kitchen to get a napkin, and will peer out a window and get the shock of their lives. But until that day comes, we must all be content to speculate with wonder just exactly what is "really" going on.

The fact that I wasn't hungry threw a monkey wrench into my "going-home" routine, and I found myself idly driving west on Colfax Avenue. It wasn't until the dome of the Capitol Building came in sight that I realized where I was "really" going.

CHAPTER 10

The face was familiar. Or perhaps "facade" is a better word. In fact—it is the correct word. The facade of Denver General Hospital was quite familiar to me due to a bank robbery, an assault, a manslaughter, etc. I can't really be expected to remember all the reasons I ever ended up driving through the parking lot of Denver's main hospital looking for a parking space—and why would anybody expect me to remember those heinous crimes anyway? None of them actually existed, in spite of the insistence of six or more plainclothes detectives and God knows how many uniformed members of the Denver Police Department. It's true that some bad things had happened, but I was as innocent as a newborn babe.

Until now.

During the past couple years, I had endured so many unpleasant encounters with my conscience that I now decided there was no point in putting off the inevitable. I would go to DGH, try to calculate the depth of my responsibility for this latest catastrophe, then go to DPD and throw myself on the mercy of the Law. In other words, it was a typical Friday afternoon.

I parked my car in a lot across the street from the main entrance, then walked into the building and up to the front desk. None of the receptionists recognized me, which annoyed me as well as pleased me. You would think that as many times as the cops had hauled me into this place I would be somewhat of a medical celebrity, but on the other hand I was not so eager to be in the spotlight since I had virtually murdered a young woman who had recovered only by the grace of God. Who says there is no such thing as bad publicity?

After stating the nature of my mission, a receptionist informed me that a Maureen Spinelli had been admitted for treatment of a drug overdose earlier in the day and that she was still in the ICU and was being monitored. I did not hear the last part of the rundown because I was unconscious.

When I heard the word "Spinelli" something happened inside my brain. Rather than try to give you the technical medical explanation, let me just say that the lights went out in Massachusetts.

Have you ever smelled "smelling salts?" Believe me, they do not smell like salt.

"How do you feel?"

I awoke on a bed-thing, or whatever they call them in the ER. I recognized the ceiling. Same cracked sound-absorbent tile, same peculiar water stain. It was the ceiling I saw on the night I delivered my first baby, but I will not dwell on that.

I decided to dwell on the question the jolly nurse asked me. Nurses drive me crazy. They grin like maniacs while they patch up broken bones. I guess it takes a special kind of person to smile while inhibiting the flow of blood from squirting arteries. I could never be a nurse. The state medical board isn't crazy.

"I feel fine," I lied. I never feel fine. But at this particular moment my lie had an edge that I did not wish to discuss. Maureen Spinelli. Was she the wife of the leader of the outlaw motorcycle gang? And more importantly, how many minutes did I have left to live? When Spinelli found out I had practically killed his wife, he would probably "do" something. I hate it when outlaw bikers do things. If I was an outlaw biker I would never do anything. I would sit in my pad and listen to the Rolling Stones. As a cab driver I sit in my pad and listen to Pachelbel's Symphony in E Major, so I would probably make a pretty good biker if I knew how to operate a hog and had no wish to conform to the uptight rules of the Squares. But this was no time to contemplate career alternatives. I had to get away from the hospital before I actually needed a hospital.

"Where am I?" I said, starting at Square One, my favorite geometric shape.

"You are in the emergency ward at Denver General Hospital," the nurse said in a somber, officious tone of voice. I already knew this of course. I love tricking nurses. But I wanted to make certain of the location of the starting block of my escape from certain death. "You fainted at the reception desk."

"Am I going to be okay?" I said.

"Yes," she said. She did not elaborate. The smugness enraged me but I put a leash on it.

"Will I be able to leave right away?"

"Just as soon as the doctor okays it," she said.

Doctor? I didn't even know hospitals used doctors anymore. Every time I ended up at the hospital as a patient or a visitor, I saw only nurses. I thought doctors were like the Loch Ness Monster. I probably do not need to explain that analogy. Everybody has seen the famous black-and-white movie clip of the doctor swimming in Loch Ness.

Let's cut to the chase. I was released from the hospital a half hour later. They did not chauffeur me to the curb in a wheelchair, which annoyed me, not only because I like to be treated "special" but because it would help me to make my exit from the hospital without Spinelli seeing me. I intended to go from the wheelchair to a Yellow Cab to Wichita in one smooth move. Instead, I had to walk out the front door of DGH and believe me, it was one of the longest walks of my life. Everywhere I looked I saw bikers. Bikers on crutches, bikers in wheelchairs, bikers with stethoscopes dangling below their beards, bikers in nurse uniforms, bikers on stretchers, even bikers seated in taxicabs waiting to kidnap me to Commerce City. Fortunately, I was so used to chronic paranoia that I knew how to handle these hallucinations. I handled them the way I handle all problems. I simply ignored them and walked across the street to my Plymouth. I climbed in and sat behind the steering wheel and stared out the front window at the thousands of bikers flying south for the winter. That seemed like a darn good idea.

Having made it to my car alive, I then did something I rarely do in my car. I started thinking. Sooner or later Mrs. Spinelli would tell her husband how she came to buy drugs, which meant Spinelli would waste no time finding out where I lived. The image of Rollo popped up in my mind, the spineless traitor who would stool on me at the first signs of a sawed-off shotgun. Ergo, I could not decide whether to go home or just drive to Wichita right now. The problem was that most of my cash was at my apartment. I have a bank account for the same reason I have a credit card, to trick people into thinking I'm real. It doesn't work very well because my credit limit is four hundred dollars, and when the police find out, they have a tendency to look at me funny. I found that out on the day of the bank robbery, but again, I digress.

I started the engine and drove out of the parking lot. It was probably best that I make a moving target of myself until I resolved this quandary, if you think of hiding out from a motorcycle gang as a "quandary." It was probably more of a "fix." The odor was unmistakable though. I was in deep.

As I drove east I thought about going to DPD and asking one of my many detective friends what I ought to do. But given the fact that I had knowingly taken part in a drug deal that resulted in near death, I realized I might find myself in a legal quagmire—or "jam," as they say in gangster movies. I continued to drive east, pondering what I now thought of as a "dilemma." I had the entire Denver Police department as well as a gang of outlaw bikers on my trail. "How did that happen?" I asked myself aloud. I realized I had made a terrible mistake. I had no business driving while thinking. Thinking and driving can be dangerous, especially if you are thinking about women, death, or algebra. Instead of thinking, what I should have been doing was talking. This was so obvious that I laughed out loud. It's funny how you sometimes can't see the forest for the trees. The solution was right there in front of me all along. I'm not talking about talking to myself, of course. That had never produced any satisfactory results. I'm talking about talking to another taxi driver, a man named Big Al. He had taught me how to drive a taxi back when I was a newbie. He was my mentor, my friend, my judge, my jury, and my executioner.

He had cured me of gambling on the dogs, and one afternoon he had even tried to teach me how to think, but he abandoned that rather quickly. Too quickly, if you ask me. I didn't know if he was a quitter or a genius, but I did know one thing. I didn't know what to do. The next best thing was to track down Big Al and ask for his advice. If he didn't want to give it to me, then I would pay him for it. That had produced satisfactory results in the past. Big Al seemed to take especial delight in making me pay for my advice, as well as my sins. He went to a Jesuit high school. I went to a nun high school. When it came to penance, nobody could outflog a Jesuit. They even knew how to perform exorcisms. That sounded like my cup of tea.

I made a U-turn and headed for the Brown Palace Hotel.

Already I felt good inside. My friend Big Al is the walking embodiment of common sense. He is the exact opposite of me in so many ways that I won't waste any trees compiling a list. He had pulled my ass out of the fire dozens of times by simply telling me what I already knew. Some people call it "The Truth." I call it "Trial by Humiliation." To be honest, I don't think Big Al has ever told me anything I didn't already know, but I always went to him for advice, or "confirmation," so that I could not be blamed if things worked out okay. By this I mean that when you end up doing something right, people expect you to do things right from then on, and that is a burden I do not wish to bear. I would prefer to do things right once in a while, and since I rarely do anything of importance anyway, it doesn't matter if I do it badly. But I do want to do the important things well, like rescuing people whose lives I have inadvertently put in jeopardy through meddling, not minding my own business, and do-gooding in general, which is why I go out of my way to consult my mobile oracle: Big Al.

Big Al once asked me why I spend so much time meddling in the lives of my fares, and I confessed to him it was because I was bored. He advised me to get a hobby. I replied, "Why should I build birdhouses when I can spend my off-hours destroying people's lives?" He was not amused. To my knowledge, nothing has ever amused Big Al, with the possible exception of existence.

There were four taxis in line at the Brown Palace Hotel. Since I was driving Blue Boy, I could not park at the cabstand. But because my life was in danger, I did not make a big deal out of parking at a meter around the corner from the Brown. Normally I turn such a maneuver into a three-hanky melodrama complete with thunder and lightning, but time was of the essence. I did not see Big Al's cab, so I walked up to the first taxi in line. An RMTC cabbie was sitting in it with his hat pulled down over his eyes. It was Jacobsen.

I knocked on his roof. He lifted his hat and looked at me, and almost lowered his hat again. This is how most people respond to my presence, but he kept the brim raised and waited for me to do whatever the hell I intended to do. I cannot say for certain that I saw fear in his eyes but I did see his hand almost yank the brim. I saw it there, a little bit of a tug before he stopped. Jacobsen is one of the few cabbies at RMTC who still talks to me. Why—I don't know. And I don't want to know.

"Have you seen Big Al?" I said.

Jacobsen blew a sigh of relief, lowered his brim, and said, "He's in Vegas."

"Do you mean Las Vegas?"

"Do you know any other Vegas?"

"Yes," I said.

This was turning into a typical Murph conversation, but Jacobsen was an old pro, so before I could parse him to death he finessed me by saying, "Big Al is on vacation. He won't be back until next week."

Oh great, I thought. By then I'll be dead and I won't be able to ask Big Al how to avoid dying. This dilemma had the quality of circular logic. I normally love circular logic. I spend so much time trying to figure out what I'm getting at that I sometimes forget what I'm trying to get at. It's better than Valium and much more cost-effective.

I came to within a hairsbreadth of asking further questions—or "stupid" questions, as I like to think of further questions—but I saw Jacobsen's body freeze up in a minuscule fashion. He knew me well enough to know that the next five minutes could become a living hell, so I decided not to pursue the conversation. Big Al was in Las Vegas, New Mexico, and I was on my own.

"Thanks," I said, which must have thrown Jacobsen for a loop because his hat fell off. I quickly walked away before the next five minutes turned into anything at all.

I cannot begin to tell you how helpless I felt as I drove to my apartment. Without Big Al to advise me, I felt like something that depended on something that wasn't there. I'm sure you've experienced this. I pulled into the parking lot behind my building, climbed out, and ascended the fire escape to the third floor, or "my" floor, as I had come to think of it, since I was the only person who lived there, to my knowledge.

When I got inside I headed straight for the refrigerator, glancing at my wristwatch as I opened the door and pulled out a Bud. It was 3 p.m. I seemed to remember something about the number three being associated with the dark night of the soul, but I couldn't make the connection. The only thing to do was reread the entire body of work of F. Scott Fitzgerald, but *Gilligan* was on at five, so I wouldn't have time to figure out what it was I was trying to figure out.

No matter. By the time I was seated uncomfortably in my easy chair, I had given up. This was usually the first step in the solution to my problems, so I did not feel entirely out of my element. That always came later, but for now I took a sip of beer, scratched the top of my head, and wondered what the odds were of calling Las Vegas on the telephone and getting Big Al. It was then I realized that Big Al could not possibly be in Las Vegas,

New Mexico, because there is no legal gambling in New Mexico, and Big Al doesn't go on vacation anywhere that does not involve coming home "flush," as he likes to phrase it with a satisfied smirk. Besides, I doubted that they even had telephones in Las Vegas, New Mexico. I knew they had a telephone in Taos, New Mexico, because I once used it—for reasons that I do not wish to divulge. It had to do with tequila and a lost bus ticket, but let's move on.

The only other place I could think of named "Las Vegas" where Big Al might be located was a place called Las Vegas, Nevada. They have legal gambling there. It all added up. Unless I missed my guess, Big Al was seated at a blackjack table in Las Vegas, doubling down, splitting tens, and tickling the chins of women who brought free drinks to the tables. The bastard. I wondered what the odds were of my calling Las Vegas, tracking Big Al down in one of the many casinos, and convincing him to take a telephone call from me. I quickly changed the "me" to "Keith Moon," and the odds increased dramatically in my favor. But still there was the problem of asking him to solve my problem without him catching on to the fact that I was not Keith Moon.

I began to feel edgy. I've never been completely comfortable with the concept of "complexity" and this scheme had all the earmarks. I was starting to get confused. Maybe I could call Keith Moon and ask him to call Big Al. That was probably the best idea I ever had. I will let you mull that one over.

I finished my beer, crushed the soft aluminum can in my mighty Irish fist, and tossed it in the general direction of the kitchen. I wished Big Al were here to advise me on how to get in touch with Big Al. I then realized that if Big Al were here, I would not have to get in touch with him in Las Vegas. While this certainly would have solved my problem, it didn't make any sense. I suddenly felt like I was talking to an idiot. Which is to say, I felt like I was having a conversation with a bartender named Harold. He works at Sweeney's Tavern in downtown Denver. He runs for fun. I've never had any fun running, and believe me, I've run a lot. One time I ran away from two men who were trying to shoot me for bollixing their plan to destroy the western hemisphere, but I won't bore you with that story— and anyway the government told me not to tell anybody about it.

The fact that I had somehow managed to metaphorically transform myself into one of the most hated bartenders west of Broadway sent me spiraling into a pit of despair so severe that I felt like lurching violently to the nearest liquor store. I don't keep hard liquor in my apartment, for reasons that should be obvious to anyone who has met an Irishman. On the plus side, it did make me forget my real problem, which was the possibility that a biker was roaming the streets of Denver looking to stomp me in a two-man rumble. The moment I realized this, I forgot about the difficulties involved in drawing Big Al away from the gambling tables. Instead I began to wonder what time the next flight to Wichita left from DIA.

"Jaysus, Big Al, what am I going to do?" I said aloud, and in that moment I heard a voice say, "Take the coward's way out."

I nearly went into shock. I recognized the voice and it was not that of Joanne Woodward. It was the voice of Big Al. Good Lord! Was he taking a vacation inside my head? Or had he devised a form of primeval mitosis that split him in two, leaving part of him in Denver and part of him in Las Vegas?

It made sense to me.

"I am not going to commit suicide," I said adamantly.

"I'm talking about the other coward in you," Big Al said.

"Do you mean the one who pretends that nothing bad has happened and goes on with his life as if everything is okay?"

"You can read my mind, Tenderfoot," Big Al said.

This confused me so much that I started to go to the refrigerator for a beer, but then I remembered that Big Al drank only Michelob, and I didn't have any.

I eased back into my chair and thought this over. If I pretended nothing bad had happened and simply went to work the next day, drove my taxi, crossed my fingers, and hoped that I was wrong about everything, maybe I wouldn't be pushing up daisies next weekend.

After all, what had I really done? I had driven a fare around Five Points and had subsequently found my fare unconscious in her house. I gave her CPR and saved her life, and she was now in the hospital being taken care of. On the surface, that was all that I had done. That was all anyone knew. If someone were to ask me about the events of the morning, I could simply—and innocently—describe my actions as if my life was a screenplay and not a gothic novel.

"I chauffeured Maureen to a number of places in Five Points, then drove her home. I subsequently realized she had left some money in my taxi, so I drove back to her house and found her unconscious. I gave her artificial respiration and called 911. The medics showed up a few minutes later and took her to Denver General."

Surface appearances.

Of course!

This is America, where surface appearances mean everything!

If a cop or a biker or a lawyer or judge or somebody asked me why Maureen wanted to cruise around Five Points, I could just play dumb. "My job is to take people where they want to go. I don't ask why they want to go there."

If I played my cards right, I just might come out of this situation smelling like a rose. My plan seemed so flawless that it scared the hell out of me.

The idea of playing my cards right made me think of Big Al. "Are you still there?" I said. I say this frequently when I'm alone. Apparently I was, because the voice inside my head did not answer. I sat perfectly still and listened for the sound of snickering. I frequently do this too. But I heard nothing.

Whether or not Big Al had actually spoken to me telepathically through the medium of a phantasmagoric version of himself floating inside my head, he had nevertheless solved my problem, and that was good enough for me.

I decided that I would stop worrying and start living. Then I realized that *How to Stop Worrying and Start Living* is the title of a Dale Carnegie self-improvement book. I wondered if I could get sued for improving my life without paying him $14.95, but I decided to take a chance that he wouldn't get wind of it. The fact that the good doctor had passed away years ago did nothing to ameliorate my paranoia.

I don't think anything can do that.

CHAPTER 11

I woke up the next morning smelling like a rose. I didn't even bother to use Right Guard. I grabbed a Coke from the fridge, made a cheese sandwich, collected my accouterment, and climbed down the fire escape. I noted that Blue Boy had not been stolen during the night. Blue Boy was stolen less often than Ol' Betsy by a burglary ratio of six to one. This annoyed me because on the days my car was stolen, I didn't go to work. It was a holdover tic from my grade school years. I used anything as an excuse to avoid going to school when I was young. Looking back on my childhood, I wonder why I never just said to my Maw, "I don't want to go to school." But maybe it was because I knew instinctively that the Truth wouldn't work. Instead, I made up insane excuses. Remind me to tell you about the time I soaked my tennis shoes in water and slept with them on all night in the hopes that I would catch a cold.

Perhaps I just did.

I hopped into Blue Boy and headed off to RMTC feeling like a million bucks soaked in rose perfume. I was three blocks from RMTC when I stopped wondering why the government doesn't print money in different colors, like pink and blue, and add a chemical like a scented candle to make taxpaying more fun.

I parked Blue Boy in the lot and climbed out. As I made my way to the on-call room I almost started whistling. But the Big Al inside me told me to knock it off. I knew one thing for sure. I couldn't accept Hogan's offer of a free lease. The word "beholden" gives me the creeps. I am a fan of routine.

When I got inside I strode up to the cage and practically tossed my seventy dollars at Rollo, but the plexiglass window made this virtually impossible, assuming I wanted to inflict a wound. But our battle of the intellects rarely came to blows, if "rarely" can be defined as "never." It still made my skin crawl to think that he had touched my hand the previous day. I might as well admit that I had spent a couple hours washing my hand the previous afternoon. "Out, out, damned spot," I kept mumbling—a holdover from English 101.

I was smiling as I shoved the money beneath the glass, and sure enough, the bastard smiled right back at me. I smiled even bigger, and he matched me mandible-for-mandible. By the time I walked out of the room I felt like Mr. Sardonicus. I only hoped that Rollo felt like The Man Who Laughs. That guy's smile was put there by horrible people with knives, but I don't want to ruin the plot for you. It was written by Victor Hugo, which is as good a reason as any to stop talking about it.

As I drove out of the lot, I called the dispatcher and told him I was on the road. I didn't crack wise. I didn't give him the opportunity to threaten to send me to the supervisor for a chewing out. The dispatcher sounded disappointed to me, but I didn't care. I was so happy I was ready to disappoint everyone I talked to.

I gassed up 123 at a 7-Eleven store, bought a Twinkie and joe, and was heading toward downtown Denver when a call came over the radio.

"One twenty-three, you've got a personal."

No I don't, I said to myself. I didn't pick up the mike. The dispatcher repeated his call. I grabbed the mike off the dash and said, "One twenty-three."

"You've got a personal in Commerce City."

I froze.

"One twenty-three, is there something wrong with your radio?" he said.

I pressed the button. "No," I said.

"Come on, Murph, stay on the ball," he said. He sounded pissed off and happy as hell.

He gave me the address. He didn't really have to. There were only two addresses in Commerce City that had any significance, and one of the tenants was in the ICU. The other was at the headquarters of The Varmints.

"Check," I said weakly, then hung the mike on the dash.

The dispatcher said something else, but I didn't hear it. I heard only a distant ringing in my ears, and a buzzing like hornets, and the sound of chain saws, machine guns, and atom bombs. I continued to drive toward downtown Denver. The "other" coward in me had taken charge. I was pretending that nothing bad had just happened and that I should go on with my life as if everything was okay. This got me as far as 32nd Avenue when a voice inside my head said, "Turn left." I don't suppose I have to tell you who said it. If I do, you haven't been paying attention. It was the voice of the man who seemed to think that his mission in life was to reform me, cleanse my soul, and do whatever was necessary to make me pay for my sins.

I turned left.

I began driving in what I sometimes refer to as a "daze." I did not think about where I was going. The cabbie inside me knew where he was going. I watched the scenery while Murph drove to Colorado Boulevard, turned left and drove to the Vasquez turnoff, and eventually turned left again and drove toward the street where Maureen lived.

When Murph saw a biker standing in the front yard with his fists on his hips, he shook me out of my reverie and dove for cover. I took over the driving at that point and pulled up behind a parked motorcycle.

The biker walked around the front of my taxi and came up to the driver's side window. He rapped on the window with a knuckle. I said the Act of Contrition and rolled the window down. Supposedly, saying "The Act" would get you into heaven if you couldn't make it to confession before the Grim Reaper caught up with you. That's what the nuns taught me anyway. I love deathbed confessions.

"Are you Murph?" he said.

"Yes," I said truthfully. I wasn't going to die with a new sin on my soul.

"Thanks for coming to get me," he said. "I'm Ted. I'm Maureen's boyfriend."

He yanked the back door open and slid in.

This reminded me of a scene from *The Godfather*. I could never forget the uproarious death of Paulie the traitor.

"Where to?" I said. For some reason I felt strangely calm. I understand soldiers feel this way during combat. I wouldn't know. I spent the Vietnam era being passed around from one stateside army base to another like a joke Christmas present.

"Denver General," he said.

I nodded and hit the meter, wheeled my taxi around, and headed back to Vasquez.

"The cops told me what happened," Ted said. "I wanna thank ya, man, for what ya did."

This was it. I knew I had to say something or I was a dead man.

"You're welcome," I said.

"If ya hadn't found my woman, she would have died," he said.

I nodded.

"I owe ya one," he said.

I nodded again. I couldn't talk. Was I being set up? That's how Al Pacino set up Paulie. Stroked his ego like a kitten, and then *whammo*.

A strange silence settled inside the taxi. I made my way to Colorado Boulevard and decided to take 13th to Broadway and go to the hospital from there.

I wanted to take 13th because it would take me past my crow's nest. I wanted to say goodbye to it.

"Mind if I ask you something?" I said.

"Ask," he said.

"I remember you from the night I . . . visited . . . the headquarters of The Varmints."

"Yeah," he said. "I remember you. Moochie got his ass kicked by Spinelli after you left."

That I did not need to hear.

Ted started chuckling, so I chuckled too. I won't go into the dynamics of acting just like my taxi fares like I usually do. For some reason I have this perpetual desire to confess to being a phony, but not right now.

"Can I ask why you didn't just drive your . . . bike over to Denver Health?" I said.

"I was drunk," he said. "Spinelli wouldn't let me. He told me to call you. He don't let us drive our bikes drunk. It just brings the heat down."

Thank God he said "bikes."

I had almost said "hog" in order to appear to be cool. I would do practically anything to be cool as long as my life wasn't on the line. I might add here that I did not recognize Ted from the night I visited The Varmints. I lied. This goes to show how rattled I was. Lying to a biker to get on his good side—who but a brilliant tactician would do such a lethal thing? I might also add that I was leery of saying "visited" because it sounded sort of candy-ass to me . . . but I couldn't think of a synonym, and I'm pretty good at finding synonyms when my candy ass is on the line.

I might also add here that when he said he was drunk I couldn't decide whether my rattle should increase or decrease in volume. I decided to "play it by ear."

"How is Maureen doing?" I said.

"The nurse told me she's unconscious but breathing," he said, peering out the side window.

"Has she . . . recovered well enough to . . . talk to anyone?" I said, feeling like the embodiment of pure evil, as usual.

"I guess. I don't know. The cops want to talk to her."

My crow's nest passed by in a flash. I barely had time to wave goodbye forever.

"Can I ask you something else?" I said.

I looked into the rearview mirror. Ted turned away from the window, cocked his head sideways, and fashioned something of a derisive smirk. "You don't have to keep asking me if you can ask, Murph. Just ask."

I had forgotten that I was not talking to a barbarian, I was talking to a civilized man. Bikers are people, too.

"Is Maureen related to Spinelli?"

"She's his older sister." He looked out the side window. "The both of them had crappy childhoods. Their father was a mean drunk and their mother was in jail a lot."

In jail a lot?

I decided not to ask.

We drove in silence for the rest of the ride. I tried not to glance at him in the rearview mirror. I was afraid I would see him pull out a pint of liquor and take a surreptitious sip. This was a common occurrence on a Saturday night but never on a Tuesday afternoon. It also happened a few nights before I was accused of kidnaping and murdering the girl I went out to Hollywood to save from a life of sin, but I don't want to get off the track here.

I pulled up in front of Denver General. The fare came to eight dollars. He leaned forward and held out a ten and said, "Keep the change, Murph."

"Thanks," I said. I hate it when potential enemies know my name. A learned thing.

In order to start paying for my own sins, I looked back at Ted and said, "Do you want me to wait for you here?" which was the last thing in the world I wanted to do. Penance always involves doing things you don't want to do. You don't even have to be Catholic to understand that, although it helps.

"Naw man, I'm going to stay here until they kick me out."

"You could sell tickets to that show," I wanted to say. This was the comedian in me, a sick persona who immediately envisioned a bunch of doctors and nurses and security guards trying to throw a biker out of a hospital. I hate that sick persona. He's more like me than I am.

"All right," I said. "Give Maureen my best wishes if she wakes up."

"If Maureen wakes up, I'll make sure to let you know so you can come visit her," Ted said just before he climbed out of my taxi.

I had mixed feelings about his statement. I don't like people telling me what to do, and he had just ordered me to visit his girlfriend when she recovered from her coma. But being told to do something by a biker made me feel like I was being badgered by a bully, even though I would have visited Maureen anyway because it was the right thing to do so that I would not look like the coward that I was, which might add a few days to my life before she told the cops and her boyfriend and Spinelli the whole story, which would subtract a few days from my . . .

I think I will stop there. That whole paragraph passed through my mind in less than one second, which was not a record for me, but a close runner-up. Large paragraphs normally pass through my mind when I am suspected of murder. This was the first time it had happened because I was an accomplice in a near-lethal drug overdose. I cannot begin to tell you how much I hate reality.

I watched Ted as he swaggered through the big sliding doors of the hospital. They were open, of course. Would it have mattered if he swaggered through closed doors? Ask Roger Corman.

I saw a man exit from the hospital on crutches, so I drove away quickly. I had better things to do than pick up handicapped persons. Okay. I'll admit it. Two empty cabs had pulled up behind me, so the "handi" did have a ride. I was just trying to sound callous. And tough. To be perfectly honest, I was practicing lying. I knew what I had to do, based on years of doing the wrong thing and then the right thing. I would have to call upon any crumbs of courage that had not been sucked from my body by my draft notice and go to Spinelli and tell him the whole story. Yes, I realized she was buying drugs, no I did not know she was your older sister, yes I am sorry, yes I would like you to not kill me. My usual line of defense in a hopeless situation. I don't like to brag, as you know, but I might be one of the world's greatest tacticians when it comes to hopeless situations.

Escape and evasion, retreat, surrender, singing like a canary, these are just a few of the charms in my bag of The Better Part Of Valor, which happens to be "discretion."

Give me a break, okay? I'm just a cab driver, I'm not James Bond—unless Octavia should . . . but perhaps I've said too much.

I heaved a sigh of resignation, which is the starting pistol of my Pyrrhic victories, then aimed the hood ornament of my taxi toward Commerce City. RMT Number 123 does not actually have a hood ornament, although it does have a large, bulbous front end with a wicked-looking grill like an old Buick. But I just like to say "hood ornament." It makes me feel like a hood. Little did I realize that before this week was over I would feel like an outlaw. In fact . . . well . . . let's not get ahead of ourselves. I tried that once in Wichita and ended up naked inside a taxicab. Getting ahead of myself usually involves beer and whimsical pranks.

I drove up to 13th Avenue and headed east. Destination: the garage clubhouse of The Varmints. I girded my loins as I drove. This is difficult to do when you wear blue jeans that are two sizes too small or sport a belly that is two sizes too large. Take your pick. But somehow my loins got girded, and I concentrated on my "speech" to Spinelli. What the hell. Today was a good day to die. Perhaps Spinelli would let me "count coup" and run away fast. He looked like a well-read young man. If you do not know what "counting coup" is, ask either Thomas Berger, Dustin Hoffman, or Black Elk. They are hip to nineteenth-century Native American jive lingo.

I drove down the alley expecting to see a gang of bikers standing around drinking beer, punching each other on the shoulders, grinning with big mean teeth, jangling with steel chains, and generally supplementing my nightmare with appropriate Samuel Z. Arkoff frills. But the alley was deserted. No bikes, no bikers. But the door to the garage was open, and inside I could see a man wearing a dirty green field jacket with black camouflage insignia. The phrase "Vietnam Veteran" came to mind as it always does when I encounter men who were almost like me in the army, men who almost didn't get shipped overseas.

I pulled up and stopped and peered into the darkness. The man was leaning over the fender of a car. I could not read the insignia. I couldn't tell what unit he might have served with. That would come later. The back of his hand would reveal it to me.

He raised his head and stared at me. He was wearing rimless glasses, had a short-cropped goatee, and was holding a greasy wrench in his right fist. Close enough to supplement my nightmare. I shut off the engine and climbed out.

"Whaddya say, Murph?" he said before I had a chance to open my mouth. It seemed like an awful lot of people had become familiar with my nickname lately. Why couldn't this have been a gang of renegade millionaires?

"You have me at a disadvantage," I said, completely losing my cool. "I don't know your name."

"Doc," he said, leaning under the hood.

His left hand was splayed on the top of the radiator. That's when I saw the tattoo on the back of his hand: 101st Airborne Brigade. Screaming Eagle.

"Is Spinelli around?" I said.

He stood up straight and frowned at me, then whipped a greasy red rag from his back pocket and began polishing the tool. Gun owners sometimes refer to weapons as "tools." I don't know why that thought ran through my mind.

He shook his head no. "I heard what you did for Maureen," Doc said.

I froze. The operative word there was "did." What did he think I "did?" I decided to play it cool and not talk until I learned what misconception was driving this conversation.

"You done good," he said.

"Thanks," I said, realizing that I would probably never have a real conversation again as long as I lived. I would be required to take notes to make sure I never contradicted myself. I would talk like a fugitive. Everything I would say in the future would be weighed, measured, and false.

I stood there watching Doc polish the tool and realized that I could not possibly live the rest of my life like that, even if my life ended this Friday. Keeping track of lies is a fool's ploy. That is one of the things I like about the Truth. It just lies there, immobile and irrefutable. That's also what I don't like about it, but let's not get into that.

"I need to talk to Spinelli about something important," I said.

Doc nodded and set his tool into a metal box, then peered at me. "Might not be advisable at the moment. I'm sure he would be glad to talk to you about what you did for his sister, but right now he has . . . more important things on his mind. It might be best if you waited until . . . oh . . . Sunday night to shoot the breeze with him. Everybody meets here on Sunday night."

"What for?" I said.

Doc grinned. "Head count. Spinelli wants to make sure he didn't lose anyone over the weekend."

"Does that happen very often?"

"Sometimes. It's mostly our guys getting busted and jailed. Spinelli makes the appropriate phone calls and squares the deck, helps the family if the jailbird's family needs it. That's part of being a leader."

I began to fidget. Involuntarily of course. Fidgeting is something I often do on purpose to distract the person I'm lying to so that I can change the subject. Odd as it sounds, it works rather well.

"Can I ask you something about Maureen?" I said.

"Shoot," he said. He went on with his work as if I wasn't there. I wish everybody knew how to do that.

"Has this ever happened before to Maureen?"

"You mean the OD?" he said.

"Yes."

"Yeah. Maureen isn't supposed to do drugs. Spinelli went ballistics when he found out she OD'd. He thought her boyfriend or one of us gave her the drugs. He threatened to stomp whoever helped her get high."

"Is she an addict?" I said.

"You better believe it. Spinelli helped her get clean, but she's backslid plenty of times. This is the third time she's OD'd."

Jaysus. "How did he get her clean?" I said. "I mean, did she go to AA?"

"Yeah, something like that. A twelve-step program for druggies. I don't buy into that bullshit, but I guess it helped her for a little while."

"Why don't you buy into it?" I said.

As an Irish/Catholic I had experienced more than my share of near misses with AA. I even managed to talk a friend into going to AA. This was back in college. He was flunking out. So was I. He graduated clean and sober magna cum laude. I ended up in Denver.

Doc looked over at me. "Ever have a conversation with an AA?" he said.

Rather than correct his shaky syntax, I simply said no.

"Buncha snobs," he said. "They act like jerks when they're drunk and they act like jerks after they get sober. They're always sidling up to you and telling you how many years since they last took a drink. I don't even remember when I quit drinking. All I know is I haven't had a drink today, and that's all that counts. Yesterday don't count and tomorrow don't count. Hell, they might be lying on their asses dead drunk in the gutter tomorrow."

"I'll drink to that," I almost said. But I sensed I was treading on dangerous ground. I had to take this further though. I felt that no matter how far I took it, I would never be in more danger than I would be when Spinelli found out I had chauffeured his sister to OD-land.

"I take it you've gone to AA," I said.

He nodded and held up his left hand. The wings of the Screaming Eagle flared. "After I got home from Nam I stayed drunk for about twenty years. Spinelli made me go to AA. I quit the program after a while. I couldn't stand the snobs. But I guess it got the job done. I don't drink alcohol anymore."

I felt a wave of envy pass through me. I wished I didn't do anything anymore.

"Spinelli doesn't let me drink," he said. "He doesn't let a lot of people do a lot of things. He's a good man. A good leader."

Spinelli was good alright. I didn't get it. An outlaw biker who acted like James Woods? Could it be that Roger Corman had steered me wrong? Why would Roger do such a thing? For money? I found that hard to believe. I found it hard to believe that Roger Corman made any money at all.

Doc stood up and lowered the hood of the car. The metal slam made me jump. It sounded like the door of a jail cell slamming shut. Don't ask me how I know what a jail door sounds like. I just do.

"I pity the poor bastard who helped Maureen get her hands on drugs," he said. He yanked the red rag from his back pocket and began wiping his hands. He smiled at me. "Is there anything else I can do for you, Murph?"

"I guess not," I said.

"Are you going on the run?" he said.

I heard this as if through a fogbank. I was barely aware of his words.

"What?" I said.

"Spinelli was talking about inviting you on the run next weekend up at Cherry Creek Reservoir. He appreciated what you did for Moochie."

"A run?" I said. "Do you mean like in the movies?"

"Yeah. The gang is going there for a picnic."

Omigod. I had to get out of there right now.

By "there" I meant the western half of the United States. And I think we all know what I meant by "now." I always mean it.

"I haven't heard from Spinelli," I said.

"Yeah, well, he might get in touch with you. Don't tell him I clued you in to the run. He likes to surprise people. The Varmints rarely invite outsiders on a run, but Spinelli says you're good people so he might give you a call. Does he have your home phone number?"

"Huh?"

"Your home phone, does Spinelli have it?"

I stood there with my jaw hanging open. I had gotten pretty good at that ever since I received my draft notice. I couldn't bring myself to answer Doc. I felt like my Fifth Amendment rights were being violated.

"I think so," I lied.

Doc nodded and tucked the rag back into his pocket. I have trouble remembering what happened next. I think I said goodbye and got into my taxi. I think Doc said goodbye. That scared me. Why would he say "goodbye"? Just because I was leaving? Or did the word "goodbye" have a hidden meaning? Doc seemed like an intelligent person. Perhaps well-read. Perhaps he had gone to college on the G.I. Bill and majored in English, where he was steeped in the dismal swamp of symbolism. Perhaps he had minored in Psychology and knew how to infect a man with a psychological tic. Isn't that what psychology majors do? They psych people out. Was I psyched out?

All I know is that I found myself back on Vasquez Boulevard trying to remember the words of a prayer that I had made up in basic training. As soon as I recalled the first eight words, it all came back to me:

"Hear me oh Lord from Heaven Thy dwelling place, fill me with an abundance of denial, that I may walk through the valley of the shadow of death like a clueless nitwit."

I devised this while I was at the hand-grenade range in basic. This was just before they handed me a live grenade and told me to pull the pin and throw the grenade as far away from myself and the drill sergeant as I could. I might as well admit it. I had "strange" thoughts after I pulled the pin. I didn't like the drill sergeant very much. He yelled at me a lot. In fact, he even yelled at me to throw the damn grenade. I threw it. I was like a mindless robot in basic training, thank God. I obeyed orders the way Robby manufactured liquor for actors.

There is much more to this story, which ends with a kind of low-level court- martial that I do not want to get into, save to say that it is all rather amusing in retrospect.

I pulled onto Colorado Boulevard and headed toward downtown Denver thinking of an addendum to the prayer that I concocted sometime after "The Incident," as the drill sergeant endlessly referred to it.

"Hear me oh Lord from Heaven Thy dwelling place, lead me along the paths of steep cliffs oblivious to the laws of physics, that I may admire the view without realizing the danger I am in."

Who says denial is just a river in Africa? Denial is the lifeblood of anybody with half a brain. I knew that my only chance of maintaining my sanity was to lose it completely. If I sat down and made a detailed list of the "problems" I was facing, I would probably lose my mind anyway. When it comes to going off the deep end, I like to keep things neat and organized.

This explains why I found myself seated in my crow's nest that evening making a list of all my troubles. I felt like a bluesman trying to write a Tin Pan Alley hit.

To wit: I had helped a woman buy drugs. She subsequently overdosed and nearly died. Her brother was an outlaw biker who was trying to find out who had helped his older sister get her hands on the drugs.

If things worked out the way they usually did, I would be facing a potential manslaughter charge when the police found out that I had been an accomplice in a drug deal. God only knew what the actual legal wording of my "accomplicement" consisted of, but it all added up to the same thing: a nickel in Cañon City.

When the Rocky Mountain Taxicab Company found out that I had used an RMTC vehicle as a "mule" to transport drugs and to take part in a drug buy, they would fire me. This was a given, of course. They always fired me. They fired me every time I was suspected of murder and other stuff, but I always got my job back because I was always innocent.

Which brings me to the fourth and final problem in this litany of sins: I was guilty. I couldn't get around it this time. I had actually done all these things, and a woman had nearly died. The guilt was like the monolith in *2001: A Space Odyssey*. It kept appearing in front of my eyes no matter what direction I looked. A big black block of guilt that blinded me to the future. A big black blob of blame. A monolithic mass of . . .

Pardon me, but I sometimes play word games when I am suspected of stuff. It helps me to forget the stuff. It is just one of the many facets of denial that help me make it through the night. It also helps me make it through the Mousetrap, which is the worst interstate interchange in the United States. It is a massive series of winding roads that allow you to switch from Interstate 25 to Interstate 70, assuming you have the ability to solve Rubik's Cube while simultaneously driving like Parnelli Jones. Whenever I am forced to use the Mousetrap, I like to pretend I am on a ride at Elitch's amusement park. Not the new Elitch's, but the old one where I once saw Mickey Rooney.

Don't get me started on Mickey Rooney.

As I sat in my apartment that evening sucking on a beer, I decided that I had come to the end of the road. I had walked away from virtually every job I had ever held, but I had never walked away from cab driving. Not for real. Sometimes I finessed my supervisor by firing myself just to save time, but I always knew I would be back. That was a given. It was back in the days when I was as pure as the driven snow. But now I was GUILTY!

See. The monolith returns.

No matter what I thought about during that night, the black monolith of guilt slammed into the earth and stood there grinning and asking me what I was going to do about this situation. It was grinning because it knew I did not have the answer. The only person who might possibly have the answer was currently winning money at craps in Las Vegas.

"Oh Big Al, what am I going to do?" I said reluctantly. I didn't really like talking out loud when I was alone. What's the point of being weird without an audience?

I didn't have an answer to that one either, but it didn't matter because the phone suddenly rang. It brought me out of my "reverie," as I like to call drunken stupors. I sat waiting for the three rings of my answering machine followed by the voice of the person who was fool enough to think I used telephones.

"Hey, Murph," a familiar voice said. "This is Spinelli. Call me when you get this message. I have something I want to talk to you about."

Click.

How did he get my number?

I had asked myself this many times before and the answer was always the same: phone book. My name and telephone number were listed. And why not? I had nothing to fear from anyone who called me because I was as pure as the driven snow. But now that I had become the walking embodiment of pure evil, I decided it was time to get an unlisted phone number.

But that was a minor matter compared to the decision I now had to make. Should I call Spinelli back? What did he want to say to me? Put your affairs in order and meet me at Riverside Cemetery? My sister squealed on you? I think you're a swell guy and want to invite you on a picnic?

I decided to go with Door Number 3. Unless I planned to leave Denver, I knew I had to call Spinelli back. As much as I wanted to go to, for instance, Pierre, South Dakota, I had no intention of leaving the only city that would have me. If I ran, Spinelli would track me down. I'm not sure when I learned it, but one of the awful rules that I live by is that I must always face the music no matter how bad the lyrics. It was a given that I would one day tell Spinelli of my involvement in his sister's OD. If I didn't, she would, and that would make me look like a wienie, and us wienies like to keep a low profile.

I picked up the phone and dialed the number.

As I listened to the ringing of Spinelli's phone, I thought about the fact that the people of Pierre, South Dakota, pronounce the name of their town "Pier" and not "Pee Air." I wondered if it would be possible for a human being to pee air. This is how most of my novels are kick-started. Big Al had once advised me to flee to "Pier" after I had gotten into another big mess. I can't recall when or what it was about, but I never forgot his advice.

"Yeah," Spinelli said, taking my mind off my new novel forever.

"Hi, Spinelli, this is Murph the taxi driver."

"Hey, Murph, thanks for calling back."

"Sure, I got your message a minute ago."

"Yeah, I just wanted to thank you, man, for what you did for Maureen. That was a righteous act. I talked to the doctor and he told me that when the medics arrived she was dead."

"Dead?" I said as if I had never heard the word before.

"He said technically she was dead, ya know, but not brain-dead. He said whoever gave her mouth-to-mouth kept her alive until the medics could inject her with some shit that got her heart started again. If you hadn't showed up, my sister would have died."

That is when the personality split that I had been fighting for years finally took place. I felt like a six-foot cell undergoing mitosis. I split into two giant jelly beans, one of which remained on the phone and one of which went into the kitchen and tried to open the refrigerator for a beer, but it's hard for ectoplasm to move objects in the physical world where I normally reside. I found it very baffling.

"Well, that is truly wonderful news," I seemed to say somewhere far away, like the living room. "I'm glad that I was able to help."

I floated back into the living room and watched my doppelganger chatting with Spinelli on the phone. They talked for two or three minutes, then Murph hung up and sat back with a satisfied smile on his face. He reached over and picked up the beer on the phone table, which made me furious with envy. Then he noticed me standing in front of the TV. He motioned me to come and sit down on him, which I did not want to do. However, I felt some compelling force drawing me toward what I knew was my own body. I was as revolted by this as I would have been revolted by the idea of sitting down on Rollo the cage man, but I was under the influence of a sinister cosmic power over which I had no control. It was a typical Tuesday.

"Well, stupid, guess what?" I said.

"What?" I said.

"You've been invited to go on a picnic with Spinelli and The Varmints next weekend. They are going to make a run up to Cherry Creek Reservoir and swill beer all night. There is going to be chicken, potato salad, burgers, and a few rollicking fistfights, as well as any possible number of fatal misunderstandings. It's anything goes when The Varmints kick over the traces."

I didn't know if I was joking or not, and I didn't want to know. I suddenly felt myself filled with a strength that I did not know I possessed. I stood up and headed for the bedroom.

"Hey, wait a minute," I said. "I didn't finish my beer!"

"Shut up and go to bed," I growled.

When I woke up the next morning I had the eerie feeling that I was not someone other than myself. I checked to make sure that I did not have four arms, then I threw my blanket off the bed and knocked over my reading lamp.

This innocuous move culminated in a twenty-minute conversation with my landlord, which is irrelevant to this topic. After I got back upstairs I swept up the broken lightbulb, dumped the eggshell glass into the wastebasket, and sat down in the silence of my living room to make a decision. Should I work today or not? If I worked, I would use my taxi to do the things I intended to do. If I did not work, I would use my 1954 baby-blue Plymouth. It was a tough call. Using Blue Boy would be like playing tennis without a net. Using my taxi would imbue my actions with a discipline that I was not used to and yet needed desperately in my life. But this was always true. By leasing a taxi, I could not flee Denver on the spur of the moment, whereas if I was in Blue Boy I could flee before I even put my futile plans into effect.

I then realized I had made a mistake. I had inadvertently put myself into a position of having to make a decision before sipping a morning coffee. I think you know what I am talking about. We have all experienced it: the brain is fresh from sleep and the mind is clear, the two worst criteria for making a decision. Without the additives of such external stimuli as caffeine, and even nicotine, the average human being stands a good chance of making the right decision, and I knew instinctively that this was the last thing in the world I wanted to do because it might put my life in jeopardy in ways too numerous to contemplate. What I needed was a blast of instant coffee and two or three quick cigarettes in order to fog my mind so badly that no matter what decision I made it would be wrong. That was my only hope of surviving the day. But I did not have a jar of instant coffee, and I had made the tactical error of giving up smoking before I began driving a taxi. I cursed myself for my discipline. If I was like most people, I would still be trying to give up smoking and would have a half-empty pack of coffin nails lying on the phone table next to my TV remote. But nooooo—I had to be one of the chosen few whose fear of death was even greater than his desire for pleasure. I know what you're thinking: Murph has discipline? A common and even laughable misconception that can be explained by the fact that I used up all of my discipline when giving up smoking. I can barely remember what it was like to have discipline. I seem to remember that it was something like wearing a brand-new pair of waterproofed leather boots. You felt like you could step outside and give the world a good swift kick in the slats. But those days were gone. As a consequence, I had to incorporate the artificial discipline of driving a taxi if I expected to accomplish anything. Following this thread of what I like to call "logic," I decided to drive my taxi that day. Something told me that if I had the sudden urge to pack up and flee Denver, the effort it would take to turn in my taxi and drive back to my apartment might give me the edge I needed to rescind my decision and make the appropriate fatal decision to stay in town and face the music.

It worked.

By the time I had paid for my lease, taken my trip sheet and key out to the parking lot of RMTC, and climbed into Number 123, I felt like I had what it took to give the world a good swift kick in the slats. This delusion lasted until I parked my taxi in the lot outside of Denver General Hospital, where reality finally set back in and I found myself wanting to flee Denver rather than go into the hospital and visit Maureen Spinelli—and face the music. By "music," I mean "Funeral March of a Marionette" —or the theme song of *Alfred Hitchcock Presents*, as it is known among the great unwashed out here in the hinterlands.

I entered DGH and spent a moderate amount of time searching for the reception. I had been here once before when I was suspected of various crimes such as bank robbery, assault, manslaughter, the usual stuff, so I didn't have too much trouble finding my way around, even though I was not being escorted by a homicide detective. Those guys really know their way around hospitals. To my chagrin, it turns out that I walked past the reception desk three times before I noticed it. The desk was situated near the front door, which threw me for a loop. I was not used to efficiency, but then I supposed that if you desired efficiency, you could not ask for a better workplace than a hospital.

I was directed to Maureen's room on the seventh floor. I somehow managed not only to find the elevators but to find the seventh floor. Fortunately, the floors were indicated by buttons that were lined up in neat rows—again—next to the doorway to the elevator. There aren't too many places to hide buttons in an elevator, but having served in the army I knew that a determined designer could probably find five or six inconvenient places to hide the buttons in a small room with a single exit.

When the doors slid open, I stepped out into a hallway and made my way down to room 777. The blood nearly drained from my face until realized that the scary number was 666 and not 777. Or is it "were"? Is 666 a single number, or three single numbers lined up in a neat row? I have never been good at math, neatness, or superstition, so I came close to panicking. Fortunately, Maureen's boyfriend, Ted, was just coming out of room 777, which annoyed me because I was sort of looking forward to "finding" the room on my own. People who are "math-challenged" like to solve simple puzzles in the hopes that they might someday master algebra. Fortunately for sick people, hospitals do not base the numerical designations of their rooms on x's and y's the way mathematicians do. I will be completely honest here: I have never understood how x and y became numbers, but that's what the bright boys tell me. I have always wondered what a paycheck for a mathematician looked like. "Hey buddy, got change for an x?" I once thought of saying this to a math professor but decided not to.

"Murph, my man," Ted said. "Good to see you."

"Hi, Ted," I said.

I felt like I had never said anything so banal in my life. Hi Ted. A baboon could say "Hi Ted". What was wrong with me?

"Hey man, listen, I'm running down to the cafeteria to buy some munchies. Can I getcha anything? It's on me."

"Oh, no thanks," I said. "I just had some munchies."

So hang me, okay? I was just trying to fit in with the local in-crowd, who happened to be an in-crowd of one: Ted.

"All right man, I'll be back in a while. You can go on in if you want. Maureen is unconscious, but I know I'm leaving her in good hands."

It wasn't until Ted walked down the hall and entered an elevator that I realized he was referring to me. I was now officially known as "Good Hands." I prayed that this would not become my biker moniker. I stepped to the doorway of Maureen's room and looked in. She was lying unconscious on the bed with an oxygen hose attached to her nose. Pure oxygen. The last thing she had up her nose was crack smoke. Before that it might have been cocaine. Noses have caused more trouble than God could have imagined when He invented them. He invented all sorts of pesky body parts. This is how my mind works when I am drowning in guilt.

"Pardon me," a voice said. I liked that. I could have used a few pardons right then. I looked around and saw a young doctor trying to get past me. I stepped into the room to let her by.

She walked over to the bed and picked up Maureen's chart. She looked at some machines that were softly beeping, monitors with EKG lines on them. The reality of what was happening was so authentic that it was just like being in a movie. I looked around to see if there were any cameras present. This was not unusual. I spend every waking moment of my life looking around for the cameras that are recording my mistakes. When I was a kid, the dailies were handed over to my Maw. I don't know who watches them now, I know only that after I die they will be edited together for Saint Peter to look at while I cool my heels at the Pearly Gates.

"Are you a member of Ms. Spinelli's family?" the doctor said, looking up from the chart and smiling at me.

"No, I'm just a friend," I said. "My name is . . . Brendan Murphy." I didn't want to tell her my "Murph" nickname. I was afraid she might recognize it and say something like, "Oh, you're the man who saved Maureen's life."

Which she did.

"I don't think I saved her life," I said. "I'm just the taxi driver who found her."

She pursed her lips and looked at the chart, then set it aside and smiled at me. She stepped close to me and said quietly, "According to the report written up by the medics, Ms. Spinelli was technically dead when they took over from you. Without your first aid to keep her system pumping oxygen and blood flowing, they probably would not have been able to revive her. She owes you her life."

Normally I liked this sort of compliment, but I suddenly felt my heart beginning to beat rapidly. My face began to grow hot. I knew my cheeks were flushing red. I began to feel faint.

"You're blushing," she said.

She was wrong. I was not blushing, I was going into shock. The Irish do everything back-asswards. County Cork Irish anyway.

"I rarely see men blush," she said. "I think that's charming."

In the best of all possible worlds, this conversation would have led to a cup of coffee in the cafeteria, followed by a movie date, followed by a courtship resulting in maniacal arguments and a tear-streaked breakup. I'm not sure how she would have reacted to the breakup, aside from disappearing from my life forever. You wouldn't believe the number of hankies I have collected over the years.

"Thank you," I said, pretending to be modest. This was not unusual either.

"Where's her boyfriend?" she said.

"He went down to the cafeteria," I replied.

She nodded. "He has been here ever since Maureen was admitted to the hospital."

"Did you . . ." I began. Then I stopped. "Do you . . ." I said, but I stopped again. "Does he stay here all night?" I said.

She nodded. "It's against the rules, but nobody around here seems to understand the rules." Then she smiled one of those "insider" smiles that are often used in the place of a wink.

I got the message. But what I really wanted to know was what happened when they tried to throw a biker out of a hospital—but I guess that will go down in history with the mystery of Bigfoot.

"How is . . . Ms. Spinelli doing?" I said.

"She's going to be all right," the doctor said.

"Has she come to consciousness?" I said.

"Oh yes."

She did not elaborate, which was probably for the best. If I learned what Maureen told the doctor, or the police, or Ted, or The Varmints, I probably would have needed a dozen EKG machines.

"I'm glad to hear it," I said. I refrained from asking all the questions that were dying to get outside of my brain, like, "Did she mention my name? Did she implicate me in any crimes? Did she incriminate me?"

I can't tell you how bad it made me feel to be worrying about my own sorry ass while Maureen was lying unconscious in a hospital room, but it did tell me something about myself that I never really knew before: I'm only human.

Let me explain: I have always felt that I was superhuman.

End of explanation.

"How soon do you think Maureen will be discharged from the hospital?" I said.

"It's hard to say, but I expect she will be back home by the upcoming weekend."

Just in time for the run to the reservoir. I wondered if her brother would let her go. I wondered if this incident would put a halt to the picnic. Incidents tend to do that. The history of mankind is filled with incidents that have postponed the picnic we call "Life." The hand-grenade range in basic comes to mind. I spent the weekend on KP while all my friends were getting pickled at the EM club.

"You should be proud of yourself, Mr. Murphy," the doctor said, patting me on the shoulder and walking out of the room.

"Should" was the operative word there. All my life I "should" have been proud of myself, but it never quite panned out that way. I spent most of my time being ashamed. I spent the rest of my time watching *Gilligan's Island*.

I looked at Maureen, then looked at the doorway. I decided that it was time once again to take the coward's way out. I headed for the elevators.

I didn't want to be around when Ted returned. I suspected that not being there would be as bad as being there, but at least if I wasn't there I wouldn't be there to find out. As soon as the elevator door opened up, Ted stepped out. My blushing face almost exploded like the Hindenburg.

"Heading out?" Ted said.

I was getting ready to tell him that I was going downstairs to look for him, but he had finessed me by colliding with the truth.

"Yeah, I'm driving today. I just wanted to drop by and check on Maureen and wish her my best."

"Thanks, man. If she wakes I'll tell her you were here."

"Don't do that," I almost said. Instead I said, "Thanks." This was the day that banality saved my sanity.

"Are you coming on the run with us next Saturday?" Ted said. "Cherry Creek Reservoir. It'll be a gas."

"Uuuuuuuh, I don't know," I said, reaching into my grab bag of snappy replies. "I might have to work on Saturday."

"I know what you mean, man. Gotta make the bucks. The eagle shits for me on Friday, so I'll be headed up with The Varmints on Saturday. I hope you can make it. Do you got a girlfriend?"

I stared at him with horror, then said rhetorically, "Do I got a girlfriend?"

He grinned and winked at me. "Bring a date. It ain't a party if you ain't got a date."

This might explain why I never go to parties.

"I'll see how things work out."

"If you can't find a date, I can set you up," he said.

"I'll keep that in mind," I said. My body was crying out for me to get into the elevator. So was my mind. So was Joanne Woodward, as well as the lawyer and a lot of other appalled entities.

"Thanks for coming by, man," Ted said. I don't know if I've mentioned this, but Ted had a gruff voice. He sounded like Oscar the Grouch. I practically grew up watching *Sesame Street*. "Practically" is the operative word there. I was nineteen when the show premiered. I saw the first show during basic training. I was in the dayroom hiding out from a work detail. When I first saw Bert and Ernie I was enraged that Jim Henson had ripped off Frank Capra. I began composing a protest letter in my mind. That's how the drill sergeant caught me. I had violated the first rule of escape-and-evasion: don't get caught.

The elevator doors shut, and only then was I able to breathe a deep sigh of relief. I fully expected the doors to open up, revealing a landscape of Hell, but it was only Denver. I walked out of the hospital contemplating the idea of bringing a date on a run to Cherry Creek Reservoir with outlaw bikers. I didn't know whether to laugh or go insane.

CHAPTER 12

It was exactly three o'clock in the morning when my eyelids flew open. I know this because I could see lights and shadows on the ceiling from a passing car. I looked at the clock to assure myself that, yep, once again I had awakened at the moment that F. Scott Fitzgerald described as "the dark night of the soul." I have never really known whether Scotty was asleep or just drunk when he made this discovery, but 3 a.m. certainly "felt" right. The reason my eyes flew open was that my think-brain was working overtime while my movie-brain was showing me this hilarious dream about mice crawling all over my body. I think it was hilarious. At least they weren't biting me. Then my eyelids flew open. "What if it's a trap," I whispered. I was referring to the reservoir run on Saturday. What if Spinelli was going to get me up there alone and away from "What Law!" as Burt Reynolds so ominously put it in *Deliverance*. I was certain that when thirty bikers burbled into the park, all the mom-and-pop picnickers would gather up their broods and go to Estes Park, which is as far away from outlaw bikers as the average individual wants to get. Don't tell Spinelli I said that.

There would be no "Law!" Spinelli might put me on trial. This had happened to me once before. I won't go into the details except it involved kidnaped girls, pot, hippies, a guru, and a potential murder charge that turned out to be ridiculous. I was put on trial for stealing a necklace, which was also ridiculous. I was found guilty, which was not ridiculous because I had the stolen necklace in my possession, and I wasn't able to hide it in time. It got complicated. The point is that Spinelli might know that I was responsible for driving his sister to Drugsville, and wanted to "disappear" me after a lengthy trial, or a beating, or a tongue-lashing, or whatever bikers refer to as "justice." Since I would not have a lawyer present, I would do my best to focus on the Tongue-Lashing Defense, but I didn't have much hope. I never have much hope, which is probably a good thing. It would be like having a million dollars. I would probably just drink it all up. I hope so anyway. I can't imagine wasting a million dollars on anything else. I would probably down my last drink while being lowered into the ground. A burp, a tossed can, and you could write on my tombstone: "Shoot low, sheriff, they're riding Shetlands." I've always wanted to die with a non sequitur on my lips. Just before Oscar Wilde died, he is reported to have said, "Either that wallpaper goes, or I do." I'll admit it. I'm jealous.

This made me think about death, and drugs, and Cherry Creek Reservoir. I wondered if Spinelli would cut me some slack for bringing his sister back to life after killing her. Which side of the scale held more weight? Annoyance or gratitude? But why ask? I knew the answer to that one. I knew the answer to that one on the day I was born.

There was no way I was going to the reservoir on Saturday. I could either call Spinelli and decline the invitation, or I could leave right now, get a motel room on South Santa Fe Drive, and hide out until Monday. They've got some great motels on South Santa Fe that were built in the 1920s. By "great" I mean they resemble the Bates Motel in *Psycho*. My definition of such words as "great," "quality," "excellence," and "flair" does not necessarily jibe with that of people who watch Audrey Hepburn movies—but to each his own I always say with a middle finger raised sky-high.

It occurred to me then that my experiences as a cab driver might make good fodder for a novel. My attempts to make money off action-adventure and horror novels didn't work, maybe I ought to tap into my real-life experiences and say goodbye to creative writing altogether. Just jot down what really happened to me and offer that as a novel to the publishers. Up until now I had held the same disdain for realism that I held for TV scriptwriting because, after all, if you wanted reality, just go look in a mirror. Who the hell wants to see that horror show? Give me a vampire stewardess from Hoboken any day. But things were different now. I now had the opportunity to write a book about the time I killed a woman and then brought her back to life. What drama! What tears! What laughter! What the hell was I thinking???

When I wasn't busy killing people, I was trying to make a quick buck off the situation. My God, what was happening to me? I was losing my mind. I was sick. I was a degenerate. I was perverse. I was practically a nonfiction writer! So what if nonfiction outsold fiction by a factor of a thousand to one. At least fiction writers had dignity. Yeah. Dignity. Try buying a cup of coffee with dignity. Try hocking your dignity at a pawnshop.

I had to bring an end to this horror show, and I had to do it now—even if it meant bringing an end to myself. I had to go to Cherry Creek Reservoir.

With those words, I stopped abruptly and decided to give it a second thought.

Altruism aside, did I really want to die? Who the hell wants to die? My philosophy has always been: Live life as if you were going to die three days from now. Not now, and not tomorrow, or the next day, but three days from now. This gives you time to watch any movies you've been promising yourself but never got around to watching, like the more obscure works of Ed Wood, if such a thing is not an oxymoron. You don't have time to read *Madame Bovary*, but maybe you can catch a wretched film version of it. At least you have three days to get ready. So live it that way. In three days it's doornail time. In the meantime, have a beer, catch up on your delinquent movie watching and unrequited pleasures in general. Then confess all your sins to the nearest bartender, and it's Heaven here I come.

Following this epiphany, I took another roll of the dice and tried for a second one. I had been driving a taxi for fifteen years, and one of the many things I had learned was that you learn a lot of things when you drive a taxi. I learned that you get every type of person imaginable in the backseat, and you have absolutely no control over how they live their lives. This is a part of what makes it so fun to be a nosey parker. The outcome is hopeless, which means it's "anything goes." Cole Porter knew what he was doing when he wrote that song. It made me feel like the opposite of Superman when I tried to help people out, because I knew that no matter what I advised them to do they not only wouldn't do it, but if they tried to do it, it wouldn't even work. I felt like Advice Bizarro. When I fired advice at my fares it bounced off their chests like rubber bullets. I could leap a tall building with a single bound and when I got back down to the ground my fare would still be brooding fitfully and staring out my side window. What I'm leading up to is the fact that neither I nor any other cab driver could have controlled Maureen's behavior on that fateful Tuesday afternoon.

The only difference is that if another driver, whether an RMTC or a Yellow Cab or a driver from any other company in town, had driven Maureen around Five Points, she would be dead now. The only reason she was alive was because I was me. I was forgetful, stupid, and incompetent, like someone so high on crack that I forgot what I did with the three hundred dollars I tucked under my seat. If it had been anyone else, they would have remembered, would have handed it back to her and sent her to her grave. But because I was perpetually distracted by the bizarre thoughts that plague a druggie experiencing the innermost depths of self-induced hallucination, Maureen was still alive! Maureen was still alive because I was deluded into thinking I would someday write a best-selling novel. Maureen was still alive because I earned one hundred and fifty dollars a week when all of my high school friends were earning one hundred and fifty thousand dollars a year. Maureen was still alive because I wasted my time trying to help people instead of taking a sane and rational approach to life. Maureen was still alive because I was me! If I wasn't me, she wouldn't be Maureen. She would be one hundred pounds of ex–biker chick a-moldering in the grave.

My diction was getting a little out of hand at this point, but I realized that was okay. That was me too. In fact, everything I did could be attributed to the fact that I was myself. I couldn't blame anybody but me for my behavior, which made me exactly like Maureen, including the "still alive" part. Metaphysically speaking, if I wasn't me, I wouldn't be me. I wouldn't be anybody else either. I would not be at all. I would simply not be. Is this what Jean-Paul Sartre meant when he wrote *Being and Nothingness*? I had no idea. I've never actually read a book by Sartre. I've read Camus, and that pretty much put a halt to my existentialism. Camus got me through a lot of hilarious beer-soaked conversations in college, but one brilliant Frenchman in a lifetime was enough for me. Too much existentialism is like too much scotch. I don't even know what I mean by that, except it has the odor of existentialism, which is good enough for me. I would strongly advise everybody not to drink too much scotch. I'm not sure if Camus or Sartre would agree with me—I doubt if they even spoke English. Who has time to learn English when the Nazis are crawling all over the Champs-Élysées? I had been accused of that by my drinking buddies in college.

Not crawling all over the Champs-Élysées, but when I reached a point of such inebriation that I couldn't speak English, it was time to head for

Winchell's donuts for a cup of black coffee. That's how most of our evenings ended. I suddenly realized that I did not want to be buried chugging a last beer. I wanted to be buried with a Winchell's donut between my lips. And hold the joe. There's nothing more irritating than waking up in a wet coffin.

Thank you, Albert Camus.

I breathed a deep sigh of relief. Due to my inability to complete a rational paragraph, I felt I had resolved my problem. All I had to do was convince Spinelli that I had in fact saved Maureen's life by forgetting about the three bills beneath my seat. I might have to do this while being crucified to an aspen tree, but maybe my words would sink in before the nails did. After all, by returning to the house, which would not have happened if any other cab driver in town had chauffeured her, I had been given the opportunity to raise the dead. I realized that crucifixion was what they sometimes did to people who went around doing the things that I did, but maybe I could change the outcome of history and avoid my appointment on Calvary.

When I was a kid I always thought "Calvary" was the same as "cavalry." When I was staring out the grade school window, I imagined Jesus being surrounded by troops from Fort Riley, Kansas. By the same token, I imagined General George Custer surrounded by Roman soldiers. This might explain the F that I got on my religion report card, which made my Maw laugh and remark, "Sure, but you are your father's son," thank God. Almost all cab drivers believe they are adopted. I'm almost convinced I wasn't.

I knew then that I would have to face the music, call Spinelli, and accept his invitation to go on the run to the reservoir. I understood that it would be like walking into The Meatgrinder, but I also felt like I would be going to confession. Either way, I would die and end up in heaven, but by doing it my way, at least I would have a clean bill of health when I checked in at the Pearly Gates. What more could you ask of death? It occurred to me then that this was Wednesday and Saturday was three days away. I was almost charmed out of my tennis shoes by this realization. In three days I was slated to die. I felt like a prophet, or a crystal ball gazer, or a Yellow Cab driver. Those guys have egos bigger than my beer belly.

I picked up the phone with a lighthearted lilt of laughter on my tongue and dialed the garage headquarters of the toughest outlaw biker gang in

Commerce City: The Varmints.

"Yeah."

This is how bikers answer phones.

"Hello, this is Murph the taxi driver, may I please speak to Mr. Spinelli?"

What a wimpy sentence, I thought. It made me smile. Apparently, I was willing to sink to any level of common courtesy just to save my ass.

"Who did you say this is?" the voice said.

"Murph. I'm a taxi driver with the Rocky Mountain Taxicab Company. Mr. Spinelli knows me. I'm returning a phone call that he made to me . . ."

"Hold on a sec."

He set the phone down. I waited. Apparently, Spinelli was busy. I could hear intriguing metallic noises in the background. Hammering sounds. Clanks. Your garden- variety garage sounds.

"This is Doc. What do you want, Murph?"

"Oh hi, Doc. I need to talk to Spinelli."

"He can't talk now. Listen Murph. Forget about Cherry Creek Reservoir. Don't call back again until next Monday. Got that?"

"I got it. What's the matter?"

"None of your business, Murph."

"Is Maureen okay?" I was buying time.

It worked.

"Yeah, she's okay. Listen Murph, I'll keep you posted if her condition changes, but don't call back here again until next week. Okay?"

"Okay."

He hung up.

That was clearly a dissatisfying phone call. For one thing, it postponed my doom for a week. If things had gone according to my plan, I wouldn't even be alive next Monday. This was not unusual, but it was irritating. What was going on? But at least Maureen was okay.

I sat down in my easy chair to give this some thought. It worked. Maybe I wasn't welcome at The Varmints' headquarters, but I had not been forbidden to visit Maureen. That's what I would do. Visit her every day. Isn't this what Jesus said? Visit people in hospitals, visit people in jails, give food to the poor. I wondered what that jail business was all about. Why would it occur to Jesus to tell his followers to visit jailbirds? What was jail like two thousand years ago? Conditions probably haven't changed much. Do people in jail really want visitors? Having never been in a jail long enough to receive visitors, I really didn't know the mindset. I'm not sure I would want visitors if I was doing time in lockup. I especially wouldn't want a visit from my Maw. That would be almost as embarrassing as having my Maw show up at school. She did that sometimes. I once forgot my sack lunch and my Maw brought it to school at nine in the morning and stood talking to the nun for five of the most excruciating minutes of my boyhood. My mother was inside my school! She was standing by the desk talking to the nun! Maw, have you no mercy! The other kids can see you!

While I have never given my brain much thought, I found it interesting to remember how terribly embarrassing it was to see my mother in my school. Why did I feel that way? I certainly never felt that way at dinnertime. I didn't feel that way when she gave me money for the Popsicle man. My Maw and the nun held their arms akimbo as they jabbered about inconsequential matters. I felt like I was watching Winston Churchill trading my best-kept secrets with Joe Stalin. Collaboration. Collusion! Will you please leave the building!!!

Yes, my brain was somewhat interesting when I was ten.

Maybe someday I will tell you about my brain vs. the wild world of puberty, but in the meantime I decided to do as Doc said and avoid contacting Spinelli until the following Monday at the earliest. Maybe Tuesday. Maybe never. I would play it by ear.

CHAPTER 13

My first inclination was to go to work every day to take my mind off my brain, but when I woke up the next morning I realized that I would not be going back to work until this awful situation was resolved. I wouldn't be able to think clearly about anything except Maureen. I might run a stop sign or fail to note the direction of traffic on a one-way street.

Let me explain:

When I was a newbie I once pulled up to a stop sign at 23rd and York. But because I was new I had not yet learned the street system, and for some reason I thought York was a one-way street. As a result, I looked to my right and did not see any traffic. Therefore I pulled out onto York, looked to my left, and saw the North Korean army bearing down on me in the form of automobile grills. They were perhaps twenty feet away. I punched the accelerator and made it across the street without being broadsided. I had come to within two seconds of losing my taxi license and maybe my life. Did I feel stupid? Give me a break.

As a consequence, I left my apartment the next morning, climbed into Blue Boy, and headed for Denver General. I won't drag you along the path through the scary forest. We will take the magic bridge.

The nurse at the desk told me that Maureen had not yet regained consciousness. She also informed me that Maureen's boyfriend, Ted, was not present. She thought he went home to take a shower. Normally I am not interested in the hygienic habits of outlaw bikers, but in this case I filed it in my mental Rolodex under "Nice To Know."

The nurse told me I could go in and sit with Maureen for ten minutes, but I was not to disturb her. I liked that. No need to have two disturbed people in her room.

I entered and sat down on the plastic chair adjacent to Maureen's bed. Ted had been sitting on it, and now I was. I felt like I was sitting on the hot seat. Maybe Ted had just left. I didn't think to ask. But I was relieved that he was not here. I had not been looking forward to talking to him. I was also relieved that Maureen had not regained consciousness. This meant that she had not told anyone that I had killed her. It was at this moment that the ten minutes turned into the longest ten minutes of my life.

I had always accepted the fact that I was the embodiment of pure evil and was able to live with it. Until now. What was I doing feeling relieved that Ted was not present and that Maureen was unconscious? What was wrong with me? What kind of a person was I? Here I was, sitting in a hospital room looking at a horizontal woman hooked up to all kinds of tubes, including an oxygen tube hooked to her nostrils. I was the reason she was there. If I didn't exist, she wouldn't be there. I felt like George in *It's a Wonderful Life*. It was not a good feeling, even though I like Jimmy Stewart. He was one of the most talented and versatile actors who ever lived, plus he flew a B-29 in WWII and dropped bombs on Nazis. Then he came home and went back to work. When I got out of the army I went home and stayed drunk for a year trying to recover from the fact that I had spent two years in what ironically turned out to be "the real world." If you have ever served in the military you might not believe that, but the army was more real than anything I've done since, which you probably would have no trouble believing. If you think cab driving is a real job, you should try it sometime. It's so unreal that I feel quite at home. I don't think I could stand it if cab driving was real. Yet here I was, sitting in a room with a woman who had OD'd thanks to me. I had overstepped the boundaries. I had made the mistake of allowing the real world to slop over into a fantasy worthy of a five-year-old seeing Peter Pan for the first time.

What if Maureen didn't recover? Looking at it objectively, this would mean that I would get off scot-free. It reminded me of the time I almost absconded to Tahiti with one hundred thousand dollars of stolen bank money. It's a long story.

I realized then that looking at things objectively might very well be the root source of all my problems. When I looked at things objectively I came to conclusions that one might expect of a typhoid germ. How dare I seek relief in objectivity? How dare I decide that if Maureen didn't recover I would become as pure as the driven snow, objectively speaking? If she quietly slipped away, nobody would know of my involvement in her coma and possible death.

I don't know if it was the clean fresh air of the hospital or my conscience waking from a peaceful sleep. My conscience always gets angry when I yank it out of dreamland. But I suddenly began to feel physically ill. I knew then that I was what I had been during the one-hundred-thousand-dollar mix-up. I was bad to the bone.

When would it end?

I glanced at my wristwatch and saw to my horror that only two minutes had passed since I had sat down. It felt like two years. I wanted to get up and walk out. "There you go again" a voice said. It might have been Joanne Woodward. It might even have been Ronald Reagan. I suspect there are a lot of actors rattling around inside my head. How else could I explain my precision phoniness? I was at the mercy of pros.

And to top it off, I was bad to the bone.

I looked at Maureen's pale face and knew that if she died it would be the end of me. Among other things, I would have to quit my fantasy job and find a real job. But that wasn't the worst part. Sooner or later I would have to go to Big Al and confess my sins and beg for absolution. Forget the Catholic Church with its Saturday night confession, three Our Fathers and three Hail Marys, followed by Mass, Communion, and a week of brand-new sins. Compared to the Catholic Church, Big Al was the Lord High Exorcist of North America. He was the only person on earth that I knew of who could get a stranglehold on my sins and cast them into the fiery furnace. He went to a Jesuit high school. The bastard actually spoke Latin. On purpose. Just to make me feel stupid.

"Nuns, huh?" he used to say to me after we first met.

That's all he needed to say.

If only Big Al wasn't in Vegas gambling like the devil and tickling the chins of scantily clad babes. If only he was here to tell me what to do.

"You know what to do," Big Al said.

I closed my eyes and pretended I did not hear that.

I opened my eyes and looked at Maureen, then glanced at my watch. I had now been in the room eleven minutes. I had broken the ten-minute rule. When—oh when—would it end?

I got up and took a last look at Maureen's prone form, then walked out of the room intending to apologize to the nurse for breaking the rule. But she seemed busy at the desk and barely glanced at me as I walked quickly by and headed for the elevator for my descent to either the landscape of Hell or else Denver, Colorado. At this point I could not have told you what the difference was, aside from the ski industry.

This caused me to start thinking of a novel about snowboarders in Hell, but fortunately it ended when I got back to Blue Boy. I had more realistic things on my mind, starting with my visit to the garage headquarters of The Varmints.

Doc had made it clear to me that I would not be welcome there. That was okay with me. I was never welcome anywhere. I felt in my element as I aimed my hood ornament toward the one place in Denver where I was not welcome this week. Last week I was not welcome at a woman's apartment, but I don't want to get into that. One time I was not welcome at Sweeney's Tavern in downtown Denver because I was a murder suspect, which was nothing more than a ridiculous misunderstanding. To my knowledge, I had never murdered anyone prior to this week, but try and tell that to an Irish bartender who believes everything he reads in the paper. He had scotch-taped a *Denver Post* article about my involvement in the murder to his bar bulletin board. For about a week I was the talk of the town. I was in the spotlight. Everybody hated me. It came as somewhat of a letdown when I was exonerated and everybody started liking me again. I still miss that spotlight. I guess showbiz is in my blood.

It took me twenty minutes to get to Commerce City. As I drove up Vasquez Boulevard I could see the dog track in the distance. A sudden urge to bet on the dogs overcame me. Sudden urges always overcame me when I'm doing something I don't want to do. Instead, I made a right turn and headed into the neighborhood where Spinelli lived. I liked driving into this part of town. It was like driving into the 1950s. WWII had just barely ended and all the GIs were living in little clapboard shotgun houses in the suburbs. The suburbs were destined to become Commerce City in the way that Aurora was destined to become Aurora, but it was the "time travel" element that I enjoyed. As I approached the alley that led to the headquarters of The Varmints, I saw a sawhorse blocking the alley. I slowed and cruised past the alley thinking perhaps some sort of roadwork was being done, the alley torn up, the sewer system repaired, but I saw no city trucks.

I drove on past and went to the street where Spinelli lived, intending to turn down that street, but instead I saw two sawhorses and two bikers standing behind them. I slowed even further thinking that I might recognize the men, but when I got close they both turned and faced me with their arms folded. It was not so much their folded arms but what I saw before they turned that bothered me. The logo on their colors read: The Varmints, Phoenix Chapter.

The two men stared me down as I rolled past. I stepped on the gas and went down to the next block wondering what Phoenix Varmints were doing in Denver, but then I remembered the picnic at Cherry Creek Reservoir. This didn't explain the sawhorses, but it did help to explain what I found at the other end of the street after I made the circuit. Two men wearing bikers' colors were standing behind two sawhorses at that end of Spinelli's block, and both were wearing colors that read: The Varmints, Rapid City.

I found it hard to believe that there were people in Rapid City, much less bikers, but there stood the evidence. They too stared me down as I rolled past. I didn't know what was going on, and as usual I immediately lost interest and started driving home. The slightest thing can cause me to lose interest in things, and since four bikers from out of town do not qualify as "slight," you can imagine how little interest I had in pursuing whatever it was I went to Commerce City to find. By the time I got back to my apartment I could barely remember where I had been. When I lose interest in something, I go whole hog.

I climbed the back steps to my crow's nest whistling a merry tune, and as soon as I got inside I rushed to my TV to see if any episodes of *Gilligan's Island* were being broadcast from Chicago or LA. The local Denver TV stations do not broadcast *Gilligan* in the daytime. They are very strict about that. I don't know if the new mayor has anything to do with it, but I'm lucky if I can get Mary Ann before 5 p.m. on a Saturday. Did I ever tell you about the time I got Mary Ann at twelve noon on a Sunday? She was doing the twist. Yikes! I don't even want to talk about it.

Thanks to my innate inability to remember important things, I was drinking a beer and channel surfing when I heard the dreaded sound of footsteps coming up the rear fire escape. The first word that popped into my head was "Harold," but it would take too long to explain. Believe me, you don't want to hear the explanation. I live for the day I forget the reason for the explanation, but I fear that day will never come because I go to Sweeney's Tavern a lot. See? This explanation is getting completely out of control, but that's what the word "Harold" does to me.

By now I was sitting up straight on my easy chair, which isn't easy because it's padded, and sitting up straight is like trying to do the funky chicken on a waterbed. The footsteps made the last of the two-tiered metal ladder that leads up to my door. No time to shut off all the lights and dive into bed. I waited for the timid knock of "H— —," but instead I heard three quick, furious pounds on the wooden door. Somebody besides u-no-hoo was requesting my attention, and I couldn't decide whether I was relieved or even more afraid of finding "hoo." You would feel this way too if you ever drank beer at Sweeney's.

"Hoo's there?" I said.

"It's Moochie, man, open up."

Oh Christ. Spinelli had sent Moochie to kill me. The irony was unbelievably pedestrian. I wondered if I had any reason to go on living, then gave up on that line of thought and opened the door.

Moochie was standing there in his colors, leathers, spangles. His bike was parked at the bottom of the fire escape. "How's it going, man," he said. "I hope you don't mind me dropping by without calling. I was down at the gym pumping arn and I wanted to show you something. Do you got a moment?"

In a moment I expected to have all eternity on my hands, so I didn't really know how to answer his question. I decided to go with the gutless but reliable "nod," and opened the door so he could enter.

He entered talking. I had noticed this about the bikers after I first met them. They seemed to do things without preamble. They get right to the point. They are so unlike real people that anyone except people like myself would have a hard time keeping up with them on a daily basis. I expected him to glance around and comment upon the cozy and sensational atmosphere of my crow's nest, but we might as well have been standing within the bland environs of a bus station.

"Hey, listen up, man," he began. "I heard you like to write stuff."

I nodded again, although I was secretly frowning on the inside. Was he setting me up for a fall? Was he going to distract me by stroking my ego—and then bushwhack me when I let my guard down? But no. That seemed too preambular. If he was going to bushwhack me, he probably would have whipped out a gat the moment I opened the door. That's what I would do if bushwhacking was my game. My only game.

"I want to read all your novels," Moochie said.

I suffered a myocardial infarction when he said that, but I covered it up by pulling a couple of Rolaids from my pocket and popping them into my mouth. I keep Rolaids in the tiny pocket sewn above the regular pocket on the right-front side of my jeans. I don't know what that little pocket is actually for. Keys maybe, or small change. Or maybe it's just there for decorative purposes, like so many useless things in this world. Have you ever been to the Museum of Modern Art in New York City? Me neither.

"I gave up trying to be a novelist a long time ago, dude," I said, hoping the word "dude" would keep me on his good side.

He reached inside his black leather jacket. I assumed he was going for a gun at last. From my experience, that's where people kept guns. The Day Of The Gunslinger was long past. You rarely see cowboys with shoulder holsters. But he wasn't going for a gun. It was something far worse.

He yanked out a sheet of paper and held it up. "The reason I mentioned it, man, is because I write poetry."

I reached for the Rolaids.

"And since you're, like, a writer, man," he continued, "I wondered if you would read my poem and tell me if it's any good."

For the first time since Maureen's OD I felt like crying.

"Poems are rather subjective," I began. "The dominant element of poetry is lyricism rather than story, which is the realm of the novel, just as melody is the . . ."

"I hear you, man," he said, shoving the piece of paper through the air toward my eyes and interrupting the speech that my poetry professor had given us at UCD. It was a required class. I needed the credit to receive my English degree. We had to write three poems in order to pass the class. My first poem was titled "Living Hell 101." It got an A. Let's move on.

Even though I was in shock, I remembered something that I had learned a long time ago about poets: if you don't read their poems today, they will just bring them back tomorrow.

Riding My Bike
by
"Moochie"

Clutch pop.
My teeth are whistles.
Air barges into my lungs
when I breathe speed.

The single-stroke warms my ankles
like a woman
gripping my boots
when I hug speed.

The table is set
with a black asphalt spread.
Faster is my feast.
It fills my gut with distance
when I eat speed.

I lowered the piece of paper with tears in my eyes.

"Don't you like it, man?" he said.

I wiped away my tears and nodded. "I like it, Moochie. It's the best poem I've ever read by someone I know."

"The best?"

"I particularly like the ambiguity of the word 'speed.'"

"Huh?" he replied.

"It can be read on two levels."

"Yeah?"

"That's one of the characteristics of art. True art can be interpreted on more than one level."

"You mean you're like, this is art?"

"You have to understand that I'm just a failed novelist and not a literary critic," I said, although I did not know what the distinction was. "But I think your poem could be published."

"Do you think *Biker Rag* would publish it?"

"What's that?"

"A magazine I subscribe to."

"Do they publish poetry?"

"Yeah. They publish all kinds of crap."

I shrugged. "Give it a shot," I said. "Who knows? This might be the dawn of a new era for *Biker Rag*."

He lifted the paper with both hands and frowned at it. "Maybe I should change the title to 'The Best Poem Ever Written.'"

"No . . . I think 'Riding My Bike' is an excellent title. It tells the reader what the poem is about without giving away anything."

"Is that good?"

"It's the best."

"Thanks for reading my stuff, man."

I tried not to think about the biker definition of "literary success."

He rolled his poem into a scroll and tucked it into his black leather jacket and said, "I probably won't be seeing you again for a couple weeks."

"Why is that?"

"The rumble. I might get clobbered."

"I'm sorry, you have the advantage," I said. "What rumble are you referring to?"

"The picnic this weekend in Cherry Creek Reservoir was cancelled. Didn't you hear about it?"

He paused and glanced at me with a peculiar eye. "Spinelli found out that the Denver Dragons are holding their Labor Day picnic at Cherry Creek Reservoir, so that's where we're going to ambush them."

I nodded and felt a chill as cold as the headwaters of the Platte beginning to creep up my spine.

"Why are you going to ambush them?" I said. I do not believe I had ever said that sentence before in my life.

"Spinelli found out that Maureen's ex–old man sold her the drugs that landed her in the hospital, so we're heading out to Cherry Creek on Saturday morning to deliver a few buckets full of whup-ass."

By now I was like one of those ice-carvings that you see at corporate Christmas parties except I didn't have swan wings and a nest of champagne bottles tucked under my butt.

"What ex–old man?" I said.

"Maureen used to date a guy with the Dragons, back when we were one club. Spinelli hates him."

"How does Spinelli know he sold her the drugs?" I said.

"Ya got me," Moochie said, zipping up the front of his leathers and pulling out his gloves. "Spinelli knows all kinds of stuff. That's why he's the leader."

Without remarking on the charm of my apartment, Moochie turned and headed for the kitchen door. He yanked it open and looked back at me. "You're probably welcome at the rumble," he said. "I can ask Spinelli if you want to make the run. You can hitch a ride on the back of my bike."

"I'll give that some thought," I said in a voice so hollow and tin-like that

I might have been made of hollow tin.

"Catch you later, man," Moochie said, and with that he was gone, along with my mind.

CHAPTER 14

I was sitting in my Fortress of Solitude drinking a Coke and staring at the dark landscape that forbade me to see any further than one inch. This was unusual. I had not hidden out in the Fortress since I was twelve years old. I first encountered the Fortress of Solitude in Superman comics, then later learned that Doc Savage had his own Fortress of Solitude. This is turn motivated me to write a letter to Kenneth Robeson suggesting that he sue DC Comics for plagiarism. But like most of my brilliant ideas, I forgot it and found myself at the age of forty-six hiding inside my own Fortress of Solitude. I figured I was legally safe because Robeson apparently never sued DC, which put the Fortress of Solitude in the public domain. In my case, it's located in my bedroom under a paisley bedspread that a hippie girl once gave me for favors rendered.

The bedspread was fifteen feet in diameter and covered me and the entire bed. I was seated cross-legged in the middle of the bed with no shoes. Neither Doc Savage nor Superman allowed people to wear shoes when they entered his Fortress, and I decided for legal reasons to continue the custom. I was hiding out from an outlaw biker gang. The fact that my hideout consisted of cotton cloth one-twentieth of an inch thick demonstrates how deluded I can be when I really set my mind to it. I knew now that there was no hope for me. My refusal to face the music and tell the truth was going to result in a gang war, bloodshed, and possible death. An innocent man would be run to ground and stomped by Spinelli and his gang. The Cherry Creek Reservoir Parks and Recreation Security Patrol would have its hands full with what I assumed would be at least two hundred crazed bikers going at it with tire-irons and chains. This was ironic because I had once applied for a job with the P&R Department. Because the job looked easy. Anybody can wear shorts. I had never worn shorts in the army, but the P&R shorts were made of khaki so I did bring that particular military skill to the job. This was around the same time that

I took the Post Office test. I failed both tests. If I had passed the P&R test, I would have been required by law to show up for work next Saturday and try to control two armies of rabid bikers. The irony lay in the fact that I was going to show up for the rumble anyway, without getting paid the minimum government wage for P&R personnel, which I believe was $12.35 an hour at the time of which I speak. I would now be dying for free.

Doing things for free always makes me feel noble, which is why I rarely feel noble. Of all the fraudulent postures that I incorporate as a cab driver, nobility is the most exhausting and stressful. It can get expensive too, especially when you start giving out free rides to people whose lives you have ruined. I prefer the posture of greedy cynic. For some reason that characterization fits me like a glove. But that's the problem with posturing—you get lazy. Pretty soon you forget how to fake it when the chips are down. When I thought back on all the messes I had gotten out of by pretending not to be me, I was surprised I was capable of remembering who I really was. I don't think it would be sufficient to describe myself as a "fraud." It might be accurate but not sufficient. I prefer to think of myself as a "survivor." A hard-core cynic might describe me as "a gutless puke incapable of taking responsibility for his own actions." It depends on your point of view: survivor, fraud, gutless puke, I was a regular Rashomon of an individual. And don't get me started on all the people who live inside my head, including Joanne Woodward. I don't know how they got there and I don't want to know.

Occasionally they helped me out when I got into a tight fix, but as I sat there in my Fortress of Solitude trying to decide what to do, I could not help but feel that the multitudes who resided inside my skull had turned their backs on me out of shame. I had killed a girl, and now my silence was going to result in the injury and possible death of total strangers. Sure, I had brought the girl back to life, but the agony of defeat always seems to leave a larger footprint than the thrill of victory. I mean, let's face it, I wouldn't have had to bring her back to life if I hadn't killed her in the first place.

"Just go tell Spinelli the truth," a voice said out loud. It was probably me but I was hoping it was Big Al, simply because he was always right. In other words, if I had said it, it would be the wrong solution—but if Big Al had said it, it would be the right solution. The internal dynamics of sheer nonsense is as impossible to trace as the loops of a Gordian knot, which is irrelevant anyway because it's only a single strand of rope. My approach had always been to try and untangle the mess, but Big Al's approach was the same as that of Alexander the Great: whip out a sword, slice the knot, and get on with your life.

The problem with the Alexandrian solution was that, in this case, the "get on with your life" part would not apply. When Spinelli found out that I had helped his sister buy drugs, he would not only kill me, he would have to apologize to the Denver Dragons for defamation of character, assuming they had any. After all, they did steal Moochie's bike.

Maybe I should go to the police and warn them that there was going to be a massive gang fight at Cherry Creek Reservoir, all because of me. Duncan and Argyle wouldn't have any trouble believing that. They were a couple of detectives in the Missing Persons Bureau who had brought me in for questioning so many times that I qualified for free air mileage points in their paddy wagon. Then it occurred to me that I would have to admit that I had been voluntarily involved in the purchase of crack cocaine. I would not be able to fall back on my hole card: "Hey, I'm just a cabbie. I get paid to drive people where they want to go, I have no interest in why they want to go there." Which is to say, I'm the "form" in the form-versus-content debate. I cannot be held responsible for what my fares do. I am a tool used by people to achieve their goals. I am the vessel, thou art the wine.

This garbage went on for a while until it started to get hot under my Fortress of Solitude. I dragged the paisley spread off my head and took a deep breath and let it out slowly—the way I like it. My face was covered with sweat. I didn't know if it was normal sweat or the sweat of guilt, my least favorite category of sweat, next to asking a woman for a date.

"You know what to do," I said as I untangled the Gordian knot of my legs and planted my bare feet on the floor of my bedroom. While that sentence was syntactically correct, there wasn't a word of truth in it. I said it only to kick-start the subconscious machinations that frequently lead me to solutions. They usually led me to Big Al, but he was in Vegas and I was on my own. My only hope was that I was subconsciously unaware that I was on my own. If my subconscious thought that I was going to get dressed and scour the mean streets of Denver in search of Big Al's taxi, maybe my subconscious would relax and start listening to Pachelbel's soothing melodies, which it had memorized from my years of lying on a beach towel in my living room and gazing at a handful of black-and-white photographs of Mary Ann that I had snapped off the screen of my TV. Don't tell Sherwood Schwartz. I'm not certain what the copyright laws are concerning the illicit reproduction of television images for private viewing, and I have no interest in getting dragged off to Hollywood to face another lawsuit. The last time I was in Hollywood I was looking for a girl that I had supposedly "murdered." I don't know what makes Denver flatfoots think I am capable of murder. Involuntary manslaughter, sure, but murder? Save it for the late show, pal.

I glanced at my clock. It was a little after 8 p.m. It had been almost an hour since Moochie had visited me, but even then I went to my kitchen window and looked down into the parking lot to make certain he was not there. This was not unusual. I spend half my time making certain that people are not anywhere. It doesn't always work, which doesn't explain why I do it. But the parking lot was empty. Blue Boy was parked in the choice "V" spot. There were no other cars in the lot. I didn't know where my belowstairs neighbors were. I never know that, but it always pleases me to know that my building is empty except for me. It makes me feel like Leonardo DiCaprio standing at the bow. I gazed out over the sea of roofs that led toward downtown Denver where the lights shone the brightest, and I thought about all the other times I had gazed at the roofs of the city during the midst of messes. I had been in the middle of so many messes during the past couple years that one would think I would be used to it, but you never get used to knowing that you live in Denver. It is somewhat of an acquired taste. The irony is that I spend half my time wishing I were somewhere else, usually Wichita, which is like Denver minus the mountains.

I felt strange. Given my circumstances you wouldn't think I would have trouble putting my finger on the crux of the problem, but I couldn't. I had never felt quite this way before. I had never helped to kill anybody before either, but even that didn't seem like the crux. Trying to find a crux is like trying to find lost car keys. Irritating to the point of infuriating if it goes on long enough.

I turned and walked back into the living room thinking that perhaps some TV would take my mind off my crux problem. TV took my mind off everything else, why not a crux? I sat down and lifted my remote off the side table and aimed it at the TV, but I could not bring myself to turn the TV on. I knew that if I turned on the TV, it would serve only to postpone my discovery of the crux, which was as appealing as the idea of postponing a dentist appointment. I have never liked the concept of postponing. Either do it or cancel it, that's my philosophy. Postponement is the purgatory of "doing things." I set the remote down and sat in the silence trying to understand this strange feeling, and as I did so my eyes fell on the telephone. Since there are some people in this world who take sentences literally, let me rephrase that. My eyeballs did not pop out of my head and land on the telephone, I merely saw the telephone. But suddenly I realized what the strange, unique, unprecedented feeling was: I was waiting for the telephone to ring.

I had never done anything so insane in my life.

It sent a chill down my spine. I leaped out of the chair and backed away from the phone, staring at it as if it was a rattler about to strike. I knew then that I was waiting for any number of phone calls: one from the hospital telling me that Maureen was either dead or talking, or perhaps a call from Spinelli, or from the police, or any other people who were directly or indirectly related to this mess. Maybe even . . . Paul!

What if the drug pusher had tracked me down for some reason which would be made clear to me only when we came face-to-face? He probably knew my taxicab number—123—and would be able to find out from RMTC who I was and possibly even where I lived. And what about all those men who had been hanging around that green Dodge? They probably took note of every vehicle that cruised their neighborhood and memorized every auto license plate number for reasons known only to people who memorize numbers on purpose.

I suddenly felt ill.

I won't say that this was unusual or not unusual. It sort of came and went in rhythms, like an irregular heartbeat on the EKG machine of my life.

I had the sudden urge to rip the telephone out of the wall. This was usual. It was practically SOP.

I knew I had to get out of there.

The rational part of my mind told me that I was not about to receive a phone call from a pack of drug dealers or anybody else that night, but the irrational part of me, the part I take counsel from on a regular basis, was telling me to amscray hubba-hubba.

I went to my closet and pulled my deep forest green RMTC jacket from a hanger and put it on as if donning armor. My taxi jacket always made me feel safe. It was an illusion that I not only clung to but wore like a glove. I did not put on one of my many caps. This amounted to a kind of "negative" disguise in that I did not want anybody to know I was a taxi driver, should anyone be looking for me. That thought was in the back of my mind, where paranoia had set up housekeeping on the day I was born. I would evict the bastard except he had warned me away from danger on numerous occasions. Paranoia was like an old army buddy who was always hitting you up for a loan, but he saved your life in the war so you have to be nice to him—and the bastard damn well knows it.

I left my apartment and worked my way down the steep fire escape as fast as possible, which was no different from normal. Fire escapes, ironically, are not built for speed.

When I got down to the parking lot, I began the swivel-headed routine that I always followed when I was certain I would be followed. Left, right. Like that. I won't belabor it until it becomes necessary.

I pulled out onto 13th Avenue and aimed my hood toward Denver General. I wanted to visit Maureen. I wanted to see if Ted was standing watch. I wanted to know if Maureen had awakened and begun singing like a canary. I didn't care if my metaphors were inappropriate. I was worried. Worry is what I do to fend off fear. It's like a vague promise to my brain. "I'll be scared later if you let me worry now." This was a little trick I used to fool my brain. I rarely if ever came through on my promises to be scared. I was usually too busy dealing with the thing that ought to scare me to indulge in fright. My brain isn't the brightest bulb on the Christmas tree.

I made it as far as Broadway when the first of the three wobbling lights pulled up behind me. When car lights wobble and weave, you know they are not car lights. You don't even have to be an asphalt warrior to know that three motorcycles are behind you. I made a sudden change of plans. If I went to DGH, I might get cornered by three bikers who were out to get me. The fact that they would leave my body crumbled in front of an emergency room did not persuade me to cooperate with their insidious plan.

But maybe they weren't out to get me. Maybe this was the kind of coincidence that never happens in real life. And since my life rarely drifted into the realm of reality, I thought I just might have a chance. I turned left onto Broadway rather than right, hoping that these three men were in fact traveling to DGH and that we had merely crossed paths by accident. My willingness to bet on long shots proved wrong once again that night. They turned right behind me and followed me south. I knew then that I was dead. The only question was where I would die. When seemed to be during the next fifteen minutes or so. Why was irrelevant. Why is always irrelevant.

I headed down Broadway and kept the sight of three motorcycle lights in my rearview mirror. Fleeing before the storm had the strange quality of putting off the inevitable, which I was familiar with. And I didn't like it. I didn't like putting the inevitable off, and I didn't like the inevitable either. There were too many other things I would rather do—like, for instance, anything. My options were running low.

I decided that the only thing to do was evade the bikers and get to a place where I could think clearly, to make my next move. As I approached Evans Avenue, I suddenly had a flash. I would hide from the bikers, and I knew just where to do it. There is a drive-in movie theater near the intersection of Broadway and Evans called the Cinderella Drive-in. It was named in honor of Cinderella City. Cinderella City is now defunct. If you are not from Denver, you are probably wondering what Cinderella City was. But I don't have time to explain the bizarre history of Denver names. Just take my word for it: the place was once called Cinderella City and now it doesn't exist anymore.

I swung a hard right onto Evans and began making my way toward the drive-in. It's built in a kind of industrial valley filled with a lot of junkyards. The path is not easy but it's real, like the paths to most drive-in movies. It involves a lot of right and left turns, and I knew that if I could evade the bikers I would be home free. I drove down into the valley and began making my maneuvers, right, left, here, there, until I was driving along the classic white clapboard fence that traditionally decorates the ugly exteriors of so many fading landmarks in this country. Joe Bob Briggs is wrong. The drive-in will die one day—but not on my watch.

I swung left and barreled down the dirt track toward the ticket booth where a young woman sat chewing gum and waiting for the next die-hard American International buffs to hand over a dollar and sneak in with a trunkful of teenagers clutching warm beer cans to their spindly chests.

It was with a sigh of relief that I pulled up in front of the ticket booth and handed over my dollar. I glanced in the rearview mirror. The three bikers were right behind me. I canceled my relief and put it in gear, drove along a wooden fence, and made a hard left into the arena where I calculated that approximately three hundred bikers were waiting for me. It was a sea of bikers. Mine was the only car in sight. Things were working out the way they usually did. I put the cap on that tradition by giving up.

It was obvious what was happening here. I was about to be put on trial by hundreds of strangers. This was nothing new. You wouldn't believe the number of times it has happened to me. Sometimes I'm put on trial by hippies, sometimes by the people of Kansas City. I never know where the jury is coming from, but the verdict is always the same. Need I say more?

Rather than floor the accelerator, I began looking for a convenient spot to set up the stand—as in "please take the stand." I was so used to this that I had no difficulty finding the ideal spot, taking into consideration the number of judges, the shape of the terrain, natural acoustics, and so forth. I pulled into a spot not far from the snack bar, figuring that during a recess I would be able to dash to the front of the line for one of those legendary delicious drive-in movie pizzas. Just the thought of all that white goo got my heart pounding. I don't care what the situation, a picnic with the family or a trial for your life, there is nothing like cardboard and mozzarella to give a meal that zing.

I was unsnapping my seatbelt and preparing to throw myself on the mercy of the bikers when the perimeter lights went out and the movie projector started up. This was a highly unorthodox procedure, but I decided to wait before voicing an objection. A moment later images began appearing on the wide screen and the words "The Savage Seven" came up.

Horns began beeping. Buzzer biker horns, the kind of horns they build into motorcycles, the exact opposite of semi-tractor-trailer horns. Men began howling. I assumed it was for my blood. I began to hear a strange rattling sound—strange yet familiar—and as I paused in my preparations for condemnation, suddenly I realized what I was hearing: pop-tops. Someone was opening beer cans. And not just anyone but the hundreds of judges who had gathered to examine the evidence, then hang me either metaphorically or really. Since these were bikers, I assumed they would take the *really* route. Bikers are very up-front when it comes to judgment, accusations, vengeance, retaliation, vindictiveness, retribution, Lordy Lordy, the list is almost endless.

The popping died down, the beeping died down, and as far as I could tell the trial was put on hold because everybody was leaning back on their bikes like cowboys in the saddle and watching the movie. I began to get the feeling that I had misinterpreted something along the way.

I turned in the seat and scoured the landscape and suddenly saw the marquee blazing in the sky beyond the big screen. It read as follows: "Dusk-to-Dawn Motorcycle Marathon. See 5 Count 'Em 5 Action-Packed Thrillers Featuring America's Two-Wheeled Outlaws On The Loose!!!!"

As an English major, I was somewhat offended by the profusion of uppercase letters. I had the urge to go to the manager's office and register a complaint about the decline and fall of the King's English, but then I realized that the marquee had probably been posted by a minimum-wage drive-in worker who didn't have a classical education in literature like moi. I decided to give the poor sap a break. Who knows—maybe he simply ran out of lowercase letters and was forced to improvise like a Green Beret living off the land in enemy terrain. People who abuse the English language often make good snipers.

Suddenly everything made sense.

I rarely say that, but in this case it was true. In my paranoid desperation to avoid the three bikers who had trailed me down Broadway, I had inadvertently taken refuge in the very location that the three bikers were headed for. It was the sort of thing that happens only in fiction and never in real life.

I breathed a deep sigh of drive-in-theater air, exhaled the odor of popcorn and bad pizza, and reached for my ignition key.

It was this precise moment that I saw something that made my hair stand on end. Penny Marshall.

Yes—one of the two immortal stars of *Laverne & Shirley* had a role in *The Savage Seven*. "Laverne," to be exact, for those of you who are unfamiliar with the cultural highlights of the 1970s. My hand froze on the ignition key and my mind began to reel. I did the only thing I could do in such a situation. I dived out of my car, rushed to the snack stand, bought a box of popcorn and a Pepsi, and rushed back to my car just in time to see Robert Walker Jr. come onstage. Yes—the son of the star of *Strangers on a Train* was also the star of *The Savage Seven*. He looked just like his father. My mind continued to reel. It reeled right up to the moment where Penny Marshall started kissing badass dudes at a biker party. At that point I sighed, burped, and started the engine. I had seen enough.

As I drove out of the theater, I wondered whatever became of Robert Walker Jr. Did he go on to star in other movies? I decided not to ask. Just seeing the son of *Train* satisfied my craving for bizarre cravings. The experiences of the past hour had calmed me down to the extent that I now knew exactly what I had to do: throw myself at the mercy of Mother Church. Whether or not I was actually going to do that remained to be seen, but at least I knew what to do. That's always a good starting point in the solution of any dilemma. Not "throwing yourself at the mercy of Mother Church" but "knowing what to do."

The next step was to find a Catholic church that was open at this time of night. I felt like Quasimodo bellowing "Sanctuary! Sanctuary!" as he raced through the teeming streets of Paris pursued by an angry mob that did resemble outlaw bikers to an astonishing degree. That Victor Hugo was quite a prophetic writer. I once knew a teenage girl whose favorite author was Victor Hugo. I was suspected by the police of kidnaping and murdering her, but I assure you that it was just another of those silly misunderstandings that can happen to any forty-five-year-old male with a checkered past.

I drove up Broadway, which turned into Lincoln in the stupid way that Denver streets often do. I continued north and came to Alameda. I recalled that there was a Catholic church on Sherman Street, so I turned right and drove down the block and sure enough, there was Saint Something with its tall green steeple. It towered over a Catholic grade school that looked just like the grade school I attended in Wichita, Kansas. This ought to have comforted me. Let's move on.

I parked in front of the church and got out of my car. The wind was picking up. The sky was overcast. I whispered a silent prayer that the rain would not ruin the dusk-to-dawn biker show, then I walked up to the big Quasimodo doors and knocked. To be honest, I was sort of hoping that nobody would be home, but since it was God's house I will let you finish the thought.

A white-haired old priest opened the door.

"Yes, my son?" he said.

"Faddah," I said. Then I cleared my throat and said, "Father, I wonder if you could help me out."

"I will do my best, my son," he said.

His syntax sort of creeped me out, but this had always been true of priests, nuns, cops, and drill sergeants, so I continued to march.

"I wonder if you could give me the address of a local Alcoholics Anonymous meeting," I said. "I need to talk to someone who is an expert at drug addiction."

"Come in, come in, my son," he said, raising a hand and reaching toward me.

I let him touch my shoulder. He guided me into the vestibule. The last time I had been touched by a priest I became a Catholic. I was only a couple months old, so I don't really remember my baptism but, strangely, I do remember the noise of the party afterwards. Irish/Catholics get a big kick out of practically everything.

"Are you in need of spiritual guidance, my son?" the priest said.

What a loaded question. It took all my willpower to strip away a dozen or so smart-aleck answers and get down to cases.

"No, Faddah . . . Father, I have a friend who is addicted to crack cocaine and I need to ask some experts how to . . ."

"There is no need to be ashamed of your problem, my son," he said, giving me the fish-eye.

I saw where this was going. He thought I was the person with the drug problem and that I was pretending I was okay. Under any other circumstances I might have taken off running, but I decided to play along. "Playing along" is one of the best ways I know of to cut a conversation short with a priest.

"I would like to attend an AA meeting tonight."

"I noticed that you parked your car in front of the church," he said. "Are you intoxicated right at this moment?"

"Oh no, Father. In fact, I was thinking about going to a bar when I accidentally drove past the church and realized that God may have given me one last chance to redeem myself."

"It's been known to happen," he said. "What is your name, my son?"

"Brendan Murphy."

"Are you a member of this parish?"

"Oh no, Father. To tell you the truth, it's been a long time since I last attended Mass."

"When was that?"

"Last Christmas. I went home to Wichita for a visit and attended midnight Mass with my mother and sister."

"Wichita?" he said. "Were you a member of Blessed Virgin Catholic Parish?"

"Er . . . yes."

"By any chance did you know Monsignor O'Leary?"

I froze.

How could this be? I looked at the white hair on this man's head and realized that he and Monsignor O'Leary were probably the same age.

"Yes," I said in a guilty whisper. Why "guilty" I do not know. You be the judge.

"What a wonderful coincidence," he said. "I served on the faculty at Blessed Virgin Grade School when I was a young priest. I taught classes in religion."

"Oh yes, I remember those classes," I said. "The priests were always brought in to teach religion."

This didn't sound quite right, but he overlooked it.

"Murph . . . Murphy . . . ," he mumbled. "I knew a Murphy when I taught at Blessed Virgin. A fine outstanding student by the name of . . . let me see . . . Gavin Murphy. By any chance are you related to a Gavin Murphy?"

I began to tremble with rage. "I don't know, Father," I said through clenched teeth. "There are a lot of Murphys in Kansas."

"To be sure, to be sure," he said. "Gavin was one of the brightest students in my class. He even received the Ad Altare Dei award in his Boy Scout troop. I had always hoped that he might enter the priesthood."

So did my Maw.

You cannot believe how happy I was when Gavin disappointed her and decided to become a rich computer jerk in California. Gavin was like John Travolta's priest brother in *Saturday Night Fever*. I was like Travolta himself, except for the looks, talent, voice, and overall persona. But this is true of every actor I resemble.

"I don't know anybody named Gavin," I seethed. "At any rate, do you know of any AA meetings that I might attend tonight, Father?"

When I drove away from Saint Something, I was clutching in my fist a list of two hundred AA meetings that were taking place in Denver that night. Criminy, what a town.

CHAPTER 15

I headed west then, past Interstate 25 toward Federal Boulevard. There was an address out toward the old Villa Italia shopping center. It was in a residential neighborhood, part of Denver that sprang up after WWII composed almost entirely of low-budget shotgun housing. I turned south off Alameda Avenue and came to Center Avenue, which ran east/west. Eventually, I came across it, a little white church built of clapboard. It wasn't a Catholic church. The parking lot was barren earth. Cars were parked on three sides of the church, nose to the wall. It almost looked like a roadhouse. But this made sense. The place was filled with the sort of people who once patronized roadhouses. This made me uneasy. Any time that anything related to alcohol starts to make sense, I get edgy.

I pulled into the lot and shut off the engine. I sat listening for a moment. I expected to hear a choir singing "Yes, We Shall Gather at the River." I always expect that when I'm around Protestants. I blame *Elmer Gantry*. The Byzantine patterns of word association that strafe my mind are too complex to explain here, so let's just say that I climbed out of my car and headed for the front door of the first AA meeting I had attended since college, when I had gone out of my way to save a fellow student from turning out like me. I had to trick him into going to the meeting. Just before the two of us entered the place, I suddenly got the funny feeling that maybe he had tricked me into going to the meeting. The Byzantine patterns of paranoia that strafe my mind are so transparent and pedestrian that I would rather not talk about it.

I entered the foyer and paused a moment to glance at the AA literature laid out on a table near the entry to the auditorium of the church itself. But in reality I was peeking into the church with one eye. The other eye was scanning pamphlets with titles like, "Isn't It Time For You To Say Hello To You?"

It sounded like one of those evil-twin screenplays that litter the highways of Hollywood. But it started me thinking about writing a screenplay, like everything I do does. It would be about a man who turned into a monster whenever he drank a certain type of chemical. I pondered the idea for a moment, then decided that idea had been done to death, both in the movies and in real life. I had been drinking certain types of chemicals since the day I got my first fake ID.

Suddenly my right eye that was scouring the auditorium saw a man walking toward me. He was smiling.

I panicked. Whenever smiling people approach me in close quarters, my billfold starts to vibrate like a cell phone.

I tore my left eye away from a pamphlet entitled, "Quitters Are Winners" and looked at my visitor with both eyes. But I have to admit that I was intrigued by the title of that pamphlet. I decided to steal one when I left, even though the pamphlets were free. By "steal" I meant slip a copy surreptitiously into my coat pocket like I do with everything that I am ashamed of. Mouthwash comes to mind.

"Welcome to the westside chapter of AA," the man said. "My name is Bill."

Bill? Wasn't that the name of one of the guys who founded AA? I immediately began to suspect that this man was a pretentious phony. I felt right at home.

Glancing at his right palm to make sure he wasn't holding a joy buzzer, I shook hands with him. I will admit it. My glance was a kind of knee-jerk reaction to shaking hands with drunks. A learned thing that I kept forgetting, especially on New Year's Eve. But then I had to remind myself that Bill was not a drunk, he was a recovering alcoholic. When people stop drinking, they stop doing other things too. If I ever give up drinking, I don't know what else I will give up, since I never do anything. Maybe I should buy a joy buzzer.

"Is this your first time at AA?" Bill said.

I almost busted out laughing. This is a problem I have always wrestled with: I find practically everything funny. I really ought to get some counseling.

"No," I said. "I attended an AA meeting in college. I had to trick a friend into going because his grades were sliding and he really needed help," I said, and kept saying and saying until Bill began giving me "the eye." I didn't find that funny. As my voice withered I realized he thought I was lying about something. Alcoholics and me often do that, so I was familiar with the "snap judgment." I stopped talking and said, "I need help."

"We're here to help you, brother," he said, completely misunderstanding my statement like everybody else in the world. This didn't bother me because I was used to it. I took a deep breath, secretly sighed, and allowed Bill to take my upper arm like a cop and gently guide me into the room where people were standing around sipping cups of coffee and smoking their goddamned lungs out. I will admit that I like the smell of cigarette smoke, ergo I had the urge to "borrow" a tuber from one of the smokers. "Borrow" is a ridiculous description of the dynamics of what I wanted to do, but I used to ask soldiers in the army if I could "borrow" a cigarette, as though I had any intention of giving it back later like a used rake. One soldier got an annoyed look on his face, then said yes— but only because I had said "have" and not "borrow." As he handed me a butt he told me that he was sick of other GIs asking him if they could "borrow" a cigarette. I was the only man who ever asked him if I could "have" one. There was a lesson in this little vignette, although I'm not sure what the lesson was. I was too busy smoking my goddamned lungs out to reflect on the irony of my linguistic error, aside from realizing that if I had said "borrow" he would have reacted with scorn and umbrage, the usual response to everything I said in the army.

"Shall we start the meeting?" someone said, and there was a flurry of activity. Normally I hate flurries, but this allowed me to escape from Bill and find a seat near the back of the room where cowards always hang out. I used to sit in the back row at church for reasons that should be obvious.

Everyone took a seat on folding chairs and settled in for the night.

"Let's begin with the prayer," someone else said. Everyone stood up and bowed their heads and held hands and recited the prayer. If you are anything like me, you are familiar with the prayer. Please don't make me repeat it.

But as I stood at the back of the room feeling smug about not having to hold hands, someone took my hand. It was Bill. He smiled a big shiny smile, indicating to me that he was going to follow me like an IRS agent for the scope of the entire meeting. I have a gift for sensing horrible situations, even ones I am not responsible for instigating, fomenting, or stumbling blindly into.

It had been so long since my last AA meeting that I couldn't remember the procedure. I wanted to ask the group as a whole what I should do about the drug-induced situation that I was in. I felt that my indifference to Maureen's drug buying made me as culpable as the dealer she bought from. I wanted them to tell me what to do. I wanted them to tell me that everything was going to be okay. I wanted them to pat me on the shoulder, and reassure me, and convince me that we were not our brother's keeper and that I should not feel the slightest responsibility for this tragic situation.

It was at this point that I began to wonder if I was possessed by a devil. At first I thought I was only joking, but for some reason being in this place made me feel as if I ought to plumb the depths of my innermost being and examine my sins. Big Al always makes me feel this way. But the deeper I looked, the more shocked I was to find that I really did want to be absolved of responsibility. I wanted to avoid being blamed for anything at all costs. I really wanted to wash my hands of the whole mess and walk away. This did not explain what I was doing at an AA meeting, but I nevertheless had to acknowledge that there was something inside me that wanted to go on the lam and never look back. It was like a creature slithering around the black recesses of the bowl of my being. It resembled Gollum. Not the Gollum of *The Lord of the Rings* movie but of the novel, i.e., the Gollum that Tolkien allowed me to imagine rather than the cyber-generated force-fed artificial image conceived during mass-market consumer group gatherings and shoved down the throat of the American . . .

I seem to have gotten off the track here.

"I'd like to start off the meeting tonight by reading from the big blue book," a man said. He was standing at the front of the room. He had a beard and looked like a poet. It struck me that most people who drank too much looked like poets. This made me wonder if there was some subtle connection between my brain and reality, but I had my doubts. I decided to wait patiently and ride this out, looking for an opening to state my case.

The man read a story from the blue book. It was about a young man whose life was ruined by alcohol. After the reading, he asked if anyone would like to speak to the group about their personal experiences. At least seven people told stories about how their lives were ruined by alcohol. I started to detect a pattern. Then the man asked if there were any new people at the meeting, and I suddenly realized he was talking about me. For some reason this came as a surprise. The first time I attended an AA meeting I was not the person with the problem. It was a college student, a friend of mine whose life was in the process of being ruined by alcohol. I tricked him into going to the meeting and I sat with him the whole time, but I didn't pay much attention to what was going on because all the stories about alcoholism made me want to run out and get wasted, which was what I did as soon as I got my friend back to the dorm. He succeeded in quitting drinking, graduated with a business degree, and went on to get rich in the world of high finance.

I moved to Denver.

My point is that I did not expect to be singled out during this meeting. I gave a moment's thought to ducking low and hoping nobody noticed me, but this proved difficult to pull off because everybody turned and looked directly at me. I realized then that I was "the new guy" in the group because nobody recognized me. I began to sweat. I knew that I had to handle this situation delicately. Most people came to AA meetings because their lives were falling apart, whereas I was there because my life was a total mess. I knew that I would have to draw upon all my knowledge as an English major to communicate the subtle difference between themselves and myself. My life was not a total mess because I drank too much. It was a total mess for a different reason, although if I had the slightest inkling as to the nature of that reason I probably wouldn't even be at this meeting. I began to wonder exactly what my problem was—not the specifics but in general. Which is to say, I had helped to virtually kill a woman, but I had no idea how I managed to get into such a goofy situation. The one thing I did know, though, was that alcohol was not my problem. My problem was not caused by something that could be bottled and sold. If anyone tried to bottle and sell the cause of my problems, they would probably find themselves sentenced to life-to-eternity in Supermax.

"What are you talking about?" a voice said.

Startled, I looked up and saw that everyone was still staring at me.

"Pardon me?" I said.

"You've been talking for almost two minutes and nobody here can make heads or tails out of what you're saying."

Ouch.

It looked like my old problem of talking out loud had caught up with me again. I will admit that most people do talk out loud, but they also do it on purpose. I, on the other hand, have a more cavalier approach to expressing my innermost thoughts. Some people call it "obliviousness."

"That's fairly obvious," the poet said. "We do understand that you are probably a little bit nervous, since this is your second AA meeting . . ."

Good Lord.

How long had I been talking out loud?

". . . but we want you to know that we have all been there and we understand what you are going through and that we care about you and want to make you feel as comfortable as possible."

This made me uncomfortable. Every time a stranger expressed a desire to help me, I usually had a dickens of a time holding onto my billfold. But I had the feeling that these people were not interested in my money. Rather, they seemed more interested in my salvation. It was as though I was in a room filled with Big Als.

"Who is Big Al?" said the man named Bill seated alongside me.

"Was I talking out loud?" I said. This was a purely rhetorical question. Again, I knew the answer. I had been inadvertently talking out loud to myself from time immemorial.

"Really?" Bill said. "Does drinking have anything to do with that particular problem?"

I chortled. His misconception truly amused me. I decided to go ahead and steal the spotlight from the group and clarify things for everybody so that there would be no more misunderstandings.

As I stood up from my chair I pinched and yanked my nose as if it itched, but in reality I was trying to control the smirk on my face, where most of my smirks occur. This was akin to "wipe that smile off your face," as my sergeants used to say. To be perfectly honest, I was embarrassed for Bill. I don't know how many times in my life people had misunderstood my position on a given topic, but it had happened so often that I must say—in all humility—that I had become something of an expert at making clear to people that they were completely wrong and that I was more than willing to set things to rights before they embarrassed themselves any further.

"First off, let me say that—"

"Why don't you tell us your name?" Bill said with a friendly smile.

"Oh . . . well . . . sure," I began, "but I want to make it clear that I'm not actually one of the—how would you say it—'candidates for reformation' or whatever it is that you dudes do here. I didn't come to get cured of drinking, so I'm not sure if I actually qualify to be one of those people who say 'my name is so-and-so.' I'm more of an outside observer, so I actually probably don't really need to tell you my name, or else I could give you my full name rather than just my first name like guys in the movies about AA do. I mean—I could play along and sort of 'pretend' to be someone in dire need of help and give my first name while keeping my last name a secret like you all do, but it would be somewhat disingenuous, since I am not really here to take part in the rites or rituals or whatever it is that you do to get people to stop juicing and so on . . ."

It was at this point that I realized that everyone was staring at me as if I had a raccoon on top of my head. This was not unusual. I glanced at Bill, who was sitting with his arms folded like an unusually patient man standing in line at the ten-items-or-less line in a grocery store while a little old lady tried to palm off expired coupons on the cashier. I am always amazed by men with that sort of patience. I usually make huffing and snorting sounds whenever little old ladies go into their act. Sometimes it works, sometimes I get hit by umbrellas. It's a virtual jungle out there.

"My name is Murph," my vocal cords suddenly said.

I grabbed the tiller and added to that statement by saying, "Or Brendan, which is my real first name. Murph is just a nickname, although I can't tell you the derivation because it might give away my secret last name, and I know how all of you ex-drinkers feel about last names. I've seen *Days of Wine and Roses* about a thousand times. It's one of my favorite movies. I like to drink pink Chablis and smoke cigars while . . ."

I stopped again and noted that the expression on the faces of all the people had not changed one iota, and I have a pretty good eye for iotas.

I suddenly swallowed hard and cleared my throat. I think it was me anyway. It might have been Joanne Woodward.

"I guess what I'm getting at is that I just came here tonight to ask for some advice."

"You came to the right place," Bill said, which I thought was rather presumptuous. How could he possibly know that I came to the right place? Maybe I had come to ask directions to Pierre, South Dakota, and maybe— just maybe—nobody in the room had heard of Pierre, South Dakota.

But I let it slide. Bill had embarrassed himself enough for one night.

"I have a friend who is addicted to drugs," I said. "In fact, it's not really a friend—it's more of a woman. But she snorts cocaine and needs help, and I want to ask your advice on how to deal with the situation."

I saw it then.

An iota.

It appeared on Bill's face, then appeared on the face of a woman seated at my left sucking on a cigarette. Suddenly iotas were popping up all over the room. Apparently, I had hit a raw nerve. I was getting through to these people at last. That came as quite a relief.

"For starters, you could bring her with you next time you come here," Bill said.

"Okay," I said, wondering where he got that "next time" jazz. "But I mean . . . afterwards. After she stops using drugs, what should I do?"

"Well, first you should understand that you cannot control another person's addiction," Bill said.

"That's preposterous," I said. "All of my plans are predicated on that idea. If I can't control her addiction, I might as well do nothing."

"Sometimes that is the correct solution," the cigarette woman said.

"What!"

"Sometimes you just have to let people go their own way until they hit rock bottom. With luck, they will seek help."

I thought of Maureen lying on the rug with drool running out of her mouth, and realized that the bottom didn't get any rockier than that.

"Well . . . I can't do that," I said. "She's already hit rock bottom, and I'm not sure she is capable of seeking help."

"Is this woman a close friend of yours?" Bill said. "Or perhaps . . . a relative?"

I sensed he was trying to find out if she was my wife. I tried to see myself the way everybody in the room was seeing me, and what I saw was a nervous dissembler trying to find the answer to a question he could barely articulate. This was normal.

"No, she's not a relative or my wife or anything. She's barely even a friend, I mean, I barely even know her."

"Where do you know her from?"

"I helped her buy some crack cocaine," I said. I didn't mean to state it that blatantly. Normally I would couch my words in feeble excuses in order to avoid blame, but I was getting the jitters.

"And she almost died from it," I said.

A silence erupted, but for the soft sifting sound of lips sucking on cigarettes.

"How's that?" Bill said.

And suddenly I realized the real reason I had come to this meeting. It was not to seek advice on how to help Maureen. It was to confess my sins and seek absolution. I would have done that back at Saint Something but the priest scared me. I admit it. If I had told him I had helped to almost kill a woman, God only knows how many Hail Marys I would be facing without possibility of parole.

I cleared my throat as I always do preamble to public humiliation and said, "I helped this woman to buy some drugs, and she overdosed. I found her lying unconscious on her living room floor. She's at the hospital now recovering from an overdose."

"So you feel responsible for her condition," Bill stated succinctly.

"Yes, I do," I replied, baring my soul. I looked at each member of the group. There were perhaps twenty people gathered in the church. Each person was looking directly at me. "I mean, I know that I can't control another person's addiction, but there are some things I can control," I said.

"Like what?" Bill said. This took me by surprise. It almost had the tenor of sarcasm. Did recovering alcoholics ever resort to sarcasm? It seemed a bit risky to me. A beginner might be scared off. But I had the answer to his possibly sarcastic question. Ironically, it was a possibly sarcastic answer, like all my answers.

"My taxi," I said. "At some point during the ride, I realized that I was getting involved in a drug deal, but instead of bailing out I just went along with it."

"Why?" someone said.

I started to answer the question, but then I hesitated because a second answer occurred to me. But before I could decide which answer was appropriate, a third answer came to me. Suddenly I realized that someone's simple little three-letter question was generating answers like sausages, and none of them were satisfying. Yet they were still answers. I went along with it because if I didn't, some other taxi driver would have driven Maureen to the drug deal. If I hadn't gone along with it, I would have missed out on a fairly large payday. I went along with it because it was none of my business why my fare was going where she was going, my only business was to take her there. All of my answers were like this. They all seemed to be revolving around a sort of black hole, like the nozzle of a tornado, like the placid eye of a hurricane, like an uncovered manhole that everyone keeps stepping around in order to avoid falling into a black void filled with . . .

I stopped thinking.

"Filled with what?" Bill said.

"Huh?"

Apparently, I had stopped thinking out loud.

"I . . . I don't know," I said.

"Sure you do," Bill said.

"No, I don't," I said. I was instantly miffed by the fact that he seemed to be calling me a liar. "If I knew, I would say it," I asserted.

"Then say it," Bill said.

Now he was accusing me of knowing something that I insisted I did not know.

"Do you want me to say it for you?" Bill said.

My shoulders drooped. I let out an exasperated sigh. I felt as if I was in the presence of a group of people who were masters at mind games. At almost the same instant, I realized that I was, in fact, in the presence of a group of people who were masters at mind games: drunks.

I suddenly felt naked. I had the sense that every single person in the room could see right through me. I quickly reviewed the past forty-four years of my vocal life, starting with the first time I said "Mama" and ending with the phrase, "If I knew, I would say it."

I was particularly struck by the predominance of lies that often made up the substance of my "vocals." Almost every one of them was linked directly or indirectly with the concept of survival. Why else would I waste my time lying to people? My utter indifference to everything that everybody said or did would preclude that possibility. However, a closer inspection of the past forty-four years revealed to me that I did not always lie in order to avoid being captured, clobbered, or justly accused. Sometimes I did it just because . . .

I stopped again.

"Just because what?" Bill said.

Again—the Talking Out Loud Syndrome that I had always had such trouble with. I suddenly wondered if I had a hearing problem rather than a talking problem, which would explain why I never seemed to hear what other people heard me say. Or maybe it was a psychological hearing problem. Maybe I blocked out the things that I said because . . .

I stopped again.

Nobody said anything.

Apparently, I had not spoken out loud. This threw me for a loop. I tried to remember what it was I would have said out loud if I had actually spoken. I couldn't seem to keep my mind on track, and I suddenly realized that I was using my audience as a crutch to keep track of my sentences for me. But why would I do such a thing? If I had something to say, you would think I cared enough about it to be aware of what I was saying regardless of the content.

"You're almost there," Bill said.

"Almost where?" I said.

"At the eye," someone said.

"At the nozzle," someone else said.

"At the open manhole," Bill said.

I looked down to see if there was a hole in the floor. I wasn't used to other people using metaphors. That was my cute game.

"Indifference," the smoking woman said.

"Don't tell him!" someone interjected.

"Why not?" the smoking woman said. "This guy is as self-aware as a manhole cover."

I felt as if I ought to get angry—but at what? The Truth? When did the Truth about my self-awareness ever bother me? I couldn't have cared less if other people knew that I couldn't have cared less what they thought, believed, or knew. I was completely and totally and utterly indifferent to . . .

"Everything," I said out loud.

Bill closed his eyes and nodded.

I took a step backwards and looked around the room. Everyone was staring at me. Some people were holding cigarettes and some people were holding coffee cups, but everybody was staring at me. To top that off, everyone looked exactly like Big Al.

The images around me suddenly became disjointed. I was hearing and seeing things that made no sense. It reminded me of the first hundred times I was bullied in grade school. The next thing I knew, I was seated behind the steering wheel of Blue Boy and driving out of the church parking lot. I was sweating bullets. I didn't know where I was going. I was just going. This is my standard approach to driving when I'm not in my taxi.

Sometimes I end up at the grocery store, sometimes I end up at a laundromat. This is good because, for reasons that are not always clear to me, I often have a pile of laundry in the rear of my car.

I tried to forget the things that had happened to me in the past hour. I never thought the day would come when I would be 86'd from an AA meeting, but I'm glad the day finally came. I could now concentrate on solving my problem on my own rather than letting someone else solve it for me, which had never actually happened before. These events served only to prove to me that I had to be responsible for my own actions, perhaps the most distasteful lesson that I learned on a weekly basis. Even when Big Al helped me, it was only in the form of advice. He never actually helped me to do anything. He usually sent me off into the wilderness armed only with words and high hopes, just like a high school graduate. The only thing missing from my car right at this moment was a mortarboard and a diploma. I was just like the scarecrow in *The Wizard of Oz*, minus the exquisite dancing ability. That Ray Bolger was a real hoofer.

I drove back up Lincoln Street toward 8th Avenue. I passed a Denver bus, the Number Zero, which I had ridden many times before. I remembered one particular rainy night when I rode it after putting the entire western hemisphere in jeopardy. I won't drag you through that mess, partly because it would take too long and partly because I am forbidden by federal law from even referring to it obliquely, although the parameters are not clearly defined. That will be my defense anyway, when Langley comes after me again.

Ten minutes later I was in sight of Denver General Hospital, where Maureen lay in a coma. I assumed she was still in a coma because I always assume the worst and then proceed from there. I am no Pollyanna. I am more of a Henry Morgan. If you don't know who he is, try Oscar Levant. If you don't know who he is, it is highly doubtful that you and I will ever be anything more than casual acquaintances.

I wanted to park at the hospital and go in and check on Maureen, but I was afraid that her boyfriend or her brother might be there. Boyfriends and brothers are the Scylla and Charybdis of disintegrating relationships. I've been chased by both. Then there are fathers, the Neptune of bad experiences, most of which were based on misunderstandings, but not all of them. I find it interesting that the anger of fathers does not seem to differ in degree whether the father is in the right or in the wrong. That truth almost seems like a violation of the laws of physics—but that's true of practically everything that has ever happened to me during a date.

As I cruised past the hospital trying to decide whether to go or not, I suddenly had an epiphany. I avoid epiphanies whenever possible because they have the quality of deus ex machina that the average person can do without in his daily life. Sudden facile solutions to difficult problems, such as God descending in a chariot and smiting all your enemies as you cower at the edge of a cliff, can upset your metabolism and leave you with the disjointed feeling that your very existence is dependent on chance—and who needs that? No, it's better to find a realistic solution to your problems that can be adapted to other miserable situations, but in this case I decided to embrace the epiphany due to the fact that it had far greater appeal than getting stomped by bikers. I realized that I was trying to solve a problem. What was wrong with me? After fifteen years of driving a taxi one might think I had learned to stay away from that tar baby, if I may be allowed to use a euphemism that is offensive to people who are appalled at the overt racism depicted in a small number of politically incorrect Walt Disney animations. How many times had I learned that sitting still and doing absolutely nothing has solved more problems than wracking my brains for a solution—or a "way out," to be more precise. Without going into detail, I once solved a problem in New Mexico by simply leaving Albuquerque and never looking back.

As I passed 8th Avenue and went on toward 13th, I decided to head back home. So far the entire evening had been a complete disaster, which I fervently hoped had not taught me any lessons. I intended to go home, climb the steps to my apartment, fall into bed, pull the covers over my head, and wait for Time to do what Action does least best, if I may be allowed to incorporate the strange syntax that you often encounter in Shakespearean plays (see: "most not difficult" from *Hamlet*, Act II, scene 5, Apollonius to Zethe).

As I drove toward my apartment I felt the burdens of the world being lifted from my shoulders as though a great bird had snatched a python from around my neck and . . . and . . . and then I noticed a motorcycle parked out front of my apartment building. It had ape-hangers. It looked familiar, and suddenly the great bird lost its grip, the python fell back onto my shoulders with a meaty slap, and I almost lost control of my bladder.

I took my foot off the accelerator and coasted past the turn-in to my parking lot. I could not see anybody lurking about. Maybe the biker had gone up the fire escape to my apartment, busted in, and was now sitting on my easy chair smoking a cigarillo and waiting for me to enter. Perhaps he was leafing through the unpublished screenplays on my bookshelf made of unpublished novels. Perhaps he was skimming *Draculina* and making notes for a screenplay of his own that he would rip off, turn into a blockbuster, and sell for a million dollars in Hollywood.

Perhaps.

Writers tend to think that way. They are paranoid about their ideas. (Note the words "they" and "their" as if I was not referring to myself. On top of being chronically paranoid, writers are also quick to avoid practically everything.)

By taking my foot off the accelerator I felt as if I had "silenced" the pistons of my car. This illusion carried me to the end of the block, where I stepped on the accelerator and continued moving. I suddenly realized how fortuitous it was that I had left my apartment and gone to the drive-in and to church and to the AA meeting. Had I not done these things I would be technically dead instead of virtually dead. This is how I chose to view things. It was already a given that I was dead. All that remained were the details, the how if not the why. I knew the why. And the answer was not as simple as "I had killed Spinelli's sister," which may or may not have been true, but why split hairs on your journey to the cemetery.

I knew that there was only one thing to do. In some cases this involved going to the police, but instead I went for the "Albuquerque Option," which consisted of finding an obscure motel and holing up. I don't have time to explain the "Albuquerque" part, except to say that a motel saved my ass that time too. My life gets fairly complicated at times, but fortunately I somehow manage to glean survival lessons from my embarrassing hijinks.

I turned north to Colfax Avenue and aimed my hood ornament east. My hood ornament is a chrome-plated naked lady with wings that looks like she was fired out of a cannon, but I don't have time to explain that either. It boggles my mind to think of all the things I don't have time to explain. If I explained everything, it would not only take forever but would clarify many of the things that perplex me, which—logically strikes me as impossible, though certainly intriguing.

It was at this moment that I suddenly realized that I was driving toward Aurora, the enchanted suburb, and this brought me back to reality in the way that "BRIDGE OUT" signs often bring sleepy drivers back to reality.

As I drove along Colfax toward the enchanted suburb, I found myself glancing at neon signs. I was familiar with this habit. It usually preceded the purchase of a bottle of liquor. I began squinting at vertical signs, looking for the phrase "Coward's Way Out." In English this is spelled "Liquor," but I was no longer in England. I was in a territory that I had visited many times in the past, but it was never as real as it was now. The fantasy landscape that I inhabited when in a similar frame of mind had the recognizable soft edges of illusion, but because I was on the run from outlaw bikers, and because I had virtually killed a woman, the soft edges had disappeared leaving the hard, cold, cruel edges that are often mistaken for reality but that are—in fact—the definitive lines of what is known in most English languages as a "nightmare."

There was only one way out of this nightmare and that was to crawl inside a bottle and hide until the nightmare has passed like a mare ridden by one of the Nazgûl. For those of you unfamiliar with the concept of a "Nazgûl," I suggest you try reading a book once in a while.

I finally saw what I was looking for. It was a liquor store near Chambers Road, a small redwood establishment that—thankfully—had a drive-up window. It had always struck me as odd that a liquor store should have a drive-up window, but then Aurora itself had always struck me as odd. It seemed to me that if a cop wanted to hand out his quota of tickets, all he would have to do is park behind a telephone pole and nab everybody who chose to purchase hard liquor from the convenience of his private automobile. The fact that liquor stores also had parking lots did nothing to dissuade me from thinking illogically, but this had always been true of parking lots.

I got in line behind a Studebaker and waited with my engine running for my turn at the window. It was like waiting for my turn to purchase a burrito at a Taco Bell—a 180 proof burrito. When my turn came I pulled up alongside the window and peered at the wall of bottles inside the store. The phrase "Southern Comfort" came to mind. As the late, great Ken Kesey once wrote, "Southern Comfort may taste like honeysuckle but it is one of the few hundred proofs that a man can drink and still not get burned by."

That was the ticket.

I did not want to get burned. I just wanted to hide out from reality as long as it took for the human body to process and dispose of one pint of hard liquor. By that time I assumed the gang fight at Cherry Creek Reservoir would have resolved itself without any help from me, and I could return home completely absolved from all responsibility for whatever might occur while I was "sleeping it off," as Rip van Winkle would say.

The plan seemed so perfect that I'm surprised red flags did not spring up all over my body and mind. I purchased my pint of booze and drove straight to a motel that shall remain nameless but that was located off Interstate 225 near 6th Avenue. The hotel stood practically on the borderline between Denver and Aurora, which had its appeal to me for reasons that make no sense except they had to do with the idea of police jurisdiction. I like performing questionable activities near legal borders. It gives me the same illusion of comfort that alcohol affords those whose abhorrence of reality drives them to seek answers in blown glass. Apropos of nothing in particular, I've always wondered what it would be like to work in a liquor factory.

I won't drag you through the embarrassing process of renting a room at a motel for the night. I won't dwell on the sleazy feeling it always gives me to sign my real name and jot down my real license plate number on a sign-in sheet. Rather, I will escort you down the sidewalk past the ice machine and quickly open the door and slip you inside room number 7 before the woman behind the desk sees you.

The lock on the door barely clicked before the first sweet rush of Southern Comfort tickled my tongue.

Let us jump ahead twenty minutes.

I was seated on my bed smoking a cigarette from a pack I had purchased at the liquor store without telling you about it, sipping on the pint, and watching the color television bolted to the wall above the chest of drawers that contained little more than a telephone book and a Gideon Bible, neither of which I planned to peruse that night, which is how most of my motel stays begin. The liquor was already streaming through my system, and due to the nature of the brand I was sipping, I felt like a little kid watching a movie and sucking on a Black Cow, which is a long hard flat caramel candy bar on a stick of the type that I used to suck on only in movie theaters.

I had not eaten a Black Cow—or a candy apple for that matter—since I was ten, but it didn't matter because this was not an all-day sucker anyway. It was an all-night sucker, and I was the suckee.

The beauty of drinking and smoking while hiding out in a motel room is that drinking and smoking itself is a form of hiding out. Combine that with a motel room that has a lock on the door and you get to experience the thrill of the "Double Hideout," like a man hiking through the vast white wastelands of the Yukon wearing two layers of clothing. Drinking hard liquor always makes me think of Jack London. And Jack London always reminds me of "To Build a Fire," perhaps the most popular and most anthologized of all of Jack London's stories, which is read by high school students and ends in frozen death. I've often wondered why schoolteachers think that such a morbid story is fit for teenagers, but I never wondered long enough for it to have any discernible effect on the way I live my life. The thing I find most interesting about Jack London is the fact that he died of a drug overdose. That was back in the days when you could buy hard drugs down at the soda shoppe and "doctor" yourself, if it is grammatically correct to refer to a job as a verb.

According to the Oakland coroner, Jack "accidentally" injected himself with approximately one hundred times the amount of heroin that a man needs to give himself a quick pick-me-up, like a glass of orange juice or a hot shower at dawn. How a man could accidentally load a hypodermic needle with exactly one hundred times more heroin than he needed has always perplexed me, as it has perplexed literary critics for the past one hundred years, but the coroner wrote off his death as a "misadventure," which has a kind of wistful poetic sound considering the nature of the man who embarked on this last venture.

This in turn reminded me of the fact that Maureen Spinelli had come close to dying from a drug overdose, which in turn had the effect of nullifying the whole point of hiding out in a motel in Aurora or any other suburb in America. I was here to forget, not to remember. But by sipping Yukon suds I had inadvertently opened the door to a place I had no desire to be, a place where my conscience stood with its arms folded, tapping a toe and frowning at me. But is there any other kind of conscience? I've never known my conscience to gleefully throw an arm around me and shout "Huzzah!" to the accompaniment of trumpets and drums. No, my conscience is like a skinny old lady, a Miss Grundy type, or perhaps a Python character in drag holding a hickory stick and eyeing my ass, which is always easy to spot because it is inevitably in a bind.

I had helped to almost kill Maureen Spinelli.

I quickly took another sip, wondering if I ought to have gone with Johnnie Walker for the burning sensation, which is not unlike cauterization, according to the works of both de Sade and Bukowski. As a Catholic, I had always held a passing interest in the concept of self-flagellation, but I had never taken it to its logical extreme. This was probably due to the fact that it was almost impossible to coax me to do something that I did not have to do, or was not getting paid to do, like cab driving. I simply never experienced the inner fire it took to pick up a cat-o'-nine-tails and flail the skin off my back like the British navy did to poor ol' Billy Budd. Ironically, I was now mentally flailing myself for having helped to place Maureen Spinelli's life in jeopardy. The "Mental Flail" is as close as I have ever come to perpetrating a self-inflicted wound, not counting an amusing incident at the hand-grenade range in basic training, which is not relevant to this story at all.

"All roads lead to self-flagellation," someone said.

It was me of course. I said it in the bathroom while taking a leak. The bathroom had a tin shower booth and a nice echo, which I would take advantage of after the booze was gone and I had only my Irish tenor voice to entertain me.

I went back into the bedroom, which—technically—was the only room and sat down on the bed next to the bottle of Southern Comfort. I picked it up and started to twist the cap off, then I looked at the TV bolted to the wall. This reminded me of the time I went to LA to save a girl and stayed in a motel near the Farmer's Market. Practically everything reminds me of something else, so I quickly put that out of my mind and spent the next few minutes trying to decide whether to take a sip of booze first or turn on the TV first. This is the sort of irritating minor conflict that I indulge in when I am losing my mind. I was dealing with priorities here. Which was more important—the TV or the booze? If I took a sip first, this meant the TV would be framed by booze for the evening, whereas if I turned on the TV first, it would frame the booze. Why this was important to me I have no idea, but I finally solved the problem by realizing that while I would inevitably run out of booze, I would never run out of TV. Therefore I decided to turn on the TV first. I would much rather run out of TV than booze, but since that was physically as well as metaphysically impossible, it made me feel good. As I sat back down on the bed and raised the bottle to my lips, I watched the images on the TV and felt as if I had turned on the faucet of a bathtub and was watching it run down the drain without any thought to the inhabitants of the world who did not have access to television. I was—in effect—wasting TV. This made me feel very American. I was a man steeped in video wealth. I could walk around the room with the TV on and not even look at it, that's how much wealth I had. I could even let the TV run all night with impunity, the sound and images observed by no one in the room, while I snored my patriotic ass away.

Yes—this is how my mind works when it isn't working very well.

But after the second sip of Southern Comfort things began to return to normal. I supposed that it was something like never forgetting how to ride a bicycle—the physical flavor of hard liquor brought back memories of parties I had attended, and the moment when I took my first drink of the evening. It reminded me of sobriety. I was always sober before I took my first drink. In this way I was different from most of my friends. They were usually three sheets to the wind when they took their first drink. I don't know how they managed it, but I was never interested enough in this neat trick to learn how it was done or to ask instructions, as I had done on the night I had asked a friend how to "do shots." He told me to toss an ounce of scotch into my mouth and then swallow it in one hair-raising gulp.

It worked.

I fully expected to experience projectile vomit, but instead I experienced nothing in particular, which threw me for a loop. The next thing I knew, I was drinking shots like it was Kool-Aid. I couldn't believe how easy it was to drink scotch straight. Later on in the evening the procedure was reversed, but I was too drunk to remember the details. My friends later told me all about it. College can be a real grind when you lose your sense of direction and have to rely on engineering majors to lead you to a bathroom.

At any rate, by the time I had taken my third sip of Southern Comfort I was beginning to feel the soothing effects of alcohol in my brain, which caused me to set the bottle on the table next to the bed, sit with my back against a pillow propped against the headboard, and gaze at the TV. There was some sort of army movie on involving airplanes and tanks. Nothing except hard liquor soothes me like gratuitous violence, and I guess I must have fallen into somewhat of a daydream that was not unlike Transcendental Meditation, in that I began to hallucinate that I was watching a TV show called *Stranger to Danger!!!* starring Brendan Murphy, which is my real name. Only a handful of friends actually called me "Murph." Strangers never called me "Murph." By the time those people did get around to calling me "Murph," they were no longer strangers, which had a logic that made me as uneasy as most of my schemes to earn a fast buck. Which is to say, it made sense that people who didn't know me would not call me "Murph" in the way that schemes never resulted in wealth. But given the fact that people eventually did call me "Murph," it seemed logical that I might be able to get rich if I could apply this truth to semantics. The only thing missing from the construct seemed to be logic itself, which was the standard "downfall" in all my schemes to get rich.

Stranger to Danger!!! was a show about a man who was never around when danger erupted. "On land, on sea, on air! You'll never find Brendan Murphy there, because he is a Stranger to Danger!!!"

Images of airplanes dive-bombing battleships, cavalrymen on the charge, and sailors racing PT boats across the Pacific appeared on the screen, and in none of these scenes appeared the star of the show—i.e., me.

I was always somewhere else when banks were being robbed or lions were escaping from zoos or orphanages were bursting into flames the way orphanages frequently seemed to do back in the olden days.

"Tune in again next week for the further adventures of Brendan Murphy in *Stranger to Danger!!!*" an announcer barked at precisely the same moment that someone slammed a motel door, bringing me out of my hallucinogenic reverie. I sat up startled and blinked my eyes a few times. I glanced at the bottle of booze and saw that three sips were missing. I glanced at the TV and saw that the war movie was over. "Whew!" I said out loud, which is something I never do when people are around because it sounds kind of corny. But it accurately summed up my feelings. The TV show that I had dreamed about—*Stranger to Danger!!!*—had seemed so real that I felt as if I actually was skulking around trying to avoid danger. I started to reach for the bottle of booze when it hit me like a ton of bricks: this was not a dream. I actually was skulking around avoiding danger. That was why I was sitting in a motel room. That's why I had dive-bombed into a bottle of liquor. I had seen a biker outside my apartment and I had made a beeline to the nearest hideout. This was second nature to me, so it had never bothered me before, not even in Albuquerque, but my evasion had never been tied to the near death of another person. It usually involved small loans, or angry women.

I closed my eyes and leaned back against my pillow and tried out a small groan, which worked rather well. I finally had to admit to myself that I was a yellow-bellied sidewinder. This was a species of coward that faded with the passing of the Old West, but I was living in Colorado where some people still wore cowboy hats and rode horses, so the nomenclature had not died out entirely. It will be a long time before Colorado catches up with the states of the Eastern Seaboard, where people are referred to by the more modern appellation of "gutless bastards." Not all the people, just the cowards—most of whom seem to hail from New Jersey, although I have been told by tourists that Connecticut has its share of spineless wimps.

I could not remember the last time I had deliberately hidden out from danger, which may sound like hyperbole considering the number of times my life has been in danger just during the past year, but running away from danger had never been my style. As I like to tell people, if it's dangerous let's just get it done and get it out of the way. I'm not the type to tantalize myself with the prospect of anticipating pain—or for that matter the prospect of nonexperience, which is a far more malevolent delusion.

I knew then what I had to do. I reached for the bottle of booze, put the cap on it, and dropped it into the wastebasket. I turned off the TV, crawled into bed, and pulled the covers over my face. It most situations this behavior would accurately be defined in military terms as a "retreat," but in this case it was analogous to the first step in the preparation of an "advance"—although in civilian terms it might simply be referred to as "getting a good night's sleep."

We often got a good night's sleep in the army before leaping with enthusiasm from bed and scarfing down that delicious mess hall food. I wrote the previous sentence in civilian language, due to the fact that the military language that I could have used for those three events is not now, nor has it ever been, covered by the First Amendment.

CHAPTER 16

Rain clouds blotted out the sun. I knew then that I was in for a bad day because every time I dreamed that rain clouds were blotting out the sun, bad things happened to me. Of course, my definition of the word "bad" is not necessarily a touchstone of civilization, but it always seemed to me that bad things happened to me on cloudy days. Sunny days too. I don't know why I even bring it up.

Then I opened my eyes and realized I had been dreaming. I was lying in the motel room near I-225, and I had the ominous feeling in my gut that I had just had a good night's sleep.

I heard the distant sound of marching boots, pounding drums, and the clink of bayonets dangling from pistol belts. The TV was still on. A bad habit I developed from staying in motels. Given the amount of time it takes to unconsciously develop habits, you can imagine how many motels I had stayed in.

"Plenty, brother," I said out loud. I was gazing at the ceiling and trying to psych myself up for death in the afternoon. I was trying to be funny. I couldn't tell if I was succeeding or not. That's because I was distracted by those thoughts of death in the afternoon. And not just anybody's death, but my death. I suppose that was probably obvious, but I thought I would clarify it anyway. When I talk about myself being annihilated, I want to make it perfectly clear to everybody on earth that I am talking about a future event—just in case somebody decides to get "helpful."

It didn't work. Not only did I not laugh, I did not even feel psyched up about death. Silver threads among the gold, darling I am growing old. At the age of twenty there was nothing that psyched me up faster than thoughts of bayonets and bullets and sergeants and Shit On A Shingle, yet there I lay in bed softly groaning and wondering if it made sense for a broke bachelor to even bother with writing a will.

If I died right at that very moment I could not think of a single item from my "estate" that would be wanted by anybody I know—with the exception of a ThighMaster. Also a computer, I suppose. And quite a hefty sum of money in the bank, which grew to an even heftier sum as a result of my living the way I have lived for the past twenty years. Some people call it "frugal." Other people have other names for it. But it all came down to the same thing. There was no getting around it. Plenty of people on this planet would like to see me dead.

I sat up in bed and stretched and yawned. This is how uncontrollable situations always affect me. I mean, let's face it—if you were attacked by a werewolf, why would you bother screaming? You know you are a dead duck and that even if bobbies chase the werewolf away, you are still doomed to lurk within the twilight world of the undead. So stick a sock in it, Olive Oyl. Your doom will not be alleviated by your milquetoast shrieks.

But to get back to my own death, as I shoved the covers away I realized I was already dressed. This made me groan with displeasure because that put me forty-five seconds closer to death. It takes me forty-five seconds to get dressed, but I won't belabor the point.

I planted my feet on the floor, planted my elbows on my knees, and closed my eyes. I began scratching my head with my fingers held stiff and poised like claws. I gritted my teeth and squinted as I scratched. This made me feel tough. I began to wonder if I could go through life with my teeth clenched and my eyes squinted while scratching the top of my head.

Would men fear me?

I stopped scratching, stood up, and dragged the curtain away from the front window. I decided I was probably dreaming but also decided not to pinch myself to make me wake up. I would let the links of a biker's tire chain shattering my teeth wake me from sleep. And if that didn't work, at least I would have experienced the thrill of feeling invulnerable (as a dream character) as I drove toward the Cherry Creek Reservoir and my impending death at the hands of who knows how many people aside from Spinelli?

I would be killed by all the people who loved Maureen and who hated The Varmints. Two hundred murderers, rough estimate. It was the kind of statistic that normally would have made me feel "special." However, that flood of spine-warming ego juice failed to make its appearance. I'm usually able to finesse any depression that comes my way because I am a firm believer in the power of positive thinking—but I guess it was the certainty of my death that rendered self-delusion ineffective. I can't tell you the number of times that I have laughed in the face of death, but my psychiatrist probably could.

Just kidding. I don't have a psychiatrist—and I don't need one. I don't need AA either, and my wardrobe might be drab but it's sensible, and I can sing like Elvis and dance like Fred Astaire, so kiss my ass, you friggin' busybody.

As you can see, I was starting to lose my focus. I knew right then that the best thing to do was just get it done and get it out of the way. Somewhere south of where I stood, the Cherry Creek Reservoir was waiting for me. And standing at the edge of Lake Styx was a group of men bent on revenge, bloodshed, and possible death. This fact did not explain why I left the motel and got into my car. I can't explain it, I can only offer one theory: the memory of Maureen Spinelli as she lay in a hospital bed fighting for her life. If it was good enough for her, it was good enough for me.

One of the things I dislike about myself is that once I set my sights on a goal, nothing can stop me. Rejection slips don't count. Even though they have the same external effect as not writing novels at all—which is to say that on the surface I appear no different from someone who doesn't write novels—I nevertheless have never been thwarted from pursuing my goal of being a published novelist. By the same token, the idea of violent death as a metaphor for a rejection slip did not stop me from driving relentlessly toward the Cherry Creek Reservoir.

This is the part about myself that I don't like. I admire it, but I don't like it. It's similar to my feelings about Jackson Pollock paintings, except that I don't understand Jackson Pollock paintings whereas I do understand self-destruction. But can it be said that a man driving toward certain death is being self-destructive? The implications of such a statement were enough to give a humanities major sufficient material to write a half dozen theme papers, but my learning days were over. If I hadn't learned to avoid self-destruction by now, the odds were good that I would never avoid self-destruction as long as I lived, which is an interesting sentence if not a metaphysical truth, which it might have been but I was too busy looking for the reservoir turnoff to give it the kind of scholarly contemplation that it probably didn't deserve.

The highway system of southeast Denver can turn into a real mousetrap if you don't know what you are doing, but unfortunately I knew exactly what I was doing because I was a cab driver who had fifteen years of scholarly investigation of Denver asphalt to back up my progress. I found the turnoff to the reservoir much quicker than I would have liked. The average person bent on self-destruction might have been so perplexed by the confusing road signs that he might have just gone home and given up on the idea of giving up, but I was not blessed with the virtue of benevolent confusion. I knew exactly where to go and how long it would take me to get there. I even knew where to find the bikers, but this was not due to experience. It was due to the cloud of dust being kicked up in the recreation area by all the motorcycle enthusiasts who had come to Cherry Creek to participate in a rumble.

The reservoir is a giant lake that was formed by the erection of the concrete dam that was built to prevent Denver from flooding, as it had done a number of times in centuries past.

Cherry Creek itself runs from the dam to downtown Denver where it hooks up with the Platte River. One of my favorite apocryphal stories about Denver is that the Native Americans, probably Cheyenne, who lived here when the white men showed up to search for gold, told the white men not to build their houses and business establishments on the dry riverbed of Cherry Creek. Being good easterners, the white men ignored this benevolent advice only to see their buildings float away in what they finally realized was the legendary "100-year flood" that the Indians had warned them about. While all the white men were running around trying to figure out how to prevent their buildings from floating all the way to St. Louis, the Indians sat on their ponies shaking their heads and wondering why white men were so impervious to good advice. To be honest, I don't really know if the Indians did this, but I am assuming they did based on all the good Colorado lumber that ended up in Missouri.

The road leading into the Cherry Creek Recreation Area is a narrow, two-lane asphalt road that winds all over the park, which must be a good two or three miles square. When I first arrived in Colorado the reservoir was practically the southeast boundary of the metropolitan area, but new housing swept past the reservoir to the south and east so that Cherry Creek is now practically in downtown Denver, if you have the vivid imagination and execrable mapping expertise that I possess. The road splits up and veers off into various parts of the recreation area, but the place I was seeking was located near the edge of the water itself where, normally, sun worshippers and bathers lay around on the sand, but as I approached the area I could see that there were no tourists mingling with the two biker gangs that were gathered at the water's edge. Sun worshippers and bathers are always half-naked, and I've gotten pretty good in my lifetime at spotting half-naked people, so their absence was noticeable. I saw nothing but wheels and leather.

Wheels and leather I hummed to myself as I guided my car toward certain destruction. This is an aspect of my personality that I do not necessarily hate, but I do find it mystifying. The closer I get to danger, the more lighthearted I act, which means to me that a person engaged in such an activity must be living in a state of complete denial. It makes me think of General Custer's troops singing a cappella as they reloaded their pistols. But most things make me think of that. I often ponder General Custer's men and how crappy they must have felt when they finally realized "The Truth."

As I drove toward the location of "the party," I noticed two things. There didn't seem to be any civilians around and there didn't seem to be any birds in the area. It made me think of how animals abandon a location where an earthquake is pending. I could understand why any tourists who happened to be around when the bikers showed up might have packed their picnic baskets and fled, but how did the birds know to flee? Truly one of the mysteries of nature. This in turn reminded me of the mysterious process by which sunlight is turned into matter through photosynthesis. Without belaboring the subject, by the time I arrived at the site I was thinking about the Bessemer process, which was introduced in nineteenth-century England in order to cut down on air pollution as a by-product of coal-burning factory furnaces. I forgot why I was even at the Cherry Creek Reservoir, which is how my subconscious liked it. But as usual my consciousness bollixed that plan when my eyes perceived two armies of motorcyclists squaring off down near the docks where, on a normal day, you can rent parachutes for sky-rides behind motorboats. But this was not a normal day, except for me, because even if they were available I wouldn't rent a parachute like some kind of nincompoop and let a speedboat drag me through the sky. What if an eagle attacked me? Would I let him peck my eyes out or would I unbuckle myself from the chute and drop two hundred feet to the reservoir?

This was the best and most distracting conundrum I had ever engaged in while moving toward certain death. I had the funny feeling that I would probably unbuckle myself rather than let my TV sensors be plucked from my skull by a bird. I could always watch TV in a hospital bed with my legs in traction, but I would have no reason to go on living if I couldn't watch TV, even as a paraplegic.

Yes—the most distracting fantasy I had ever engaged in.

I was pulled abruptly out of my TV/eagle fantasy by four bikers who suddenly drove into the middle of the two-lane blacktop, thus blocking my access to the rumble. I knew then that I had come to one of those bridges that you cross only when you come to them. I could have used their blockage as an excuse to go back home and get on with my life and let the bikers fall where they may.

But I had already done that once.

The biker's name was Maureen. Whether she was an actual biker or not I didn't know, but I did know a bona fide metaphor when I allowed one to OD on hard drugs.

I brought Blue Boy to a halt and stared at the bikers. Two of them were Denver Dragons and two of them were members of The Varmints. Apparently, their job was to halt all traffic like a construction defile until the rumble was over and traffic could be allowed to flow freely again, assuming all the blood and spokes were cleared from the roadway. I didn't envy the bikers whose job it would be to clean up after the rumble. Probably new guys were given that job, like privates in the army. All the older bikers—the sergeants as it were—would probably stand around laughing while the newbies got their hands all bloody. Old pro cab drivers did that too, whenever the opportunity arose, although it didn't arise that often, but when it did, they milked it.

I rolled my side window down as one of the Dragons wheeled his bike toward my door. It came back to me then—the TV show that I had dreamed: *Stranger to Danger!!!* "What would Brendan Murphy do in a situation like this?" I asked myself. It was rhetorical, like most of the questions I ask myself. I already knew what I was going to do, and acting like myself was not on my agenda.

"Road closed," the man said. "This party is for bikers only."

"I understand," I said, "but you see, I am a member of The Varmints. I cartwheeled my hog on Interstate 70 last night, so I was forced to drive my car to the rumble. I hope I'm not too late."

I wish you could have been there to see his reaction to what I said, because I sure didn't see it. He just stared at me like a mannequin. He had a black bandanna on his head that was decorated with little white skulls. Both of his ears had golden earrings, and his beard appeared to be stained with chewing tobacco juice. Other than that, he looked like a normal person wearing biker's colors, blue jeans, engineer boots, and an extremely large folding knife attached to his three-inch-wide belt. I was particularly struck by his fingerless leather gloves. I don't mean he struck me, I just mean that the silver brads on the knuckles sparkled in the morning sunlight. I imagined that they would make quite a dent in an opponent during a melee. I also imagined that if I stuck around long enough I wouldn't have to imagine such a thing. In theory, I might experience it.

"You're a Varmint?" he finally said, thank God. I knew that if it went on much longer I would lose the staring contest.

"Yessir, so you see I need to get through the roadblock and join my chums over there by the lake." I pointed toward the gathering of Varmints near the dock. I could see Spinelli standing astraddle on his bike talking to two of his people.

The Dragon didn't bother to look where I was pointing. I had to assume that he was paranoid, was too afraid to take his eyes off me for fear of getting ambushed. I had to assume this because any alternative assumption would have drained me of courage. Pretending I was a badass was all that I had left in my arsenal of false courage. I don't know why it didn't occur to me to bring along a bottle half-filled with scotch. By "half-filled" I am implying that the other half would be inside my stomach and headed toward my brain with the speed of liquor, whatever that is. I wondered if Einstein had ever made a formal study of the speed of intoxicating beverages. I wouldn't be surprised, based on photographs I had seen of his hair. It would not only be interesting, it would even be useful, to know how long it takes for alcohol to magically turn a coward into a mean mother.

"What's your biker name?" the Dragon said.

"Diablo," I replied.

This rolled off my tongue quickly and easily because "Diablo" is the name I always employ when I play computer games. I use it to intimidate my twelve-year-old opponents.

The Dragon's lips parted revealing an unholy grin of rotten teeth. "I'll be looking for you, Diablo," he said.

He motioned for me to drive on through.

I put Blue Boy into gear and stepped on the gas. I was perplexed by his statement. It was as though I had somehow insulted him and he had chosen to throw down a verbal gauntlet. Why would he be "looking for" me? Was he just bluffing, or would he truly be glancing around during the melee, searching through the mud and the blood and the beer for the sight of a Varmint wearing a T-shirt and a green cap? Or was he just trying to intimidate me by his threat? Why would he do such an immature thing? He looked to be in his early thirties. Why would a man that age resort to "taunting" someone he had never met before? I shook my head with exasperation as I drove toward the lake. The guy reminded me of a bully I had met on my first day of grade school who had told me to give him my lunch money. At the time, I thought he was an employee of the school whose job it was to collect lunch money every morning. It turned out that I was half-right. This set a precedent for the next twelve years—or "the lean years," as I came to think of them.

As I cruised toward the lake I looked off to my left toward a rocky landscape where the largest group of Denver Dragons were gathered, either sitting on their bikes or standing next to them. Some of them were drinking beer. Some of them were French-kissing their "mamas." It was like a scene out of a Roger Corman movie, which normally would have cheered me up. I hate it when reality too closely resembles the movies. I never expected to be in the presence of King Kong or Godzilla or Dracula, yet here I was, in the presence of characters from some of the most violent films ever produced.

It was either Edmond Rostand or Carl Foreman or José Ferrer or Cyrano de Bergerac who once said, "Is the prize not worth the danger?"

I couldn't decide whether the prize was my dignity or Maureen Spinelli, but as with most things I undertake, it didn't seem to matter at this point.

"What would the stranger to danger do in a situation like this?"

The phrase kept running through my mind like that lightbulb message thing that runs around the building in Times Square. Pardon me for the soft imagery, but "lightbulb message thing" was as close as I could come to naming the thing that I was being reminded of by my mind. Sometimes there is a disconnect between my brain and words, and sometimes there isn't.

Spinelli turned and looked at me as I drove Blue Boy toward the gathering of The Varmints. There was no question in my mind that he knew I was responsible for the near death of his beloved sister. The only question remaining was whether or not he was going to make me fight on the side of the Denver Dragons, which would not have worked to my advantage by any means because one of the Dragons was going to be "looking for me" during the rumble, and being on his side would make it all that much easier for him to do whatever he planned to do after he saw me. This is what I hate about bullies. They can be so vague at times—but then this is probably part of their strategy. Keep the enemy off-balance. Keep your victims guessing. Don't let on about the things you are going to do to them after you get your knobby fingers around their scrawny Irish throats.

Or maybe Spinelli would just dispose of me right here before getting on with the fight, like an audience teaser prior to a boxing match. Leave me like a pile of broken bones the way Sergeant Snorkel always does to Beetle Bailey. I remember how relieved I was when I learned that sergeants were not allowed to beat up on privates in the army. You would be too if you are anything like I am. I used to get beaten by nuns, fer the luvva Christ, so you can imagine what a sergeant trained in hand-to-hand combat could do to a disruptive student. Did I ever tell you about the time in sixth grade when I stood on top of my desk and the nun caught me? It's an awfully long story with some amusing highlights, but Spinelli un-straddled his bike and began walking toward my car, so I don't have time to tell you the story except that the nun somehow managed not to kill me.

"Murph," Spinelli said, leaning down and looking in my window. He was wearing sunglasses, or "shades," as the badasses call them. He looked like that cop who woke up Janet Leigh when she fell asleep out on that lonesome California highway before she checked into the Bates Motel and was subsequently disposed of by Tony Perkins' mama.

I seem to be having trouble focusing on my meeting with the gang. You could practically smell the testosterone in the air, and I guarantee you it was not coming from the exhaust pipe of my 1954 Plymouth.

"Spinelli," I replied.

"What are you doing here, Murph?" he said.

"I'm doing what I always do," I said.

"What's that?"

"Trying to fix a mess I created."

"What mess did you create?" Spinelli said.

I eased the car door open and stepped out onto the hard rocky earth of CCR, and I don't mean Creedence Clearwater Revival.

"This," I said, raising my arm and sweeping it left to right, encompassing the landscape containing two hundred bikers champing at the bit to commit mayhem.

Spinelli reached up and began rubbing his lips with an open palm. He peered at the tableau, then looked at me. "How do you plan to fix it?" he said.

"One step at a time," I said.

"What's the first step?" he said.

"Don't rush me," I said. "I'm still working on it."

Spinelli started nodding. I couldn't help but feel it was a nod of sarcasm, but how can you tell with a nod? A nod has no nuances, no inflection, no telltale undertone of mockery.

Or does it?

"Where were you last night?" Spinelli said.

I stopped working on it and looked at him. "Last night?" I said. "That covers a lot of territory. What time last night?"

"Ten o'clock," he said.

"Oh. That time," I said. It was the worst time he could have named. It was the time that his bike was parked in my backyard.

"I came by your pad to talk to you," Spinelli said.

Did he say "pad"? I squinted at him to see if he was now being sarcastic. "Pad" was a word used by hipsters in movies, but I didn't think real people used it. Did Spinelli know that I secretly thought of myself as a hipster and was making fun of the way I think? I froze then. I was so used to accidentally talking out loud that I wondered if I had said that out loud. If so, then he would know that I secretly thought of myself as a hipster. That was just one step away from making fun of me.

"I dropped by to thank you," Spinelli said.

Thank me? For what? Was he now making fun of me? Was he setting me up for a big fall? Was I one step away from meeting my Maker the hard way?

"What are you mumbling about?" Spinelli said, leaning toward me and turning his head so that his ear was lined up with my mouth.

"Nothing," I said quickly. "What did you want to thank me for?"

Spinelli glanced around at the two armies waiting for a signal to start the war. He looked back at me. "Maureen told me everything," he said.

My soul began to depart my body, but I reached up with my cosmic fingers and grabbed hold of it before it could float away like The Red Balloon. Have I ever told you about my cosmic fingers? Remind me to do that someday.

"Maureen told me how you drove her over to Five Points to score some crack," Spinelli said.

I released my soul but it remained inside my body, which disappointed me because it left me wide open to pain. Dead men don't feel pain—or so I've been told. I would hate to think that cremation actually "hurt."

"She told me that the pusher who sold her the dope tried to put the moves on her and that you put a stop to it."

My jaw dropped open an inch and I raised my line of vision until it was looking at the frosted white peaks of the Rocky Mountains in the distance. I was trying to remember the details of that incident, which had seemed so minor to me that I would never have remembered it if Spinelli hadn't mentioned it.

"Oh yeah," I said. "I do remember doing that."

"If I had been there I would have killed the guy," Spinelli said in a tone of voice that made me wonder if he had ever killed any other guys.

"I try to avoid killing my customers," I said. "The City would probably take away my taxi license."

"Maureen told me that the guy scared her, but that you put a stop to it," Spinelli said.

I nodded. The "guy" was the pusher who had sold her the crack, but Spinelli did not seem to be focusing on that aspect of the transaction. The situation began to go slightly out of focus. This was normal. I felt like I was back in my element.

"Part of my job as a taxi driver is to ensure the safety of my customers," I said. "Putting a stop to situations is just all in a day's work," said the stranger to danger.

"I came by last night to thank you for doing that," Spinelli said. "And to find out who the guy was."

"What do you mean?" I said.

"The pusher. I was hoping you could tell me who he was."

I started to freeze, but then stopped myself. I didn't want Spinelli to know that I was picking up on what he was getting at. "I never saw the guy before," I said. "He was just some pusher."

"Do you think you could point him out to me if you saw him again?" Spinelli said with a piercing gaze that made my blood run cold. And it wasn't just because he seemed to be making me an accessory to premeditated murder, it was the certainty I now felt that Spinelli had killed men in the past.

"I doubt it," I said, mustering as much insouciance as I could. "Insouciance" is a word that generally means "fake calm." I knew that if I said the wrong thing, my "fake calm" would magically transform itself into "real panic."

"Why is that?" Spinelli said.

"I see so many people in a day's work that all the faces tend to blend together. I doubt if I could identify the pusher again."

Spinelli stared at me long and hard. I sensed what he was doing. He was trying to decide whether or not I was telling the truth, or if I was lying in order to avoid the death sentence. Did it make sense that a man who saw hundreds of customers every week would not be able to identify a specific customer who needed to be singled out for retribution?

That was the $64,000 question.

Spinelli stuck out his lower lip and started nodding. I think he bought it. This put the cap on one of my all-time favorite activities—lying to the leader of a biker gang.

He peeled his eyes away from mine and looked out across the low-scrub landscape of the Cherry Creek Reservoir. One hundred feet away stood a lone biker at the head of the Denver Dragons. I assumed he was their leader. I assumed he was waiting for Spinelli to give the go-ahead for the start of the bloody punchfest. This brought me back to the reason that I was there that morning. The reason, of course, was "hubris." That's the reason for almost every bad idea I ever had.

"I can't let this rumble take place," I said.

Spinelli's eyes locked onto mine again.

It was at this point that I experienced something that had happened to me only one time before in my life, an experience so bizarre that I had never mentioned it to anyone, in the way that the victim of a UFO kidnaping will refrain from speaking of it, or a hunter who stumbles across Bigfoot will keep his sighting a secret from his drinking partners. It happened on the day that I arrived in basic training. As the busses pulled up in front of the barracks, drill sergeants began hammering on the side of the bus with what appeared to be excessively long nightsticks and shouting, "Get off the bus! Get off!! Get off!! Get off!!!"

After we got off, they told us to get back on again and start over. But the weird part was my out-of-body experience. As the drill sergeants slammed their nightsticks against the metal sides of the bus I felt my soul leave my body. It drifted out to the parking lot and seemed to float among the nightsticks and Smokey Bear hats. I sensed that my soul was trying to get back to Wichita. I suddenly came to consciousness seated on the bus while all about me men were scrambling to get off the bus for the third time.

And now, twenty-five years later, I felt my soul leave my body as my mouth was explaining to Spinelli that I could not allow the rumble to continue without my intervention.

As my "ghost" drifted away from my body I heard myself saying as from the deep recesses of an empty fifty-five-gallon oil drum, "I am placing all of you under citizen's arrest."

Even my soul was startled by the audacity of that remark. It looked back to see a taxi driver named Brendan Murphy standing face-to-face with the leader of an outlaw motorcycle gang and casually explaining that everyone within the vicinity of the Cherry Creek Reservoir was now required to follow me back to Denver where I would process them into jail for attempting to create a disturbance in a public park.

My soul somehow managed to pull a swift one-eighty, and I began traveling back toward the body of the taxi driver as Spinelli slowly placed his curled fists on his hips and frowned deeper than anybody had ever frowned in the entire history of dog-track racing.

"So if you will just get on your motorcycles and follow me back to Denver, I believe we can finish this business before lunchtime," my voice said as I snapped back into my body like a bolo ball striking a paddle. There was a distinct "snapping" sound as I came to consciousness too late to prevent myself from saying what I had just said.

I had done something similar to this once before. It's a long story and ends happily, and as I stood there staring at Spinelli I realized that this was where the similarity ended. In the earlier version, I was not confronting a group of bikers but a group of taxi drivers who apparently liked me, so there was another dissimilarity. I knew that if I stood there long enough comparing and contrasting the two events, I would doubtless finds dozens of ways that these two events differed. Then it occurred to me that the last time I led a group of men through Denver, the journey ended up at Denver General Hospital. It suddenly seemed like all the roads of my life ended up at the hospital. I began to seriously wonder if there wasn't something wrong with my roads.

"You're arresting us?" Spinelli said.

"Yes," I said simply, in order to get this over with quickly, the way you rip off a Band-Aid to get it over with quickly. Another similar dissimilarity. I would have given anything right at that moment to stop comparing and contrasting, but I had a degree in English, and this is what English majors do.

Spinelli stepped back and looked around at the vast sea of bikers who were poised on the edge of battle. It was like standing in the middle of the Coliseum on a really crowded day, or like a Super Bowl game between the Denver Broncos and the Oakland Raiders. When the Broncos battled the Raiders you couldn't buy a ticket to Mile High for love or money. But even on a dull football day it was a sellout crowd because Denver fans are the biggest fans in America. Given the thin track record of the Broncos going back to the formation of the NFL, it's easy to see why so many Denverites would show up at a football game just to see something as rare and amazing as a victory.

"That's probably not a good idea," Spinelli said. "A lot of these troops are two-time losers, and another arrest might put some of them away for good."

"They should have thought of that before they became outlaws," I wanted to say, but didn't, because Spinelli interrupted me, thank God.

"What if we compromise," Spinelli said.

"How do you mean?" I said.

"What if me and Diablo followed you to the police station and you tossed us in lockup as a symbolic gesture of both gangs."

I pursed my lips and looked at the damp, sandy earth and began nodding. Then I looked up at Spinelli and said, "Who is Diablo?"

"The leader of the Denver Dragons," he replied, pointing toward a large fellow wearing a black vest that had silver spangles and feathers and various baubles decorating his leathers—but then you've seen bikers decked out in full combat regalia, unless you don't own a television. Roger Corman practically owns late-night TV in Denver.

"That might work," I said, pretending that it might work. I knew it wasn't going to work. I knew that I was a dead man speculating, and I wondered why Spinelli was toying with me because I had thought that he liked me. He once described me as "good people," which I had been led to believe was biker lingo for "don't stomp this cat."

"Let me talk this over with Diablo," Spinelli said, but before I gave Spinelli permission to leave the "area of arrest," he walked over to the leader of the Denver Dragons and began conferring with him.

As Spinelli spoke, Diablo glanced over at me, then began rubbing his jaw. I couldn't hear what they were saying. The incessant ringing in my ears drowned out everything else at the reservoir, including the silence. I glanced around at the hundreds of bikers standing next to their hogs, and they made me think of an army made out of life-size jade warriors, but then everything makes me think this. Spinelli strolled back toward me and cleared his throat.

"I told Diablo that you planned to arrest all of us but that you would settle for jailing me and him, but then he offered a compromise."

The toying would never cease. I no longer felt that I was good people. I assumed that Spinelli and Diablo had been discussing the best place to sink my cement-booted feet into the Cherry Creek Reservoir. Out near the handsome concrete apron of the dam would have been my choice.

"Diablo wanted to know if you would call off the arrest if we called off the rumble."

I didn't even hear myself say yes, but apparently I did. I would imagine that this was due to the fact that a small but influential part of me had been looking for an escape from this mess while I had been admiring my final resting place.

Spinelli motioned Diablo over to the spot at the edge of the symbolic waters of death where we were standing. Water and death always went hand in hand in ancient literature. Even a drinking fountain would have sufficed at this point, given the century that we were living in. I had to assume that I was living in the twentieth century, although I had been accused of doing otherwise by various people including Big Al, who seemed to think that my literary ambitions were quaint and belonged in the era of Bret Harte. I wondered what Big Al was doing right at that moment. Gathering up his take in preparation for leaving Las Vegas, I supposed.

"This is Murph," Spinelli said. "He drives a taxi. He's good people."

"Hey, Murph," Diablo said. "My mother drives a taxi for Yellow. Are you with Yellow?"

"No, I drive for Rocky Cab."

He didn't remark on that, he just nodded, like it was okay with him that I drove for RMTC even if he didn't completely approve. In this way he was like my own mother, not counting the Harley. My mother drives a British Racing Machine.

CHAPTER 17

Not really.

I have often found that when I make jokes about my mother, people don't always get the joke, especially Maw. She can be quite a stickler for facts, the bane of comics, stand-up or otherwise.

After the rumble was called off, I watched as the Denver Dragons pulled away from the reservoir and drove out toward Parker Road, one of my two favorite pioneer trails. The other is Leetsdale Drive. I don't know who Parker and Leetsdale were, but with your luck I will probably get back to you on that.

As the dust of the departing Dragons faded, The Varmints started up their own bikes and began filtering out of the recreation area. Pretty soon it was just me and Spinelli standing at the edge of the water watching the gang disappear. When the noise of their single-piston engines dwindled to nothing, Spinelli looked over at me and said, "You look like hell. Where did you spend the night?"

I shrugged. "Denver," I replied.

He nodded. I think we connected metaphysically. The word "Denver" explains a lot of things to a lot of people.

"I waited outside your apartment until midnight, then I called Rocky Cab to see if you were working late," Spinelli said. "But when they told me you weren't working at all, I decided to call it a night."

I nodded at him but said nothing. What was I going to tell him? The Truth. Not likely. If he found out that I had seen his bike parked outside my apartment and that I ran like a scared rabbit, it might have played havoc with my rep. I might not qualify as good people anymore. I might have been redefined as "one of them" in Spinelli's eyes, which was true but he did not have a "need to know," as Senate investigating committees say.

"I'm glad to hear that Maureen recovered," I said. "I'm sorry about helping her get drugs. I didn't understand the situation."

"Don't worry about it," Spinelli said as he slowly pulled on his fingerless gloves and flexed his naked fingers like a pug getting ready to make short work of a speed-bag. But instead of using my head to work out his frustration, he just climbed onto his bike. "Maureen is going to be okay," he said. "We talked about it. She's enrolling in a twelve-step program, and I'm going to see that she stick with it."

I nodded and started to say something, then stopped myself. It seemed like half of the people I ever got involved with ended up joining a 12-step program. I decided not to follow that thread of conversation. Instead I just said, "I'd like to visit her again."

Spinelli nodded. "She'll be getting out of the hospital in a couple days. I'll let her

know that you want to see her."

"Listen," I said. "If she ever needs a ride to her recovery program, I'll be glad to drive her there for free, even if I'm not working that day."

Spinelli sat back on his bike and looked me up and down. Then he started nodding. He reached out to shake my hand, but it wasn't just an ordinary shake. It was the "secret biker handshake" that Pee-wee Herman incorporated just before he drove through the billboard: the full-forearm grip. It's similar to the ninety-degree-angle "hippie handshake" but more forceful.

"You're good people, Murph," he said. "Maureen will probably take you up on that."

A sinking feeling blossomed in my gut. I had—in effect—arranged a personal, which meant that I might be called on at any time day or night to drive Maureen to her program. Most likely it would take place in a church basement, which was hardly the frosting on the cake, but don't get me started on the horrors of responsibility. All things considered, I felt willing to help Maureen recover from drug addiction, since I had once helped her overdose. It seemed to possess the quality of balanced karma, which I had never been interested in exploring.

"Catch you later," Spinelli said, then he stood straight up on his starter and dropped like a sandbag. The hog roared. Spinelli put it into gear and raced off down the road leaving a wide trail of dust that pointed toward the exit to the Cherry Creek Recreation Area.

I climbed into Blue Boy and followed his dust, feeling about as sickly as I usually feel after getting involved in the personal life of a fare. The sickly feeling stayed with me all the way back to my crow's nest, which was unusual. It usually fades by the time I turn off Colorado Boulevard onto 13th Avenue.

I drove to my apartment and parked in the rear, and when I climbed out I could see the tread marks of Spinelli's Harley in the dirt lot near my staircase. I thought about getting a whisk broom and erasing the marks, but erasing reminders had always been one of my bêtes noires. I needed to start remembering things that were worth remembering: some people call them "lessons."

As I climbed the fire escape to my apartment I felt as if I had not been home in a long time. This could be attributed to the fact that every time I got involved in the personal life of a fare I experienced anywhere from one to three lifetimes, so it felt good to be returning to the ol' homestead. It was like the time I received my army discharge and returned to Wichita, which had never felt good before. But after two years in the army, practically everything feels good.

I entered my apartment and started to turn on the lights because it was dark in the apartment and the lights were not on. Logic dictates all my actions. But then I decided to leave them off. It was not totally dark, but the sun was painting the opposite side of the building, or "the bedroom side," as I think of it, so I sat down in my easy chair and contemplated turning on the TV.

Problem?

To my knowledge, there were no episodes of *Gilligan's Island* on at this time of the morning. I had an itch to pick up my remote-control device, but what was the point?

What was the point?

It seemed like every time I got involved in the personal life of a fare, I ended up sitting in my easy chair wondering what the point was. I always attributed this to the "drained" feeling I experienced every time I completed a difficult task. When I was in college I used to wonder what the point was every day, but I had a lot of time on my hands and I took a lot of courses in philosophy and existentialism. On the other hand, when I was in the army I never wondered what the point was because I didn't have time. You would not believe how much time and energy a soldier can expend dodging details. It almost equals the amount you spend pulling details. Karmic balance, as it were. By the time I got my discharge, it was too late to wonder what all that was about. It was time to head home, climb into my bed, and wait for Maw to bring me breakfast in bed. I had a long wait. It wasn't until I began going to college on the G.I. Bill and paying her rent from my monthly checks that she gave me kitchen privileges. That's probably why I went to college. My pitiful facial expressions of hunger didn't motivate Maw to let me open the refrigerator. My pitiful facial expressions of confusion didn't motivate her to type up my theme papers either. She gouged me on that deal. I spent a few minutes trying hard not to think about the near-death experience that I had just gotten shut of out at the reservoir. By now I had gotten pretty good at denying the reality of my latest bungle, but the thought of all those bikers parked at the reservoir staring at me silently, and the image of Maureen lying in the hospital hooked up to IVs, came crawling back like a ground fog, as its cousins used to do. I knew there was no point in going to bed. I knew I would just lie awake staring at the ceiling and wondering how I had managed to once again nearly get myself killed. I wanted desperately to blame it on taxi driving, but I knew that even if I was a janitor I would still end up getting involved in people's lives. Then I started thinking that, in a way, I was a janitor. Ever since I had started cab driving, it seemed like I had gone around cleaning up people's messes. By "people's," I mean my own. A friend of mine named Big Al once described this phenomenon as my "inability to operate a taxi without driving it off a cliff."

I know what you're thinking.

Gomer Pyle.

Maybe that's what my brain was thinking when I told Spinelli that I was making a citizen's arrest. The citizen's arrest episode was one of the greatest *Andy Griffith Show*s ever, but I can only tell you that this did not occur to me until I was seated alone in my crow's nest making a fearless inventory of my brain for the two thousandth time since I left home. And in thinking about citizen's arrest, I started thinking about Don Knotts—or more specifically, Barney Fife—and how pathetic he was. Every time he got into a terrible mess, Andy Taylor figured out some way to bail him out, and half the time it was through a . . . ruse.

Ruse.

As I sat on my chair thinking about the sheriff of Mayberry, a cold feeling began to sprout in my gut. Having faced up to what I thought of as "reality," it occurred to me that maybe there was another way of looking at this latest fiasco. And the more I thought about it, the colder grew the ice cube in my gut.

I had gone out to Cherry Creek Reservoir to solve a problem without a plan, as usual, and ended up thinking on my feet, the worst part of my body to incorporate as a tool of problem-solving. Whether it was the ghost of Don Knotts or a few moldy brain cells activated by the absurdity of the situation, something made me think of citizen's arrest. I had thought of this as serendipity at the time. Serendipity had more to do with saving my ass than thinking ever did. I thought that I had saved my own ass. But then the ice cube solidified in my gut and hit me like a ton of bricks. I had not solved the problem at all. Spinelli had solved it.

I suddenly realized that he had taken on the role of Andy Taylor and merely "played along" with my ludicrous threat to make a citizen's arrest of hundreds of bikers. As my gut froze, my shoulders drooped. The odds of hundreds of bikers—much less their leaders—being intimidated by a rattled cab driver were so small that I was forced to acknowledge their virtual nonexistence.

"Welcome to the real world, Tenderfoot."

I was staring at the blank screen of my TV. I did not look up when I heard these words. I did not even pretend that I did not hear them, which was unusual. It was as if Big Al himself had entered my living room, sized up the situation with the same velocity and aplomb with which he judged the ever-changing odds on a tote board at a racetrack—and articulated for me that which I already knew: I was a dupe.

Spinelli had Barney Fifed me.

I did not bring that rumble to an end. Spinelli had already known that none of the Denver Dragons were responsible for Maureen's overdose because Maureen had already told him the truth in the hospital, which meant he must have gone out there to make peace with the Dragons and call off the rumble. And in the midst of their palaver, I had shown up unexpectedly and threatened to jail the whole lot of them.

CHAPTER 18

It was at this point that I realized Spinelli had made a fool out of me.
What point? you might ask. As a reader that is a valid question, and I will get back to it. But first let me describe my reaction.

I watched with fascination as my left arm arose like a snake mesmerized by a Hindu flute and began doing something it had never done before in its life: weaving toward the telephone.

I was so shocked by this unorthodox move that I deliberately stopped my left arm in midair. My telephone resides on a table to the left of my easy chair. I refer to the table as my "beer table" since I use it more often to place beer cans than to use the telephone—otherwise I would refer to it as my "telephone table." As I say, it is located on the left side of my chair, which is an overstuffed easy chair aimed exactly at my television at a ninety-degree angle. After I bought my television and set it up in my living room, I used a compass to shoot an azimuth to make sure that my chair was positioned at exactly a ninety-degree angle in front of my television, which is located approximately twelve feet across the living room from my chair. I was unable to adjust the physical distance between my TV and my chair due to the internal dynamics and logistics of my living room. By this I mean that I could not move the TV any further away from my chair due to the fact that a wall was in the way. I couldn't move it any closer to my chair because it would have blocked the doorway to the kitchen, thus impeding my ability to go to the refrigerator and retrieve cold beer from the fridge.

Why I am telling you that I do not know, but to get back to my snaky arm, I stared at it with a kind of horror because it had volunteered on its own to pick up the telephone and make a call to Spinelli to ask him if he had set me up as a dupe. Which is to say, had he treated me in the same condescending manner that Andy Taylor treated Barney Fife whenever Barney had placed himself in a psychological position where he needed to act like a badass?

I knew the answer.

That is probably why I regained control of my left arm and brought it back down to the overstuffed arm of the easy chair, where it settled softly to the fading music of a Hindu flute. I had just experienced what some people might refer to as an "epiphany," although I prefer the phrase "grim realization." I get those about four times a month on average, but it does fluctuate depending on whether or not I have gotten involved in the personal life of a fare. Ergo, I was used to experiencing this phenomenon and it did not send a shock wave through my system as it did when I first began having grim realizations at approximately the age of ten. That was the age I was when I got hold of a set of oil paints and produced a picture of a genuflecting man with his left arm wrapped around his head hiding his eyes, and his right arm pointing at something off the canvas. I title the picture "The Grim Realization." I don't remember what inspired me to draw such a picture, but I was raised Catholic, so my vision is pretty wide open to interpretation. I still don't know why I painted the man's body green.

But to get back to the point, which I sometimes do, I realized that Spinelli had called off the rumble before I had even arrived at the Cherry Creek Reservoir. I realized that his acquiescence to my threat of arrest was all an "act." I realized that I had been "Fifed."

Spinelli had not gone to the reservoir to have a fight. He had gone there to make peace with the Denver Dragons because he had wrongly believed that a Dragon had been involved in the near-death scenario of his sister. After Maureen had awakened from her coma and told Spinelli the truth, he knew he had to make the appointment at the reservoir as planned, but only to tell the leader of the Denver Dragons that he was mistaken.

I sat on my easy chair staring at the blank TV and running this scenario through my mind until it was as if I was reading a television script of an episode of *The Andy Griffith Show*. I don't know if you have ever seen a TV script, but they differ from movie scripts in that they are divided into two columns. One column contains dialogue and the other contains the camera shots, and both are almost impossible to read. But that's beside the point, like most things I say. In this script, I read that Spinelli was in the middle of apologizing to Diablo for the false accusation at the precise moment when I was driving into the Cherry Creek Recreation Area and that I had interrupted a powwow orchestrated to prevent that massive bloodshed that frequently accompanies biker rumbles.

Spinelli had condescended to me and made it appear as if he had been intimidated by my threat of arrest, when in fact he did not have any intention of creating a disturbance at Cherry Creek for which he would have been arrested. He had simply "played along" with me in the same way that Sheriff Andy Taylor played along with Barney's moronic behavior and his need to seem like a badass: the "Karate Episode" comes to mind, but I don't want to stray too far from my point, assuming I have one.

A sense of melancholia subsequently overcame me, thank God. I can deal with melancholia, whereas I have never really gotten a handle on "humiliation." But maybe we're not supposed to. Maybe humiliation is the one experience that nobody gets used to. Maybe humiliation is "the Great Leveler" that is always preceded by a grim realization, and serves to keep mankind humble. That's quite a job, considering the fact that the history of mankind is not a history of humility. It's mostly about war, the very thing that I had deluded myself into thinking I had prevented by my attempt to make a citizen's arrest.

I glanced at my watch and noted the time, just to see how long it would take for Phase 3 to kick in. Phase 3 is "blue funk" and usually arrives five minutes after melancholia.

Bingo.

Mussolini's trains had nothing on my brain. As I settled into the blue funk, I began to think about what an abominable failure I was. I had never succeeded at anything in my life, but for one brief shining moment I had thought I had succeeded in preventing massive bloodshed. But that was just a delusion, like every other success I misinterpreted. It seemed like the only thing I was good at was failure.

I began to hear the ticking of my wristwatch.

That is how quiet it was when my second or third epiphany of the day began to blossom: failure was the only thing in life I had ever succeeded at. It's true that I was a successful taxi driver, but does that really differ from being a successful failure? While the irrelevant part of my brain was thinking that over, the rest of it was wandering around this latest epiphany as if it was a statue by Rodan. Excuse me, Rodin. Rodan was a famous Japanese sculpture made out of rubber and cheesecloth.

Maybe the reason I was such a successful failure in life was because I was so good at it. Almost immediately I began thinking about writing. Every time I think about failure I think about writing, only in this case the thought came from a completely new direction. I was reminded of the cliché that is taught in every creative writing class on earth: "Write what you know about."

Epiphany Number 3 hit me like a ton of bricks. I had spent my entire adult life trying to become a successful fiction writer, even though I knew nothing about writing fiction. What I ought to have been doing was writing what I knew about. In other words, I should have been concentrating on nonfiction. If it could be said that I had an area of expertise that might be exploited in print, it was How To Be A Failure.

Those bricks were crashing down all around my easy chair and kicking up such a cloud of dust that I was forced to rise and go to my RamBlaster 400 and sit down and switch it on. While I was waiting for the screen to warm up, I began to think about all the lessons I had been taught in English about writing essays, i.e., tell them what you are going to say, say it, and tell them what you said.

Beginning. Middle. End.

I began snapping my fingers at the computer screen to hurry it along. I couldn't wait to get started. Ideas were strafing my brain as if it was King Kong about to make his swan dive. If I could write a how-to book on failure, I just might clean up.   The first thing I told myself was that if a person wanted to be successful at something, even failure, he first had to:

"Know thyself" — since nobody else wants to know you.

Yes.

Don't look at things the way they are supposed to be, look at them the way they really are. It was all I could do to keep from running into the bathroom and taking a long hard look at myself in the mirror. I had been doing this for years but never in preparation for writing a book. I did it for the same reason that all losers take long hard looks at themselves in the mirror, and I'm not talking about hubris. Hubris deserved a chapter all to itself.

I tell you, ideas were coming at me left and right. But I knew that I had to walk a tightrope. I knew that if I approached nonfiction in the same way I wrote fiction, I would fail. I knew myself well enough to know that this was my last chance to succeed. If my book on failure failed, I would be a failure, and I wanted to be a success.

The three steps to becoming a successful failure:

1. Try (but not too hard).
2. Quit (too soon).
3. Blame (everyone but yourself).

Having typed these three sentences, I sat back in my chair and sighed with relief. Try, Quit, and Blame, the unholy triumvirate of the successful loser. I had been practicing these exercises since first grade, yet it never occurred to me to write what I knew about. No wonder I was a failure.

[NOTE: My failure did not extend to kindergarten because kindergarten was all about stick-ponies and nap time—and let's be honest—what taxi driver ever failed at stick-ponies?]

I leaned back in my chair and began groping at my T-shirt pocket for a cigar. I never keep cigars in my T-shirt, but I sure could have used one right then. Cigar I mean, not T-shirt. I quit smoking T-shirts when I left college. It's a long story—a lot longer than the nonfiction book I had just completed.

In my attempt to teach people how-to become failures, I had written a book only three sentences long, i.e., I had written a one-page book, the dream of all commercial writers. I envisioned hundreds of my books stacked up next to a cash register where all the fad books were kept at Barnes & Noble. At a buck a copy I would probably make a million bucks in the first week.

And if I charged two bucks per copy—oh baby, this was kismet!

I have to be honest. It has now been fifteen minutes since I wrote my first nonfiction book, and I cannot think of another thing to add to it. When it comes to failure, I've said it all. The only thing left to do now is open my *Writer's Market* and start looking for a publishing company that specializes in fad books. Scribner? Oxford? Penguin? The choices seem limitless! I feel like a kid going nuts in a candy store. I'm going to be rich!

Yes, Virginia—it's great to be back in harness.

The End